With Love,
Marjorie Ann

and Other Dangerous Stories

With Love,
Marjorie Ann

and Other Dangerous Stories

MARCIA TALLEY

Crippen & Landru Publishers
Cincinnati, Ohio
2025

Marcia Talley Stories copyright © 2025 by Marcia Talley

Introduction is copyright © 2025 by Elaine Viets

For information contact:

Crippen & Landru, Publishers
P. O. Box 532057
Cincinnati, OH 45253 USA

Web: www.crippenlandru.com
E-mail: Info@crippenlandru.com

ISBN (softcover): 978-1-932009-79-8
ISBN (clothbound): 978-936363-93-3

First Edition: March 2025

10 9 8 7 6 5 4 3 2 1

Contents

Introduction

Red-haired Marjorie Ann was a head cheerleader, home-coming queen and femme fatale. She couldn't help herself. She was raised that way: "Mama always said it was a good thing that I was born beautiful," she said, "because I must have been standing behind the door when the brains were handed out."

But Marjorie Ann wasn't dumb. She knew how to marry well and how to eliminate inconvenient husbands. Marjorie didn't kill them—nothing so crude as murder. They just . . . died.

Much-married Marjorie Ann is a survivor, even if her husbands weren't.

She is the creation of mystery writer Marcia Talley. You'll meet Marjorie Ann in this collection of short stories.

You probably know Marcia from her Hannah Ives mystery series. In *Sing It To Her Bones*, the first Hannah mystery, Ives is recovering from breast cancer at the home of her sister-in-law on Chesapeake Bay. Hannah stumbles onto the body of a girl who disappeared from a high school dance almost a decade earlier. Hannah starts asking questions in a town where everyone wants the unpleasant past to stay untouched.

Marcia, like Hannah, is a cancer survivor.

I first met Marcia at the Festival of Mystery in Oakmont, Pennsylvania, a book fest that was a writers' dream. Busloads of readers lined up outside, waiting for the doors of a church hall to open. And they bought mysteries, bless 'em. I never saw so many upstanding citizens eager to glom onto a good murder.

The Oakmont festival drew so many writers we were seated alphabetically. The church hall was stuffed with long cafeteria tables, starting with Donna Andrews. That year T (Talley) was seated next to V (Viets) and I wound up next to Marcia.

As a kid I hated to be seated in alphabetical order, because I was always stuck in the back of class. But this time, it worked out fine. I met Marcia, and we've been friends for more than twenty years.

At that festival, Marcia was waiting for a call from her agent, to find out if her Hannah Ives series would be picked up by a new publisher. When she got the call, Marcia ducked under the table to take it, so she could hear in the noisy hall.

The news was good. Hannah had a new publisher. Her series has survived the many storms in the publishing world, from publishers killing whole divisions to corporate giants gulping publishing houses. Good thing we write about murder, because it's a bloodbath out there.

Marcia won the Malice Domestic Grant, a literary award given to support unpublished writers of traditional mysteries. The Hannah Ives series was born with *Sing It to Her Bones*. The series has grown to twenty novels, most now in hardcover.

This durable series shows no signs of fading. Marcia is still getting starred reviews, and Booklist magazine wrote: "Some long-running series have their ups and downs, but the Ives series has been remarkably consistent."

Marcia is generous with her time in the mystery community. She's a former president of Sisters in Crime, and has served on the National Board of the Mystery Writers of America. She has been Toastmaster and Guest of Honor at the Malice Domestic mystery conference.

In her spare time, she wrote the short stories for this collection. Two of them have won Agatha Awards.

I'm partial to Marjorie Ann, but I like the sly wit in Marcia's other stories, including the witch in the award-winning Too Many Cooks, who concocts an impotence cure using "blue salts from the pools in the Sildenafil Hills." Marcia also improves on Shakespeare and Dickens, twisting plots and endings. (You'll see what I mean.)

And green-eyed femme fatale Marjorie Ann continues to lure men to their doom.

The people in Marcia's short stories get what they want – whether it's to stay in their home, or save their favorite stand of mangroves, or a weekend in New York City.

Marcia and her husband, Barry Talley, are sailors and spend part of the year in a cottage on Elbow Cay in the Bahamas, giving some of her stories offbeat tidbits about island life.

So step inside the worlds Marcia has made in *With Love, Marjorie Ann*, where you will meet determined husbands, fishermen who do more than kill fish, and of course, red-haired Marjorie Ann, batting her eyelashes at her latest husband.

Oh, and how is Marcia's own husband?

Barry's just fine.

At least he was the last time I spoke to him. Which has been a while.

Elaine Viets
February, 2025

With Love, Marjorie Ann

MAMA ALWAYS SAID it was a good thing that I was born beautiful because I must have been standing behind the door when the brains were handed out. I did okay in school—I never flunked a grade or got held back or anything—but it was a struggle. I just couldn't seem to pay attention for any length of time.

"Marjorie Ann!" Miss Saunders used to bark in tenth grade English. "You're wool-gathering again." I'd just smile and flash my dimples at her, pretending that I actually cared about David Copperfield and that ditsy little wife of his. I often think that if I hadn't been elected captain of the cheerleading squad or been crowned homecoming queen in my junior year, I probably would have dropped out of high school long before graduation. But I don't suppose Mama would have let me do it.

"Even pretty redheads need high school diplomas," Mama insisted. "Take something useful. You don't need algebra to balance a checkbook, for heaven's sake, so I don't know what earthly good it is. Take typing," she suggested. "Or home ec. Those are skills that will last you a lifetime."

Mama expected me to marry someone respectable and rich like a doctor or a lawyer. "A beautiful woman is a crown to such a man," Mama said, "an asset to his career." I didn't exactly object to the idea but pointed out to Mama that I didn't know where I was going to meet any doctors or lawyers when all the smart guys I knew were going off to college.

So Mama called one of her old sorority sisters who got me a job after graduation working as a receptionist at Williams and Lightner, a big accounting firm in Washington, DC. Mama thought it would be just a matter of time before one of the young VPs took a special interest in me. "There is very little difference between one man and another, but what little there is is very important," Mama told me. "I can't recall who said that, Marjorie Ann, but it's certainly something to consider." Mama was always quoting famous people, but she usually got confused over exactly who had said what.

In the end, I found Harrison all by myself while standing in line at the supermarket. He was very GQ—clean-cut, athletic and poised, with a wide, friendly smile and a big Rolex watch. Wearing gray trousers, a yellow tie and a leather pilot's jacket, he was waiting in line at the gourmet counter to buy a stuffed pork chop and a small plastic container of tiramisu.

Mama was thrilled. "A good man is the noblest work of God," she quoted for the umpteenth time. As she said this, I could see her gazing, almost tearfully, at the picture of Daddy on the mantel. Poor Daddy never got much older than that picture, taken when he was twenty-two. He would stand forever in that silver frame, looking smart and handsome in his army uniform, under a clump of ragged palm trees that Mama said was in Vietnam. Marrying a lawyer like Harrison is especially important for a girl like you, Marjorie Ann." Harrison had a lot of money because his father had been a self-made millionaire, although a fat lot of good it did him because he earned it by working himself into a fatal heart attack when Harrison was just ten years old.

At first, life with Harrison was a dream, like one of those romance novels you buy in the grocery store. For a month we honeymooned in Europe. We spent three days in our hotel room in Paris and never got out of bed except to go to the bathroom or ring for room service. We ended up in Italy where Harrison tipped the boatman to look the other way while we made love in his gondola, then he brought me home to a spacious townhouse in downtown Alexandria, Virginia.

I adored him. Harrison was six foot three and lean, with a tight stomach and cute little buns. Even with all the food we'd eaten on our trip, he looked like he hadn't gained an ounce. I thought I needed to weigh myself, but Harrison wouldn't have a scale in the house. "It's how you feel, Babe, and how good you look," he'd say, "not how much you weigh." We had just gotten up and he was standing in front of the full-length mirror, naked. He looked like a god. When he turned to me, I could see little square muscles under the skin on his stomach and the dark hair curling on his chest and I forgot all about cooking breakfast for a while.

Weeks later, when I complained that I hardly ever saw him anymore, Harrison explained that he had to make up for the time he had lost on our honeymoon by putting in longer hours. I'd rent videos or watch TV while he was at work, but there's only so much of "Dr. Phil" or "Oprah" you can take in one day. I tried to follow "Days of Our Lives," but even I'm not that brain dead.

"I'd like to go back to work," I confided to Harrison one evening.

"There'll be time for that later, Babe," he whispered into my ear. "We need our time together first."

"But Harrison," I begged, "it's so lonely when you're not here. Can't I get a job, please?"

"You have a job, Babe, an important job. Taking care of the house, the shopping, the meals, and me. Especially me." He held my face between his two broad hands and looked so deeply into my eyes that I felt like I was suffocating, as if we were two parts of the same person and I couldn't breathe until he did. It was easy to forget everything when Harrison looked at me like that.

One day when I went out for the mail, there was a catalog from the community college in our mailbox. It was addressed to "Occupant" so I nearly tossed it into the trash, but the picture on the cover caught my eye. Two students carrying books were walking side by side down a tree-lined path and in the background, near a modern building, a small group appeared to be discussing something important; but what I noticed most of all, was how happy everybody looked! I didn't have anything particular to do, so I brewed a cup of tea and took the catalog out onto the patio.

There were classes in computers and gardening and boating and cooking. They offered art courses of all kinds and even one in stargazing! Who would have thought college could be so interesting? I circled a few entries with a red pencil and when Harrison came home that night, early for a change, I mixed his scotch on the rocks just the way he liked it and waited until he got comfortable in his leather chair. I showed him the catalog, pointing to where I had marked a course about personal computers.

"I see all the PCs I care to at the office every day," Harrison said. "When I come home, I don't want to look at anything but you." He slipped his hand inside my blouse and gently massaged my back, making small circles down the bumps along my spine.

"But Harrison! I'm so bored cooped up in this house all day!"

He must have seen the disappointment in my face because he took the catalog gently from my hands. "Here, Babe. Let me look at that." He smoothed it out on the ottoman and leaned over, pulling me down to sit on his knee. "Now here's something useful: Classic French Cuisine." He smiled up at me, his green eyes full of mischief. "'Discover the best of France as you explore classical cuisine from some of its most famous regions.' I'd like that. Your cooking will be as beautiful as you are." His lips brushed my cheek. "I'll register for you right now, shall I?"

Harrison took a pen from his shirt pocket and filled in all the blanks, a single letter or number in each square: my name and address, social security number, VISA card number, the number of the course. "I'll fax it to them in the morning, okay?" And he folded the application in quarters and put it into the pocket with his pen. "Now, tell me what else you've been up to today."

But before I could answer he had put his mouth to mine with his tongue just tickling my lips in the way that makes me crazy.

Harrison was so good to me! I had a VISA and Master-Card with $500 limits that the bank paid off automatically every month. I used them to buy just about anything I wanted. When I shopped for clothes, though, Harrison usually tagged along. One day in Laura Ashley I found a beautiful black dress, a soft knit silk with a mid-calf skirt, jewel collar and long, slim sleeves. "Color, Marjorie Ann, color!" Harrison commented as I emerged from the dressing room. He looked out the shop window as if he were bored.

"But Mama always said I looked smashing in black!"

"Black is for fatties, Marjorie Ann. Try that red one over there."

I didn't want to argue with Harrison. I was afraid he'd change his mind about the cooking class, and if I couldn't go to class, I knew I would just die!

In our first class, Chef Martel demonstrated how to make *potage ambassadeur* and a dish I couldn't pronounce that turned out to be sirloin steak with green peppercorns. My first homework assignment was a gourmet breakfast of pancakes made out of wild rice flour. When Harrison came down to breakfast, I proudly arranged three pancakes on the plate in front of him. While I went to the refrigerator for the fresh-squeezed orange juice, he measured some butter off the stick in quarter-inch squares and put a huge pat on each pancake.

"Butter's so fattening, Harrison! Why don't you use just one of those big pats and spread it around a little?"

"Goddamn it!" He was in the middle of pouring the syrup when his hand shot across the table, knocking his plate to the floor. My perfect wild rice pancakes sat in a sad little pile next to the kitchen door while one-hundred-perecnt pure maple syrup from Vermont dripped down the woodwork.

"If I want to eat butter, Marjorie Ann, I'll eat goddamn butter!" and he stomped out of the house. I heard the gears crunch as he backed his MG out of the drive. When he came back an hour later, his hair smelled like McDonalds and he didn't speak to me for two whole days.

When Harrison gets this way he pouts and leaves me little Post-it notes all over the house. After I had finished crying and gotten up enough nerve to return to the kitchen, "Clean up that goddamn mess," with an arrow drawn pointing to the floor was stuck to the glass door of the microwave. It was my fault again. I should have known better than to nag him. Being a lawyer is such a high-pressure job. So I swept everything into the dustpan and threw it over the fence for the neighbor's dog. That night Harrison slept in the guest bedroom to teach me a lesson.

I called Mama and sobbed quietly into the telephone. I told her that we'd had a really big fight, but I didn't go into any details. "Don't snivel, Marjorie Ann." Mama sounded exasperated. "'The silliest woman can manage a clever man. As long as you remember that most men are like children, you know everything.' Coco Chanel said that, Marjorie Ann, so you think about it."

I thought about it for a very long time.

The next day, as a surprise, I got up early and made Harrison an *omelette aux fines herbes* and sent him to work with a packed lunch of *pâté de fois gras* with Carr's water biscuits to spread it on. I made smoked salmon and cucumber sandwiches with the crusts cut off and put a Post-it note in the little crease where the wax paper folded over the sandwich—"With love, Marjorie Ann."

When Harrison came home at 7:00, I was wearing the red slacks he'd bought me in Rome and a white blouse with a ruffled V-neck. I had used my VISA card to buy a bread machine and the air was full of the aroma of baking cinnamon bread. Harrison put down his briefcase as if nothing had happened, crushed me to his chest in a great hug and breathed into my hair, "God, you are so beautiful. I need you, Babe," and we made love right there on the oriental carpet in the foyer.

The following day, I surprised him with a Cadbury chocolate bar I'd been saving for myself. I carefully slipped the paper wrapper off and wrote on the foil with a toothpick: "With love, Marjorie Ann" and put the candy into his briefcase. For dinner I made puff pastry cases with salmon and asparagus topped with a special lemon butter sauce. Harrison said he loved it, which didn't surprise me one bit because the recipe called for almost a cup and a half of butter.

When my cooking class was over it was like going through withdrawal until I discovered all the cooking shows on PBS. One afternoon Jacques Torres demonstrated praline bars with orange confit. The next day they went to work with Harrison. When he got home that evening, Harrison told me that the guys he worked with were all jealous. They'd hang around the lunchroom, waiting to see what I'd packed for him each day. As he told me this, he was standing in the bathroom, ready to step into the shower.

"Do I look fat to you, Babe? Tell me the truth now," and he turned sideways in front of the mirror.

"Well, sweetie," I said, "there are those little love handles—" and I watched in the mirror as his handsome, smiling mouth turned into a mean, thin-lipped line and the back of his hand stung my cheek because I didn't see it coming and wasn't able to duck in time. It was my fault for teasing him like that, I suppose. He must have been more worried about his weight than I thought. While Harrison showered, I whipped up a pan of lemon pudding cake, a favorite recipe I'd gotten from his mother that was practically foolproof.

Sometimes, though, I'd experiment with a dish that wouldn't turn out right. One evening I made such a mess of the pastry fritters with apricot sauce that after our company went home, Harrison called me stupid and shoved me against the wall so hard that I broke my elbow. I took Tylenol for the pain and remembered what Mama once said when she was teaching me how to be clever with a needle—"A stitch in time saves nine." I never thought it might mean saving stitches in me.

Mama taught me that if you look inside a pair of trousers where the waistband joins the lining, there's always a bit of extra cloth at the back, right between the two belt loops. A few snips, a few stitches will give a little more room in the waist and a careful pressing with a steam iron will hide all traces of your work. I fixed Harrison's trousers that way, but didn't bother telling him. I figured it was one less thing he needed to worry about.

Finally when there was no cloth to spare in the seams, I bought identical trousers a size larger, snipped out the labels and sewed the old size 32 labels into the new size 34 pants. While I stitched the labels in, I watched a Jacques Pepin rerun on TV, so Harrison got smoked pork with mustard-honey glaze and braised sour cabbage for dinner. Dessert was a chocolate mousse with hazelnuts and whisky. I stuck a little toothpick flag on top of the mousse and printed, "With love, Marjorie Ann," on it.

When he had finished eating, Harrison folded his napkin carefully and placed it beside his plate. "You take such good care of me, Babe. That dessert was a masterpiece!"

The day Harrison began to complain that the laundry couldn't possibly shrink his oxford cloth shirts so badly, I packed him a plastic container of caramelized fresh plums with prune tart Armagnac and wrote, "With love, Marjorie Ann" in black magic marker on the lid. Then I went to Brooks Brothers and bought some shirts with 16-inch collars and sewed the labels from his 15-1/2 inch collars inside.

* * *

Harrison keeled over in the courtroom last Monday. It was a heart attack, the doctor said. His coronary arteries were clogged with plaque, very surprising in such a young man, particularly as he seemed to be in such good physical condition. But he didn't suffer much, they told me. He was probably dead before he hit the floor.

Mama cut short a vacation in Cancun and flew home to help with the arrangements, her nose all red and her eyelids puffy from crying. While she was at the funeral home picking out Harrison's casket, I ordered a wreath of spring flowers. I asked the florist to put in poppies, like we'd seen in France, and to add a bright red ribbon and write "With love, Marjorie Ann" on it in gold.

Then I got my outfit together. I laid my black velvet hat with the veil next to my black patent shoes on Harrison's side of the bed, then pulled the black Laura Ashley dress out of my closet where it had been wrapped in a plastic garment bag and hidden under a green velour bathrobe that Harrison had ordered me to throw away. When I slipped the dress over my head and smoothed the soft fabric over my hips, I knew that Mama had been right. I looked smashing in black.

She was right about something else, too. The way to a man's heart is through his stomach.

For Sale by Owner

STANLEY VIEWED THIS the way he did having an appendectomy or paying income taxes — something you had to do. Grin and bear it. He stood at the customer service counter of *The Jefferson County Pilot* sucking on the end of his pen, studying a pre-printed 4 x 5 index card as if it were written in Serbo-Croatian instead of his native English.

From her seat near the water cooler, his wife, Millie, glared at him. Sweat had soaked through the front of her pink cotton blouse and she dabbed at her face with a ragged tissue. Flecks of white clung to her damp forehead, but Stanley didn't intend to mention it.

"Mr. Hudson." Betty Sue leaned toward him over the counter and transferred her gum from one side of her cheek to the other with her tongue. "If you get that card filled out in the next ten minutes, we can get your ad in the Thursday edition."

Stanley gazed up at her with tired, gray eyes. "Do I pay you now?"

"Five lines, five days, five dollars," Betty Sue drawled. She slapped the Formica in front of her with a flat palm. "Cash on the counter." Stanley scribbled with his ballpoint pen on the back of the card to get the ink flowing, then began filling it out in neat, block letters:

FOR SALE BY OWNER, SPACIOUS BUNGA-
LOW ON LOVELY LOT, 3-BR, 2BA, MOD KIT,
CAC, W/W CARPET...

While Stanley considered what to write on the fifth line, Betty Sue busied herself by thumbing through an untidy Rolodex. GAS FIRE IN LR Stanley concluded.

Stanley smoothed out a crumpled five dollar bill on the stained and pitted counter, placed the completed card on top of it and slid them both toward Betty Sue's impatient, well-manicured fingers. Before Stanley had time to turn around, she had snatched them up and disappeared through a door in the back.

Millie gathered up her shopping bags and struggled to her feet. As he held the door open for her, Stanley could feel the cold air being pumped out by a single, struggling air-conditioner rush past him and into the street.

"It's about time!" Her face was dangerously red. "I thought you'd never finish. Anyone would think you were Ernest Bloody Hemingway, writing your next novel."

Stanley crossed to their car. "Well, I *did* it, didn't I? Come on. Let's go."

Millie climbed into the passenger seat, drew the seatbelt across her chest and held it there for a moment without fastening it. Stanley observed this maneuver in silence and found himself imagining an accident on the way home with Millie hurtling through the windshield at fifty miles per hour, still grasping the buckle of her seatbelt.

"I'm not sure I want to sell the house," he said for the hundredth time.

Millie scowled at him, a look of exasperation deepening the wrinkles between her eyes. "You're old, Stanley. I'm old. You know we won't be able to manage the stairs or keep up the yard work much longer." Stanley heard the seatbelt click into place.

At the stoplight at the intersection of Main and Jefferson, Millie pulled down the sun visor and reapplied her lipstick with elaborate care. "Anyone would think you weren't looking forward to seeing your only daughter more often." She flipped the visor up with a snap, leaned back against the headrest and closed her eyes. "I *like* Florida."

Florida. Stanley thought that if he heard one more word about Florida he would puke. He grunted and turned right at the stoplight, heading down Jefferson Street. Heading home.

***

Response to the ad wasn't overwhelming. Thursday night the telephone rang only three times. One caller wanted to know if the master bath included a Jacuzzi. Stanley sputtered and laughed so hard into the receiver that the caller hung up. Just after dinner, Millie took a call from a couple in Perry County and arranged to show the house the following day.

Hours before their appointment, Stanley began experiencing a sense of loss, as if the house had been sold and he and Millie were already on their way to Boca Raton and the seaside condominium Carol had picked out for them. While Millie vacuumed like a madwoman and fussed every time he put a glass down, Stanley fretted and prowled unhappily about the premises as if visiting everything for the last time — the blue-flowered wallpaper in Carol's bedroom that they had picked out and hung together one rainy January afternoon; the pencil marks on the kitchen door where Carol had stood each year on her birthday, back straight, stretching tall while he steadied a ruler on her head and recorded her transformation from a chubby tot into a lanky teen; and in the garden, his roses. How could he leave the tall, warm-pink Queen Elizabeth, the orangey Tropicana, the deliciously fragrant red Chrysler Imperial, the salmon pink Chicago Peace or the white Pascali that had been Carol's gift to him on his seventieth birthday?

By Sunday, no one had visited but the couple from Perry County and only two telephone calls, one from a telemarketer, had interrupted their weekend routine. On Tuesday, the first day the ad was scheduled not to appear, Stanley's mood noticeably improved. Millie could hear him whistling in his workshop which was tucked into a corner of the basement. That's why he didn't hear the doorbell when it rang.

"Stanley!" Millie was calling from the top of the basement stairs. "Stanleeeee!"

Stanley tightened the clamp that held together two sides of the birdhouse he was building, wiped his hands on a paper towel and trudged upstairs, following the sound of Millie's voice into the living room. There he found Millie bending over, demonstrating the gas fire to a petite, flame-haired woman wearing a microscopic black skirt and a close-fitting blouse the color of Key lime pie. Stanley shifted slightly to the right until he could glimpse the curved edge of a lacy black bra through the gap between the buttons

Millie straightened. "Stanley, this is Sheila Mason. She's interested in the house."

Sheila crossed the room unsteadily, her spike heels catching in the thick carpet, leaving raised tufts. The hand she extended in Stanley's direction was decked with rings. Too many bracelets for Stanley to count jangled at her wrist. "So pleased to meet you, Mr. Hudson. Your wife tells me you're moving to Florida. Such a nice state, Florida." She ran her hand absent-mindedly along the top of Millie's green velvet Victorian chair. "I used to vacation down in Clearwater, before Jake and I were divorced, that is."

In the adjoining dining room, Stanley watched while Sheila parted the red damask curtains that Millie bought at Montgomery Ward twenty-five years ago, the day Stanley got his last promotion at the refinery. Sheila peered out into the back yard, then turned to Stanley. "Are you selling the curtains with the house?"

Stanley looked confused. They hadn't thought about that.

"Of course we are!" Millie's voice, a little higher-pitched than usual, carried over the sound of the dishwasher kicking in.

Sheila wandered into the kitchen, examined the appliances and peered into the sink. "Garbage disposal?"

Millie shook her head. "Afraid not."

Stanley trailed behind in pained silence, watching Sheila's gold hoop earrings bounce back and forth against her chubby neck as Sheila and his wife strolled down the hall to Carol's old bedroom. "This is perfect for my office, Millie. Of course this hideous wallpaper will have to go." She waved an arm.

Stanley stepped aside to let them pass, a cold hard knot steadily tightening in his chest.

Sheila paused at the door leading to the basement. "Closet?"

"No, that's the basement. Not much to look at down there, I'm afraid. Just Stanley's old workbench and a dirt floor."

But Sheila had already found the light switch and was half-way down the stairs. "Too bad the basement's unfinished." She leaned over the wooden railing, her skirt riding high over her thighs. "This would have made a fine family room."

From a step near the bottom, she regarded them with a wistful smile. "We never had any children, Jake and I. Maybe that's why he took up with ..." She chuckled. "But I made him pay, though. Cash enough in the divorce to buy just about any house I want." Stanley saw her teeth gleam in the stark light of the unshaded bulb. "Is there someplace we can sit down?"

When it was all said and done, in spite of the home's numerous deficiencies, which she painstakingly enumerated on a sheet of lined notebook paper, Sheila offered them the full asking price. The neighborhood was quiet, she said, and near her health club. "I'll have my lawyer contact you."

Stanley signed some papers and accepted a check for the deposit without any obvious show of reluctance, but stared at it for a long time after she had gone. The figures seemed to vibrate before his eyes: $16,400. Sixteen thousand four hundred and no one hundredth dollars and the signature, Sheila Kenny Mason in a bold, elegant hand with the "Y" looping through the numbers printed at the bottom of the check.

"What do I do with this?"

"Put it in the bank, Stanley. Don't be such an idiot."

Stanley removed his tweed cap from the hook beside the back door, planted it on his balding head and wandered down to the bank on the corner only two and a half blocks away. Alison, his favorite cashier, regarded him curiously as he endorsed the check and slid it across the counter. She fixed her intelligent blue eyes on the signature and then looked up at him sideways through a fringe of frizzy blond hair. "Jeez, Mr. Hudson. You win the lottery or somethin'?"

"Sold the house. Me and the wife are moving to Florida." The words surprised him and his voice sounded strange, as if they were coming out of someone else's mouth.

"No kidding! I went to Florida once. Disney World." Her fingers danced over the keys of her adding machine. Stanley watched as it spit out a receipt. That's the trouble with Florida, he thought as he plodded home. Too many tourists. A whole damn state designed by Walt Disney. What would he do down there, for Christ's sake? Millie could shop with Carol, she could play bridge, but if they expected him to trade in his bowling ball for a tennis racquet or a bag of golf clubs, they were crazy.

By the time Stanley returned home, the Mason woman had called and Millie had set a closing date in one month's time. They'd have to visit some fancy lawyer's office downtown. Millie relayed this message jubilantly. She had already pulled everything out of the hall closet and was sorting through it. His favorite fur hat lay on top of a pile of woolen garments that included his U.S. Navy bridge coat and a comfortable, well-worn, red plaid hunting jacket. Millie patted the pile. "We certainly won't be needing these anymore," she crowed. The raccoon coat she had inherited from her mother, Stanley noted sourly, was in the "Keep" pile.

Stanley saw his life spinning out of control. He felt as if he had boarded a speeding train, doomed to watch the scenery whiz by, powerless to get off. "Maybe her financing will fall through," he offered hopefully.

"Stanley, weren't you listening? Ms. Mason is paying cash. She got it in her divorce."

"Well, don't count your chickens before they sign on the dotted line," Stanley shot over his shoulder as he left Millie to her sorting and descended to the basement. Only when the last coat of red paint had been carefully smoothed over the roof of the birdhouse did he turn out the lights and climb wearily up to his bed.

***

Millie had gone on an overnight bus trip to Mall of America with her book lovers' club when Sheila showed up unexpectedly three weeks later to measure for draperies. This time she wore a turquoise jump suit in a noisy, puckered fabric that went *swish-swish* when she walked. A large, polished pink stone on an elaborate silver chain bounced against her breasts as she stooped and stood and stretched. "Here, hold this for me a minute, will you, Stanley?" Her mouth widened in a smile, revealing straight, white, lipstick-smudged incisors. Before he could think to refuse, Stanley found himself holding the dumb end of the tape measure, standing stupidly at one end of the living room windows while Sheila circled the sofa to the other end, pulling the flexible tape along with her. "Sixty and a half," she observed, and jotted the figures down in a small, red notebook.

"I thought at first these curtains would do, Stanley, but just look at the sun damage." She extended a long, elegant finger, hooked it in the open-mesh weave and pulled down. The fabric tore easily, leaving a four-inch gash.

Stanley opened his mouth to protest, but nothing came out. She left him gaping like a beached fish and proceeded to the dining room. He heard the door to the china cabinet open and close and then her voice, unexpectedly strident, that grated on his nerves like a saw hitting a nail. "A chair rail. That's what I'm putting up in here. If you'd done that years ago, Stanley, you wouldn't have all these marks along the walls."

Stanley didn't want to look at any marks on the walls. From his spot in the living room he started to call, "Please, make yourself at home," but the last two words caught in his throat and came out *eh hum*. "I'll be in the basement if you need me," he said instead.

Stanley was repairing a kitchen chair and had just lined up the glue-covered rung with the hole in the leg when Sheila appeared at the foot of the stairs. Stanley gently tapped the rung in with his hammer.

"It's a shame you didn't finish the basement. The house would have been worth much more with a finished basement." She peered into the gloom beyond Stanley's workbench where dark shapes seemed to gather in the uneven light. She pointed at one of them. "Is that the hot water heater over there?"

If it hadn't been just the two of them standing there, Stanley would have sworn it was someone else who swung the hammer he was holding, someone else who heard it hit the back of her skull with a sound like a melon being dropped from a great height. It was Stanley who had to decide what to do, though, when Sheila crumpled to the floor with a quiet sigh and lay there, like a bag of gaudy laundry, eyes open and dark as coal in the dim light.

Stanley dug a hole to fit her small body, rolled it in and covered it over with dirt, spreading the extra dirt over the entire floor so that no one would notice. He had to go outside for the rake to smooth it out, the teeth leaving trails in the soil that Stanley fashioned into calming, swirled, circular patterns like he'd once seen in a picture book about Japanese rock gardens.

Later, when he thought about it, he was surprised how remarkably easy everything had been. It may have taken him a little longer to dig the hole than a twenty-five year old, he confessed to himself, but he found he was barely out of breath from the effort and his back didn't hurt at all. Nobody saw him as he drove Sheila's BMW to the airport and left it in long-term parking. Nobody noticed the ordinary little man who caught the shuttle bus to the terminal and rode the hotel van to the Holiday Inn where he threw Sheila's car keys into a Dumpster out back and walked home.

He certainly deserved this drink, Stanley thought, as he added ice to his bourbon and stirred it with an index finger. He carried the tall glass into the backyard where he settled his broad bottom into a plastic lawn chair. "Easy," he told his roses between sips. "Piece of cake." Stanley was proud that he had taken a small briefcase along so he'd look like a businessman coming home for the day and that he'd remembered to wear gloves and readjust the driver's seat of Sheila's car after he got out.

The following week, Stanley drove Millie in their 1988 Mercury to the underground parking garage of the law offices of Pride and Jacobson. Millie slurped at her coffee and Stanley had started on his third diet Coke with lemon, served to him by a nervous paralegal in a navy blue mini-skirt, before it was clear to everyone that Sheila wouldn't be coming.

"I'm so sorry, Mr. and Mrs. Hudson." The paralegal gathered her papers into a tidy pile and stuffed them into a yellow folder. "We'll have to reschedule the closing for another time. I can't imagine what's happened to delay Ms. Mason. As soon as we get in touch with her, I'll give you a call."

That phone call never came, of course, and after a time, Stanley learned that the contract was in default and that Sheila would forfeit her deposit. In silent celebration, Stanley called Progressive Construction and spent Sheila's deposit hiring them to pour a concrete floor in the basement, panel the walls and install drop lights in the ceiling.

While Stanley put the finishing touches on their new woodwork with a narrow brush, Millie sat on the basement steps and read to him from the newspaper. The police had found no trace of the missing woman, the article said, but because of the divorce and because nothing seemed to be missing from her apartment, the police were searching for her ex-husband.

Stanley smiled. "Don't you think the semi-gloss white enamel was a good choice?"

"Yes, Stanley, I do. It really brightens up the room."

***

Millie waited for Stanley in the same chair she had occupied several months ago. This time she wore a colorful, flowered shirt and matching shorts purchased at a specialty shop selling resort and cruise wear. Privately, Stanley thought that Millie's legs were not ready for prime time, but Millie didn't seem to care that her varicose veins stuck right out there for all the world to see. She thumbed through a magazine while Stanley tapped the "Ring for Service" bell and waited for Betty Sue to appear.

"Real sorry the first ad didn't get results for you, Mr. Hudson." She handed him another card.

Stanley shrugged and penciled on the 4 x 5 card:

FOR SALE BY OWNER, SPACIOUS BUNGA-
LOW ON LOVELY LOT, 3 BR, 2BA ... FINISHED
BASEMENT.

He turned to his wife who was reading a tattered *People* magazine with Goldie Hawn on the cover. "Say, Millie, if we don't sell
the house this time around, do you think we should add a patio?"

Conventional Wisdom

IT WAS AFTER eight in the morning, yet the day was still dark, the sky a uniform gray that shrouded the earth like a wet sweatshirt. It wouldn't be correct to say the rain fell; rather it hurled itself against the window, beading along the glass in plump droplets. Caroline watched one skitter down the oval pane, swallowing the smaller drops in its path. As her eyes gradually refocused further away, she observed the airport routine going on outside her window. It reminded her of a silent movie and she amused herself by providing dialog for a workman wearing ear protectors like bulky headphones as he waved the plane forward with laser wands. Lights reflecting from the terminal building shimmered in an immense puddle then shattered as a luggage train splashed through it. "So much for sunny California," Caroline thought. "I might as well have left my bathing costume back in London." She tried to remember whether she had packed an umbrella. She'd set one aside in her flat, ready to stuff into her bookbag. She recalled putting it in, then taking it out again in order to fit in a last-minute paperback. In her mind's eye Caroline saw the umbrella, still sitting on the hall table right where she left it. "Damn!" she whispered, turning her head deliberately away from the gloom outside the window. "Stephen had better be here to meet me."

"I beg your pardon?" Her seatmate, a scrawny woman clutching a Marks & Spencer carrier bag on her lap like a precious object, turned dark, serious eyes on Caroline.

Caroline blushed. "Oh, nothing. I was just hoping my brother wouldn't be late picking me up. He's flying in from New York." She sighed. "You can never tell with Stephen. He might be sitting in the coffee shop reading a book and have forgotten all about me."

"Don't worry, dear. I'm sure he wouldn't let his little sister down." She removed her reading glasses and dropped them into her bag.

"We're twins, actually," Caroline explained. "I'm slightly older, by a few minutes."

"Twins?"

"But we're not all that much alike." She fumbled for her purse. "Would you like to see?"

Her companion made encouraging noises so Caroline opened her wallet and flipped through the plastic sleeves containing her credit cards. She turned to a snapshot of a young man with a determined chin, squinting into the sun, his rather ordinary face split by an engaging grin. A shock of red hair was combed straight back over his scalp; an errant strand hovered over his left eyebrow. The woman's eyes moved from the photo to Caroline's face and back again. "I see what you mean, although there's a certain resemblance around the mouth."

"That was taken eight years ago when Stephen graduated from university." Caroline closed the wallet and stuffed it back into her book bag. "Stephen takes after our grandfather—they used to call him 'Carrot Top'—while I," Caroline tugged at a ringlet of her own dark brown hair. "I'm supposed to look like my grandmother." Caroline settled back into her seat and waited for the captain to turn off the seatbelt sign. In spite of the disappointing weather, she was anxious to get on with her journey. Anything was better than sitting around in her flat feeling sorry for herself, hoping that something interesting might happen. After the accounting firm she worked for had declared her redundant, Caroline had retreated to Swallow's Nest to be comforted by home cooking and buoyed by her mother's supportive and upbeat attitude. She'd thought about visiting Rosalie in New Zealand, but a visit to her sister was a nonstarter unless one of the jobs she'd applied for actually came through.

"Are you going to *MysteryCon?*" the woman asked.

"Hmm?" Caroline glanced up. The woman pointed. "I couldn't help noticing your bag."

"Oh!" Caroline guessed her bookbag was, so to speak, a dead giveaway. Against the black silhouette of a revolver, last year's *Mystery Con* logo was printed in stark white letters. She smiled. "Yes I am, actually. My brother and I are presenting the Blenkinsop Partners in Crime Award." Noticing the woman's puzzled expression she quickly explained, "It goes to the best crime novel featuring a detecting duo."

"You mean like Holmes and Watson? Or Hart to Hart?"

Caroline nodded. "Exactly."

"I never read mysteries myself," her seatmate stated flatly. "But I watch that Jessica Fletcher on TV." She bit her lower lip thoughtfully. "Blenkinsop! That's a funny name for an award."

Caroline grinned. "Isn't it? It's related to a practical joke my grandmother once pulled on my grandfather. My uncle Derek established the award in their honor." Caroline heard the *ding* of the seatbelt signal and the clicking of hundreds of buckles as passengers leapt up and scrambled for their bags in the overhead compartments. Caroline waited for her seatmate to step out, then snaked down the aisle behind her, through the business and first class sections, past the flight crew muttering their *buh-byes*, and along the passageway into the terminal.

As she had feared, Stephen was not at the gate, nor anywhere in sight. Caroline loitered for a few minutes near the bank of telephones, shifting from foot to foot, searching up and down the concourse for her brother's familiar face. After ten minutes, she gave up and followed the crowd to the baggage claim area. She watched a bag of golf clubs go three times around on the carousel before her own flowered suitcase eventually appeared. She set it on its wheels, pulled out the handle, and dragged it and herself into the gloom of the San Diego morning.

Caroline's usually cheerful face was still set in a scowl when the blue and yellow SuperShuttle deposited her in front of the Puesta del Sol on Mission Bay. She made her way to the reception desk and checked in. "Are there any messages for me?" '

The desk clerk tapped at his keyboard, studied the screen for a few seconds, then shook his head. "Sorry, Ms. Greene."

Caroline shouldered her bookbag and leaned once more against the counter. "Has Stephen Greene checked in yet?"

The clerk executed a few additional keystrokes, then, happy to please her at last, exclaimed, "Oh, yes." He pointed toward the restaurant. "You can use the house phone over there to call his room, or if you prefer, I could take a message for you."

"No, thanks," Caroline said. In the past hour she had dredged up hundreds of four-letter words with which to blister Stephen's ears, but this relentlessly perky fellow seemed only a decade on the north side of *Sesame Street*. Certain words beginning with the letter *F* might not be in his vocabulary yet.

Caroline headed toward the elevators, weaving through the lobby crowded with nametagged conventioneers who sat on every chair and sprawled on every sofa, purses, brief-cases, and bookbags heaped at their feet. Through a haze of cigarette smoke, Caroline noticed that the lobby was decorated with dozens of Halloween pumpkins, their elaborately carved faces grinning at her from the planters that divided the lobby into more intimate conversational areas. She smiled in spite of herself, feeling immensely cheered. As she passed the last alcove, one pumpkin head stood up.

"Stephen!" Caroline dropped her bookbag, controlling the urge to hit him with it. "Where on earth have you been?"

"Waiting for you, ducks."

"You were supposed to meet me at the airport, you dunce!"

"I thought we agreed to meet at the hotel."

"Airport, Stephen. We said the airport. Honestly, you do try my patience." She pushed her suitcase toward him. Stephen grabbed the handle, then kissed his sister on the cheek. "Sorry for the confusion, love, but all's well that ends well. Have you had anything to eat?"

"Nothing to speak of, except for the peanuts they gave me on the plane."

The elevator arrived and carried them to the tenth floor. "I'll make it up to you," Stephen promised. "Freshen up and meet me in the lobby and I'll feed you a proper meal." He checked his watch. "In thirty minutes." The elevator doors closed leaving Caroline alone in the hall a good two hundred feet from the door with her number on it.

Once inside her room, she pressed a hot washcloth over her face then leaned close to the mirror and examined her gray eyes for puffiness. Satisfied to see little sign of jet lag, she fluffed up her flattened hair with her fingers, applied some lipstick, and returned to the lobby. Having ten minutes to kill before Stephen was scheduled to appear, she registered for the conference, pinned her nametag on her jacket, found a vacant table near the lobby bar, and ordered some tea.

"Hello. Mind if I sit down?"

Caroline glanced up from the *MysteryCon* program booklet she was reading and shifted her chair a few inches to the right. "I'm saving a chair for my brother, but the others aren't taken." The man standing before her wore chinos and a striped shirt under a denim jacket. His lank, yellowish hair was caught back into a ponytail and he carried a backpack. Caroline stole a peek at his nametag—Lawrence Townsend from Alexandria, Virginia.

Mr. Townsend settled himself into the chair and studied Caroline over the tops of his round, steel-framed glasses. "You an author?"

Caroline smiled. "Not exactly. I'm one of the presenters."

Townsend patted his backpack which now rested at his feet. "I'm here to meet my editor."

Caroline noticed no author ribbon attached to his name-tag. "Really? Have I read anything you've written?" She smiled brightly.

Townsend gazed at her shyly from beneath long, pale lashes. "I'm not exactly published yet, but I hope to be soon." He leaned over and rummaged in his backpack. "This book, do you know it?"

Caroline groaned inwardly, recognizing a popular selfhelp book widely advertised on a home shopping channel by its author, the flamboyant Jeremiah P. Jackson. *Write It! Sell It!* screamed at her in raised, red letters from a cover otherwise unadorned except for a head-to-toe shot of the author in an Armani suit, holding a copy of that self-same book and grinning toothily.

"I've read the reviews," she admitted at last.

"It's my bible." Townsend unzipped the breast pocket of his jacket and extracted a small, square notebook. He showed Caroline page after page of neat columns containing notations in infinitesimal print, the columns dotted with checkmarks. Caroline sipped her tea and nodded mechanically while Townsend rattled on about how he hoped to get published by following the author's advice. He'd attended conferences, networked with authors, schmoozed with publishers, and so on and so on. Caroline found herself growing sleepy. If Stephen didn't appear within the next five minutes, she decided, she was going to ditch this bore and eat alone.

"I've written a mystery based on my experiences in the Gulf War," Townsend told her.

"Hmm." Caroline returned to studying her conference program, hoping, vainly, that he'd take the hint.

"Started writing in a foxhole in the desert. Wrote much of the rest on the Metro riding to my job at the Pentagon. But then I said, what the hey! Decided to take a leave of absence to finish up. Been living off my savings."

Caroline regarded Townsend with a sudden spark of interest. "Must have been hard on the wife and kids."

"Ex-wife," he said. "No kids." His face grew serious. "I have it all planned out." He turned the notebook in Caroline's direction. "See, here's where I've checked off all the steps in getting an agent."

"I hear it's hard to get an agent."

"Not really. Just followed what the man says in here." He fanned the pages of his "bible" with an ink-stained thumb, stopping about half-way through. "He suggests reading the acknowledgments in books written by authors you admire. They usually thank their agents. Then you come to conferences like this and contrive to meet them." Townsend's eyes swept the bar. "There are lots of agents here right now."

"Clever," said Caroline.

Townsend shrugged. "It's all in the book. Got my agent at *MysteryCon* last year and he sent my manuscript out to several editors. This particular editor's had my book for three months."

Caroline was searching for a reply when she saw, with relief, Stephen's tall figure approaching. She stood. "Well, good luck..." She looked pointedly at his nametag, "... Larry."

Townsend smiled up at her. "Thanks, Caroline. But I have a feeling this one's practically a done deal!"

Stephen hustled Caroline quickly away from the lobby bar and into the restaurant. "Why were you talking to that kook?"

"He wasn't a kook. Just some guy desperately trying to sell his book."

"I don't know about that, Caroline. He looked rather shady to me. While I was waiting for you earlier, I overheard him talking to someone on the telephone. All very hush-hush and Tom Clancy-ish. 'Meet me in the lobby bar, I'll be wearing glasses and carrying a backpack' kind of stuff." Stephen studied the menu while they waited for the hostess to locate a table for two. "Wonder whatever happened to the good old days when you wore a red carnation in your lapel and carried a copy of *The New York Times* folded under one arm?"

Stephen carried on with his spy-among-the-fans-and- authors theory. Caroline half-listened until she felt the soft jab of his elbow in her ribs. "Hot-cha!" Stephen croaked. A certain well-endowed writer of American mystery cozies, clad in a low-cut blouse and a tea towel passing for a skirt, squeezed between them. She held a wine glass by the stem between her thumb and forefinger.

"Ha!" Caroline chided. "I'm surprised you notice anything going on around you."

"I'm a man of many talents, my dear. Why just now I've noticed that our wait for a table is over. Mavis!" Stephen grabbed Caroline's hand and dragged her through the crowded restaurant to a table near the window, already occupied by a pair of diners. Caroline observed with pleasure that the table overlooked the bay. Outside the clouds had broken up and bright sunlight was transforming the day into a Kodacolor postcard.

A middle-aged woman, attractive in spite of a thatch of too-black hair, beamed up at Stephen as he bent over the table and kissed the air next to her cheek. "Mavis! Good to see you. And George! How are you doing, old bean? I'd like you both to meet my sister, Caroline. Caroline, George writes those true crime books our brother Andrew is so fond of reading." Stephen snatched two vacant chairs from an adjoining table and Caroline soon found herself sandwiched between Stephen's friends. She hoped the waitress had noticed their arrival because the sight of the Belgian waffle sitting on the plate in front of George, decorated with fresh strawberries and dollops of heavy cream, was making her stomach rumble noisily.

"How's tricks, Mavis?" Stephen inquired while waving a hand in the direction of a passing waitress. Mavis slapped her forehead, a look of mock panic on her face. "Overworked, as usual. Spending most of my time dealing with the merger and my conglomerate bottom-line bosses. Publishing's a crazy business now, not like the old days." She tapped the contents of a pink packet into her coffee, stirred, and tasted it. "Thank God I've got a capable assistant."

George raised his water glass and said, "To the indispensable Tiffany Carswell!"

Mavis plucked a pair of reading glasses from where they rested on top of her head, settled them on her nose, and peered at her watch. "Can't imagine what's keeping her. She was already dressed when I left the room." She scowled. "The bean counters strike again, Stephen. Never thought I'd be bunking with my assistant." Mavis relaxed into her chair, enjoying the last of her coffee. "But the girl's a jewel. Don't know what I'd do without her."

"Knows better than to call in sick every Monday like the last one you had?" Stephen teased.

Mavis closed her eyes and shook her head. "Don't remind me!"

A waitress had finally appeared to take their order when Mavis stood and laid her napkin on the table. "Well, it's been fun, folks, but I gotta go. My panel starts at noon. Coming, George, or do you leave me to face the unpublished masses alone?" She departed in a cloud of White Diamonds with the faithful George at her heels.

Stephen picked up the copy of *USAToday* that George had left behind and began reading aloud from the "Money" section. Caroline, who was used to having the news interpreted for her by her brother, munched happily on a piece of dry toast. She was half-way through her California fruit cup, wondering which of the panels she was going to attend, when a large black object hurtled past the window behind Stephen's head, glanced off the flowering shrubbery, and crashed to the terrace below. "My God!" a waitress screamed. "Somebody's fallen!"

Caroline, her stomach in turmoil and her brunch quite forgotten, rushed outside with the other diners and hovered at the edge of the gathering crowd with Stephen's arm wrapped protectively around her. Paramedics arrived within a few minutes and were attempting to revive the victim. From the pool of blood underneath the woman's head and by the odd angle of her neck in relation to her shoulders, Caroline was skeptical. But then, she had never seen a dead person before.

Sirens screamed, followed in short order, by the police. "She was pushed!" a man at the edge of the crowd shouted when the first officer appeared. "I saw him. Up there!" The witness waved a wild finger in the direction of the balcony. Caroline's eyes followed. The balcony stood empty, but hanging plants dangled in ragged tendrils from where they had been torn away when the woman went over.

Two uniformed officers held the crowds aside, making way for the EMTs carrying the victim on a stretcher. Caroline swallowed a sob as they passed. An oxygen mask covered the woman's beautiful, surprisingly serene and unmarked face. The sea breeze ruffled her ash brown hair and lifted the nametag clipped to her jacket.

Caroline shuddered, then clutched Stephen's arm so hard he winced. "Stephen! I've got to talk to the police! Now! I think I know who pushed that young woman and why."

* * *

"So that's how it happened." It was after dinner and Caroline sat with Stephen and George in the lobby bar where a Jack-o-lantern grinned mischievously from the planter behind her brother's head. Stephen stirred his martini. "Clever of you to notice the nametag, Caroline."

"Well, I knew the person on the stretcher wasn't the real Mavis Grant because we'd just had brunch with her! Tiffany must have thought she'd be doing her boss a favor by giving Townsend the bad news about his rejection. Mavis said when she went to brunch she left her nametag sitting right next to the telephone. So when Townsend called the room..."

George shook his head. "Mavis told me she'd never met the bloke, just talked to him on the phone. She's despondent, poor old dear. Claims it will be impossible to replace the girl."

George stared into his lager, a look of profound sadness on his suntanned face. "Want to know the ironic thing? Mavis said that chap's book wasn't half-bad. Needed a bit of punching up is all. But he was such a colossal pain in the ass—calling her up two or three times a week—she'd decided to give it a pass."

* * *

A few weeks later, in Stephen's New York apartment, Caroline took a brown envelope out of a desk and addressed it in a loopy, flowing hand. Stephen observed his sister in silence, watching over her shoulder as she affixed six stamps to the envelope. "San Diego Central Jail? Caroline, are you crazy?"

Caroline looked up, a half-smile on her lips. "Paradoxical, really. When 'Mavis' rejected his novel, Townsend flew into a rage. It wasn't part of his plan, you see. But now, think of all the time he'll have to write." She picked up a copy of *Writers Digest* and turned to a page she had marked with a yellow Post-it note. "Here, in the 'MARKETS' column." She tapped a neatly manicured finger on the page. "It says prison fiction is big these days." She slipped the magazine into the envelope and smiled up at her brother. "I think it's a good idea to encourage aspiring writers, don't you?"

Stephen took the envelope from her outstretched hand, licked the flap, and sealed it securely. "I do. And I'm sure Grandma and Grandpa would thoroughly agree."

To Catch a Fish

I DON'T WANT anyone to think that just because I'm sitting at the Pisces Bar & Grill every day with goddamn Saturn —rings and all— dangling over my head from a string that I believe any of that astrology crap. Sure, I read my horoscope in *The Island Packet* every day, but I read the obituaries, too, and I don't hear anybody saying I must be harboring some sort of death wish. The reason I'm sitting here, day after day, is because Mary Beth makes the best damn coffee in the Bahamas, and that's no lie.

Of course, she serves advice with her cappuccino. "When you gonna get a real job, Hon?" (She calls me "Hon," although my real name's Stuart.) "You know you'll never make any real money with that old boat of yours."

Mary Beth is right. All I want to do is write, but until I sell my novel to the movies—ha, ha, ha, pardon me while I laugh— I gotta take it as I can get it, which means sitting in the Pisces Bar & Grill most days at noon and dinner time, nursing a sandwich and a coffee, and scribbling in my yellow, college-ruled, three-subject notebook.

Mary Beth's place started life as a conch shack, growing higgledy-piggledy over the years until it morphed into an open-air restaurant, sprawling untidily over the Swiss-cheese limestone that makes up the island of Bonefish Cay. There's a hand-painted sign swinging from a wrought-iron rod out front—two fish chasing each other's tails—and inside, exposed pipes and electrical wires snake around the ceiling, connecting all the lights and overhead fans, but everything's painted black so you aren't supposed to notice. She's got a menu written on a blackboard in colored chalk, except I hardly ever look at it any more. Grouper, mahi-mahi or conch, served with peas and rice and the best damn slaw—nothing changes. And Mary Beth has new age music playing—singing whales and that rain forest crap— but it doesn't dry up the creative juices like some I can think of. Whitney Houston, for example. The way she yowls, if a dog sounded that miserable, they'd put it down. But most days, when she sees me coming, Mary Beth switches off the CD so I can get some writing done.

This one day, I'm sitting there as usual, listening to the waves slosh against the shells piled outside the window, munching on a pretzel and trying to write my heroine out of some perilous corner she'd painted herself into when in she walks. Really. Patience Bledsoe, my heroine. Same hair, same eyes, same dimpled chin and tip-tilted nose. She was standing at the bar, studying the menu, so I knew she'd never been to the Pisces Bar & Grill before.

"A skinny latte," she says to Mary Beth behind the bar, just like Patience would have done.

I leafed back to the beginning of my notebook. It was like Patience had walked right off the page. I half expected to find a blank spot on page twenty-seven, but, no, she was standing right there at the bar, no doubt about it at all. I couldn't take my eyes off her, Patience, I mean. She had long hair the color of caramel syrup, and she'd braided skinny strands of it at each temple and fastened the braids at the back of her head with a silver barrette. Then she turned her eyes on me, gas blue and about as hot, and I had to thump my chest to get my heart beating again.

"New on the island?" Mary Beth asked.

Patience shrugged. "Just passing through." She picked up her latte, moved sideways to the fixings table and tapped a packet of sugar— the brown stuff—into it.

"Thanks for stopping in," Mary Beth said with a note of disappointment in her voice. I could see Mary Beth sizing her up. Hell, Mary Beth could probably tell by the way Patience stirred her latte, little finger sticking out like that, that she was a Capricorn ruled by Saturn with her moon in the tenth house. Give Mary Beth two days and she'd have your whole life mapped out—zodiacologically speaking.

I'm a Pisces, for example, although what the hell difference that has ever made in my life I couldn't say. I was married to a Capricorn once, which was supposed to be perfectly compatible—like beans and franks or rum and Coke—but she ran off with a day trader from Boca Raton, a Sagittarius, not a compatible sign at all, so go figure. Mary Beth says it's because Saturn was in my seventh house, but that's bologna. The day trader had money, and my ex always liked men with money because they had bigger, uh, toys.

But, I got over that a long time ago.

So, that's why I was sitting there in the Pisces Bar & Grill, sending telepathic messages to Mary Beth—find out her name—hoping she was tuned into the cosmos that morning, particularly since her dishwasher still hadn't shown up.

"Come back and see us," said Mary Beth.

Patience sipped at her latte, testing it. "Oh, I'll be back," she drawled, then pointed with her cup to The Blue Dolphin across the street, one of our island's few B&Bs. She strolled over to the window with her latte and sat down under a picture of the Maharishi Mahesh Yogi. Mary Beth liked to hedge her bets.

Patience unfolded a copy of *The Island Packet*, our local fish wrapper, spread it out on the table in front of her and began to read. I tried to get back to my writing, but now that the girl had stepped off the page, what could I do? I fantasized that huge chunks of my novel had disappeared—the cop would be arguing with dead air and Patience's boyfriend would wake up in a big, empty four-poster bed. Mama taught me it wasn't polite to stare, so I turned in my notebook to the courtroom scene and worked on Todd Blackburn's cross-examination for a while, looking up every now and then to make sure Patience — the real one— hadn't vanished. She hadn't One time she caught me looking at her and her eyes smiled at me over her cup. When I could breathe again, I smiled back. *Say something. Tell me your name.* But there must have been static in the ether that morning because Patience finished her coffee in silence. I watched as she tossed away her empty cup then strolled out the door and across the street. She disappeared into the Blue Dolphin, stayed inside about ten minutes, then left again, walking east along Queen Street toward the market. Good. No luggage.

I paid for my breakfast, waved to Mary Beth and took off for the Blue Dolphin. I stood at the desk and banged my palm on the bell until Mrs. Brozman waddled out. "That girl," I said, "the one that just left, with hair like honey. I think I went to school with her. Patience somebody?"

Mrs. Brozman's white curls trembled. "Nope. Her name's Lily. Lily Farmer."

Lily. I stood on the Blue Dolphin's porch and rolled the name around on my tongue like fine wine. Lily. It suited her. Better than Patience, if you want to know the truth. I pointed my big, flat feet down the dock to my boat, powered up my laptop and did a Find and Replace—Patience replaced with Lily.

Lily scowled at the officer. Sounded okay.

With her heart pounding in her ears, Lily crouched behind the tree. That worked.

But I'd forgotten and set the blasted software to Replace All, so Captain Faraday showed remarkable Lily with the D.A. I leaned back in my chair and laughed until I got a stitch in my side.

I had dinner with Lily that night, so to speak. She was already there when I arrived, sitting at my table under Saturn, eating a veggie club sandwich.

"Hi, Stu," Mary Beth called when I walked in. "What will it be? The usual?"

"No," I said, feeling reckless. Lily was doing that to me, pulling my chain in some cosmic way. "What about the portobello burger?"

"Sure thing, Hon." She plopped a bottle of Kalik on a paper coaster and slid the icy brew across the bar. I took a grateful swig and was just trying to figure out where to sit when Lily drawled, the voice of a goddess, "Stu? Why don't you join me?"

"How . . . ?" I stammered, wondering for a mad moment if I were wearing my bowling shirt with my name embroidered on the pocket when I remembered that Mary Beth had just shouted it out for everybody and his brother to hear. "Uh, sure," I bumbled—oh so suave I slipped my notebook from under my arm, threw it on the chair opposite Lily and sat down. "Thought I'd have to sit at the bar."

"No problem." She took a bite of her sandwich and chewed thoughtfully. "Mary Beth says it's because I'm a Virgo. Always trying to manage others."

"She's gotten to you already, huh?" I laughed out loud. "Usually takes a couple of days. She must like you."

Lily shrugged and sipped an iced tea, her plump lips forming a delicious "O" around the straw as she drew the amber liquid, slowly, into her mouth. I imagined the tea sliding over her rough, pink tongue and slipping down her gorgeous throat. My fingers itched for a pen, but it was tucked into the spiral notebook now digging uncomfortably into my butt like the princess and the pea. "Watch it," I said, my forehead feeling suddenly hot. "If she gets out the tarot cards, run like hell. It means she wants to adopt you."

Lily smiled around the straw. "I'll try to remember that, but

I don't think I'll be on the island long enough for the adoption to go through."

Even the arrival of my portobello burger, plump and juicy with melted mozzarella oozing over the sides of the bun, the whole delicious mess sitting on a bed of fat, hand-cut fries, did little to cheer me up after that news.

"Are you a vegetarian, too?" she asked suddenly.

"Huh? Oh, the burger. No, I just like it is all. I'm not into sprouts and bean curd, if that's what you mean." I laid down a fry. "Where are you from?" I asked her.

"Pittsburgh."

"What brings you to Bonefish Cay?"

"I needed a break."

"When do you leave?"

"In a week or two."

I munched on a fry, trying to look blasé, hoping disappointment wasn't written large all over my face. I had this insane feeling that if I followed Lily around, my novel would write itself.

"I'm Lily, by the way."

"Huh?" I must have sounded a pretty dim bulb, then I remembered she didn't know I knew her name. "Nice name, Lily," I said, thinking it suited her much better than Patience.

"What do you do, Stu?" she asked.

I stared into the trap of her bottomless eyes. I felt the muscles in my tongue go slack. "Manage investments," I lied.

Lily jerked her head toward Mary Beth who was washing glasses behind the bar. "I have more confidence in astrology than I do in the stock market," she said, her blue eyes seriously boring into mine.

"If you could get the two of them in synch," I offered, stunned by the thought, "it could be dangerous."

"Uh huh," Lily said. "Dream on."

Mary Beth suddenly materialized at my elbow with a fresh pot of coffee. "Stu also runs a charter fishing business," she said. I was grateful that she didn't add that business was in a deep slump. Hurricane Floyd had wreaked havoc with the island and tourists were staying away in droves.

I pointed down the long pier to a thirty-two foot cabin cruiser tied up in a slip. "That's my boat." Reel Life was also my home, but I didn't tell her that. Or the fact I was fishing mostly for myself lately, trading my catch of mahi-mahi, grouper and snapper with local restaurants in exchange for meals like this. I sank my teeth into my burger.

"Mary Beth tells me you're a writer."

I nodded, my mouth full of cheese. She sat there, one eyebrow raised, waiting politely for me to swallow.

"Stu's writing a murder mystery," Mary Beth called out helpfully.

Lily smiled a slow, seductive smile. "If John D. MacDonald can do it, so can you, Stu," she said. "There's a memorial to the *Busted Flush* in Fort Lauderdale, you know."

At that precise moment I fell hopelessly in love with Miss Lily Farmer.

While I stared at her with a goofy expression on my face, Lily finished her sandwich, polished off her chips, laid a ten dollar bill on the table and slipped past me and out the door like a lavender-scented breath of spring. After she left, Mary Beth sauntered over with the coffee pot again. "What's the *Busted Flush*?" she wanted to know, refilling my cup.

"A boat. MacDonald's detective, Travis McGee, lived on it."

"Oh," she said.

"Of all the gin joints in all the towns in all the world, she had to walk into mine," I growled.

"Stu? Earth to Stu?" Mary Beth poked my arm. "Your eyes have glazed over."

"Sorry. I was busy channeling Bogart. Been receiving movie dialogue through my back fillings lately. Might be sun spots."

Mary Beth opened the *Island Packet* to the inside back page where the cartoons and crossword puzzle always appeared. With a stubby finger, she tapped the horoscope column. "Check out what Madame Zara has to say today."

"As if you didn't know," I chuckled. Mary Beth *was* Madame Zara. Wrote the silly column every day. It was probably the worst kept secret on the island.

Mary Beth ignored me. "Sudden romantic encounters are quite likely," she read. "Get out and mingle. You may find an ideal partner." She pushed the paper across the table until it rested against my cup.

I grinned up at her. "Maybe there's something to this horoscope business after all," I said.

* * *

The next morning, I got to the Pisces early. Lily hadn't come in yet and I was feeling unaccountably bereft. Mary Beth refilled my coffee, looking over my shoulder as I read my horoscope: Don't be shy. Turn on your seductive charm and make a play for that passionate partner you've been dreaming about.

"Go for it, Hon," she said.

I don't need to be hit over the head with a two-by-four. Over the next couple of weeks, I put Patience Bledsoe on the back burner and spent every waking minute with Lily Farmer, that bewitching lady from Pittsburgh, Pennsylvania. I showed her the Cays. We snorkled along the north shore of Man-o-War, got tipsy on rum punch slushies at Nipper's Beach Bar on Guana, and at the top of the red-and-white striped lighthouse in Hope Town, with the Sea of Abaco framing her lovely face, I tipped up her chin and kissed her lips for the first time.

We were looking forward to a romantic weekend in Port Lucaya when an old customer from Miami Beach called to book a week-long charter. At five hundred dollars per day, I could hardly turn the man down. So I picked him up at Marsh Harbor airport, packed him and his buddies aboard Reel Life and spent the next week with four beer-guzzling, cigar-smoking guys, each deliriously insane at being away from his bride. I was fishing, back-slapping, telling dirty jokes and peeing off the rail with the best of 'em, hopping from island bar to island bar and thinking that this male-bonding stuff is all well and good —especially with somebody else picking up the tab—but I'd trade it all in an island minute for one hour back home with Lily Farmer.

When I finally ditched my clients and hustled Reel Life back to her slip at the Pisces Bar & Grill, Mary Beth told me she hadn't seen Lily since I left. I called in at the Blue Dolphin and learned she'd checked out, leaving no forwarding address. Low as a dead man's blood pressure, I wandered the streets of Bonefish Cay looking for her, but Lily was so thoroughly gone that I almost convinced myself that I had made her up.

Except I hadn't, of course. As Mary Beth reminded me as she shoved a second cold one across the bar. "She wasn't for you, Stu. She's a Virgo."

"Virgo, schmirgo," I said.

"Let her go."

Easy for Mary Beth to say. She had a wife at home—good-looking, too—and before you start beating me about the head and shoulders for political insensitivity, it's Mary Beth who calls Kathy "the little woman," not me. I thought it'd be easier to fill up the big, black hole in my notebook than it would the big, black hole in my life.

Then I got the letter. Dropped through the hatch one day, plop on the galley table, envelope covered with stamps like seashells and written in her familiar backhand.

"Stu," she wrote:

> Please understand. I like you, I really do, but I've met this guy, Jack Browning, and we clicked right away. I hope you and I can still be friends. Love, Lily.

What else could I do? I dragged myself to the Pisces Bar & Grill and tried to fill myself up with the spirit of understanding.

By the third margarita, I came clean. "She's left me, Mary Beth. Run off with some bozo named Jack Browning."

Mary Beth swiped a damp rag across the bar. "God, Stu. Browning's twice your age and worth millions. Has a place over on Egg Island. Hell, he owns the whole island."

Holding my glass in both hands, I stared at her over the salted rim. "That's supposed to make me feel better? That's she's ditched me for some rich S.O.B.?"

"Better to find out now, rather than later," said Mary Beth philosophically.

"Yeah," I said and I thought about the way Lily's hair fell like a waterfall over her left eye and how small and soft her hand felt in mine and I wanted to put my head down on the bar and bawl.

Mary Beth pointed out that my horoscope said: Sudden romantic connections may be short-lived. Keep alert for deceptive statements. Just walk away. So I walked. I got over it. So much so, that a month or so later, when Lily hailed me on Channel 68 inviting me to Egg Island for dinner, I heard myself coolly accepting.

I put on clean chinos and my finest T-shirt, fired up the engine, cast off and pointed Reel Life down the channel and into the bay, curious as hell about the competition. At Egg Island, I expected to see Lily waiting for me at the pier, but two dockhands stood there instead, identically clad in tan shorts and blue polo shirts, waiting to help me slide Reel Life into a slip next to Browning's boat, one-hundred pretentious feet of gleaming wood and chrome, a yacht that made Reel Life look like something you sail around the pond in Central Park. His lifeboat, hanging from davits over the stern, was bigger than my boat. It was embarrassing.

"Thanks," I grunted to one of the guys as he caught my line and looped it in a neat figure-eight over a cleat. Browning's boat had Liquid Asset painted in large, gold letters on the stern. In smaller letters underneath the name it said Georgetown, C.I. A Cayman Islands registration. Why was I not surprised?

I grabbed a six-pack of cold brews and a fresh-caught, ten pound grouper—never let it be said that Stuart Anderson, model guest, had arrived empty-handed—stepped gingerly out onto the dock and hustled up the stone steps that led to Browning's villa.

Lily met me at the door, a fantasy in a crisp white cotton sundress, A red flower was tucked behind her ear, and her feet were bare. While I stood there like a dummy, clutching the beer and worrying that the fish might drip on the carpet, a maid appeared to relieve me of it. Lily kissed the air next to my cheek, grabbed my hand, and dragged me into the garden to meet her friend.

Jack Browning was old. Way old. They must have hauled him out of his wheelchair and propped him up with pillows just for the dinner. I managed to make it through the evening somehow, with Lily fetching and toting for the old fart between bites of her pasta primavera even though there was a houseful of servants to do it for her. Then I high-tailed it home and poured half a six-pack of Bud Lite over the Kansas City steaks, salad and red wine the old guy and I had eaten, not to mention the cognac. Next morning I had a hangover the size of a satellite map of Hurricane Floyd. Can't say I felt much like writing.

Two days later, my radio crackled to life.

"Reel Life, Reel Life, Reel Life. This is Liquid Asset. Over."

I was up on deck cutting new dock lines and melting the ends with my dad's old Zippo lighter so they wouldn't fray. I jammed my big toe painfully against a cleat as I hurried below deck to answer the call. "This is Reel Life," I panted into the microphone. "Over."

"Stu!" Lily's voice was high-pitched and hysterical. "Jack's sick. Real sick. We're taking him to the clicnic in Marsh Harbor. Can you meet me there? Please?"

"Sure," I said, grateful that my services were being required.

I powered up the engines and screamed across the bay, but by the time I got to the clinic it was too late for Jack Browning. I found Lily in the waiting room, tears streaking her face. "He's gone," she wept. "I can't believe it."

I handed her a napkin I had folded up in my pocket and she blew her nose into it, hard. "The nurse said the doctor would be out to talk to me soon."

We sat in silence for a while, knees touching, my hands cradling hers. "He took sick after dinner last night," she sobbed. "Nausea, vomiting, stomach cramps, diarrhea. I gave him some water, but he complained that the ice burned his lips. Oh, Stu, I'm so afraid they'll think I poisoned him or something." She looked up at me, her pale lashes beaded with tears. "He rewrote his will, Stu," she whispered. "And it's in my favor."

"Jeez ..." I began, but the doctor straight-armed his way through the swinging door just then. When Lily saw him, she leapt to her feet. I did, too. We stood there together, my arm wrapped protectively around her shoulder. "Ciguatera," the doctor told us. "Common in these parts."

'What's ciguatera?" Lily asked, tiny lines attractively furrowing her forehead.

"Fish poisoning," he explained. "Ordinarily, it's not fatal, but in someone so old and frail..." He shrugged.

"But, how?" she asked, dabbing at the corner of each eye with the napkin. "The grouper was fresh." She glanced at me sideways. "My husband said it was the most delicious ..." She choked back a sob.

"You get it from eating certain kinds of reef-feeding fish," the doctor explained. "Especially big ones at the top of the food chain like grouper, or amberjack and red snapper."

Lily squinted, clearly puzzled. "But restaurants serve those kind of fish every day! You can buy them in the market. How can you tell what fish is safe to eat and what isn't?"

"It's difficult," the doctor said, "because there's no effective test for ciguatera. But to be sure, ask any local fisherman. He'll know."

Lily's shoulder stiffened under my hand. Then relaxed. She leaned against me, curving her body slightly to fit mine. "I'll remember that," she snuffled.

Like I said, I'm not much into horoscopes, but when Madame Zara tells you plans may not go as you wish, so prepare for delays and make adjustments if you want to succeed— well, why take any chances?

Too Many Cooks

History is not what you thought. It's what you can remember.
—W.C. SELLER AND R.J. YEATMAN, *1066 AND ALL THAT*

MERAB WRAPPED HER fingers tightly around the neck of the burlap sack and, with her free hand, gathered up the skirts of her gown and scrambled over the stile. Once over the wall, she relaxed against the smooth stones, grateful for their warmth as it penetrated the light fabric of her cloak. She closed her eyes, turned her face toward the sky, and inhaled deeply, delighting in the sweet smell of new-mown hay baking in the afternoon sun. A blissful moment later, she glanced back the way she had come, the hint of a smile on her lips. It had been only a small incantation, after all, but powerful enough to topple that ruffian, to send him sprawling with a satisfying *splat*, facedown into a puddle of mud that hadn't been there only seconds before.

A pity she hadn't been able to remember the spell before that other rogue had hurled an egg at her. She picked at the yolk spots on her plain, gray gown. She shrugged—a small matter. They would hardly be noticed among the other stains—brown and tan and iridescent green—that speckled the panels of her skirt.

Dragging the sack and stepping high, Merab crossed the field. A soft breeze lifted her hair, sending the dark, tightly coiled strands dancing about her shoulders and drifting lazily across her cheeks. Overhead, a sparrow circled leisurely. "Later," she sang to the bird with a friendly wave of her hand. "Zipporah's expecting me and it doesn't do to keep Zipporah waiting."

The field ended at a dirt track deeply rutted by the wheels of the king's wagons. Merab followed the track for half a mile, then veered left at the three-trunked birch tree that marked the path through the wood to the cottage she shared with her sisters. "Cottage" was perhaps too grand a word for the elaborate lean-to of lashed timbers that made a shallow vestibule just outside the entrance to their true living quarters: a deep natural stone cave. In a sunny clearing to the left lay the garden, stoutly fenced to discourage the deer, and just beyond it, the hives.

As she emerged from the trees, Merab noticed white smoke drifting lazily from the roof hole and she feared she would be late for dinner. She slipped through the door and leaned, slightly breathless, against the jamb.

"There you are!" Zipporah set aside the mortar and pestle with which she had been grinding herbs for the stew, now cheerfully bubbling in an iron pot-hanging from a spit over the grate. She wiped her hands on her apron. "I was beginning to think I'd have to send Little Miss Feckless out to find you." She nodded toward the hearth where Merab's younger sister, Dymphna, sat on a stool busily shelling peas into her skirt. "As much good as that would have done."

Merab flinched as Zipporah snatched the sack from her hand and snapped, "Let's see what you've brought us today, sister." Holding the sack by the bottom corners, she upended it, sending a cascade of small parcels, wrapped in brown cloth and tied with rough string, spilling over the tabletop. Zipporah felt along the edges of the sack, then shook it vigorously until the last packet, a small leather pouch, dropped out. She began sorting through them. "Dried whelk, laver, lizard's toe, shark's tongue, wolf teeth ..." She looked up. "Where's the pepper?"

Merab picked up a twist of cloth, sniffed it, then placed it next to a small loaf of sugar. It wasn't always easy to separate the items they used for cooking from those they would need for spells. She sneezed.

"Bless you!" Zipporah muttered, barely pausing in her inventory. "Tiger gut, eye of newt..."

Merab froze as Zipporah untied the packet and fingered the small, dried pellets it contained. Newt eyes had grown so expensive that Merab had substituted toads' eyes for their slightly smaller and scarcer cousins. The bat wool she'd scraped from the inside of her own cloak, and although she couldn't say for sure, the Turk's nose the old leech had sold her that morning bore a remarkable resemblance to the nether end of a chicken. The pennies Merab had been able to save weighed heavily in her pocket, but oh! how she wanted a new gown. And how else to afford the fine wool, soft as eiderdown and blue as the Highland skies, she'd been admiring each week at the market?

While Zipporah refolded the packet of toads' eyes and continued sorting, Merab inched toward Dymphna, whose head was bowed, her face nearly invisible in the smoky room. She'd been oddly silent.

"Dymphna?"

Dymphna shuddered, and when she looked up, it was with red and swollen eyes. To Merab's utter astonishment, the girl's cheeks and chin were covered with a straggly beard the same cinnamon color as her hair.

"Dymphna!"

Her sister's face was a hirsute mask of misery. "It was the baldness remedy," she whimpered.

Zipporah's voice sliced through the haze like a scythe. "Silly hen got too close to the cauldron."

"You asked me to stir it!" Dymphna wailed.

Zipporah turned, hands on broad hips, eyes like currants in a plump Easter bun. "At least we know it works!" She threw back her head and roared with laughter, sending the chickens scurrying from under the table and into the yard.

Merab fished a small knife from her pocket. "Here. Let me cut it off."

"No!" Dymphna raised both hands. "I tried. It just comes back all the thicker."

Merab thought back to the big leather book the leech kept chained to his wall. She'd read something about this. "Southernwood boiled in barleymeal?"

"That's for pimples," Zipporah snorted. She shuffled across the room and loomed over the dejected Dymphna. "So much ado! It'll probably be gone by morning. In the meantime ..." She pointed toward a small table set in a corner near the cottage's only window. "There's the book and there's the quill. Write down the recipe before you forget."

Holding her skirt out before her, Dymphna struggled to her feet. She dumped the peas, bouncing and pattering, into a wooden bowl, then, dragging her stool along with her, crossed to the table and sat down. She turned the book to a fresh page and smoothed it out carefully with the flat of her hand. After a thoughtful moment, she dipped the quill into a flask of ink and wrote "Receipt for Baldness" in a precise, round hand.

Truth to tell, there weren't many recipes in the book. In the year since Squire and Mistress Weird had perished in a tragic encounter with a wild boar, leaving their three daughters with nothing save two gold coins and this rude cottage, the women had struggled to support themselves with spell craft, conjuring, dowsing, and the occasional exorcism. Hecate dropped in from time to time to offer advice, but Zipporah had little patience for the hag's old-fashioned ways.

"Surely, to be profitable, magic must be put to more practical use," Zipporah was fond of saying. "Moon drops!" she had sniffed after Hecate's last visit. "If I listened to her, we'd soon be dancing around our cauldrons like fairies in a ring!"

Under their older sister's guidance, then, they'd turned their eyes toward practicalities. Six months ago Merab had witched a well for Lord Lennox, and the news of her success had quickly spread. They'd had a recent commission from Lady Macbeth, and the baldness potion had been for King Duncan himself. "A royal charter!" Zipporah had enthused, rubbing her work-roughened hands together. Thinking about Dymphna, Merab hoped King Duncan wouldn't mind looking like a monkey.

Her musing was interrupted by the hollow pounding of hooves and the barking of dogs. The cat napping on the sill near Dymphna's scribbling hand arched its brindled back and hissed at something outside the glass. Zipporah was halfway to the door when the knocking began.

"Mistress! Open up!"

Merab's fingers curled tightly around the knife she still held while Zipporah reached for the broom, then cautiously lifted the latch. She eased the door open and, with one piercing black eye, peered through the crack. "Oh! It's you." Her shoulders relaxed and she threw the door wide to a young man Merab recognized by the badge on his tunic as a messenger from Inverness. "Come in, Zipporah held up a hand. "But wipe your feet first. I've just laid clean straw."

The messenger balanced unsteadily on their threshold, first on one foot and then the other, using the edge of his dagger to scrape layers of mud from his boots. "The Lady Macbeth sends her compliments," he wheezed. "She is riding this way and begs that you speak with her."

"We await her pleasure," said Zipporah.

Merab and Dymphna exchanged worried glances. Perhaps the potion hadn't worked. Soon they might be practicing their art from the bottom of the loch.

At Merab's invitation, the messenger dipped his drinking horn into a cask of barley water and drank deeply. Meanwhile, Dymphna threw another log on the fire and busied herself with the bellows.

But even before the messenger could drain his horn, Lady

Macbeth stood tall in the doorway before them. She wore a blue robe, trimmed with pearls, and an overskirt embroidered with fine silver thread. A silver fillet held a square of pale gauze in place over her hair, which Merab could see was the color of burnished gold. "Greetings, Weird Sisters." The hand Lady Macbeth raised in salute was milky white, the fingers almost too narrow and delicate for the heavy rings they wore. "I've ridden all the way from Inverness to thank you."

Zipporah whisked a stool from under the table and bid their visitor sit. Lady Macbeth complied, settling her skirts prettily around her. Then she leaned forward, her voice low. "On Candlemas Eve, while my husband's servants were occupied preparing their master for bed, I slipped the potion you concocted into my husband's wine. Later when I crept into his chamber ..." Astonishment sparkled in her violet eyes. "Never was there such a marvel! A veritable tent pole beneath the sheets!"

Lady Macbeth snapped her fingers and the messenger, who had been lounging negligently against the doorframe, sprang to attention. "See to the dogs," she ordered. The youth scurried away. After he had gone, the lady continued. "As my lord is so fond of saying, 'Drink provokes the desire but takes away the performance.' But not that night. Saints, no! I think he was nearly as astonished as I."

Her eyes alight with joy, Lady Macbeth laid a hand on Zipporah's arm. "And now, I am with child, Mistress Weird!" She stroked her belly. "And I desire that this child shall be King of Scotland!"

"But, Lady!" Merab exclaimed. "Your husband is Thane of Glamis. The Thane of Cawdor stands between him and the kingdom, and both the Thane of Cawdor and King Duncan still live!"

Lady Macbeth's lips drew back in a smile, her teeth flashing white in the gathering dusk. "Exactly."

Merab's hand flew to her mouth, stifling a gasp.

Lady Macbeth drew her cloak more closely around her. "There must be some incantation, some potion to aid in our noble purpose."

Zipporah aimed a silencing glance at Merab, then bowed to the Lady. "Your wish is our command, dear Madam."

Lady Macbeth's gaze fell on each of the sisters in turn, then she winked. "My husband will be abroad tomorrow, hunting with his nobles on the heath." She rose from her stool and glided to the door as if she wore wheels rather than boots. Zipporah followed, bobbing up and down like a cork.

At the door, Lady Macbeth turned. From beneath her cloak she withdrew a small leather purse, shook it so the gold coins it contained clinked dully together, then placed the purse on Zipporah's upturned palm. "See to it, then." She smiled. "I can be very, very grateful." Waving a beringed hand, she caroled, "Farewell, my lovelies!" and in a miasma of sweet Arabian perfume, she was gone.

Zipporah latched the door and fell back upon it, both hands, still holding the purse, pressed over her heart. "What a triumph!" Suddenly her eyes narrowed. "Dymphna! Where are you?"

Dymphna emerged from the shadow of the wardrobe. Zipporah skewered the hapless girl with her eyes. "You did write it down, didn't you? The impotence cure? Tell me you wrote it down."

Dymphna's shaggy chin dipped to her chest. "The quill needed sharpening."

"You didn't write it down?" Zipporah's face grew dangerously red.

Dymphna shook her head. "But I'm sure I can remember!" she added brightly. "I have an excellent memory." She closed her eyes for a moment, then began speaking, as if reading the formula off the inside of her eyelids. "Mandrake root ground with seed of lemon, a pinch of St. John's wort, blue salts from the pools in the Sildenafil Hills ..."

Zipporah's eyes grew hard. "How much salt?"

"I don't remember."

"A handful," Merab offered.

"And honey," Dymphna concluded. "That's all."

Zipporah sighed. "I pray you are right, sister. If not, it could take another one thousand years to recreate that formula!"

* * *

The next morning, two hours after the sun had gently nudged aside the moon, the Weird Sisters sat around their table amid a jumble of parchment scrolls and leather-bound volumes. Dymphna glanced up from the *Herbarium of Apuleius* she was perusing. "No poisons, Zipporah."

Merab nodded, her ebony curls bobbing vigorously. "I agree. No killing. I draw the line at killing."

Zipporah rested her chin on one hand. With the other she tapped her long fingernails on the tabletop.

"Maybe we can drive King Duncan away," Merab suggested. "Far, far away."

"But where?" Zipporah's nails clicked annoyingly against the wood.

"To England. I hear his son, Malcolm, is already there, petitioning King Edward for support."

"So?" Dymphna wanted to know.

"Macbeth is King Duncan's half-brother," Merab explained. "With both Duncan and Malcolm out of the country, Macbeth might well be declared king."

Dymphna stared at her sister, her eyes wide. "But Lady Macbeth expects us to meet her husband on the heath. Today!"

"We can still meet him..." Zipporah said.

"With no ready spell? No incantation? No potion?"

Zipporah smiled. "Remember when you fell into the loch and I gave you that bolus for leg cramps?"

Dymphna nodded.

"Sugar."

Dymphna's eyebrows disappeared under an untidy fringe of hair. "Sugar, you say? But it worked! It cured my cramps!"

"The sugar cured nothing more than your mind, dear sister. So, until we can brew the proper potion, let us play with his mind."

"But will he believe whatever nonsense we tell him?" Merab watched as her older sister crossed to the cupboard, opened a carved wooden casket, and withdrew a leather pouch and a looking glass that had once belonged to their mother.

Zipporah propped the mirror against a candlestick, spread the contents of the pouch on the table in front of her, then began fastening rounded pellets of sap to her forehead and chin, smoothing out the edges and blending them seamlessly into her skin. She reserved a particularly large and misshapen pellet for the tip of her nose. "He will, dear sisters, if we dress the part."

Zipporah turned and Merab fell over backwards, laughing, at her sister's transformation into a crone.

Zipporah's eyes darted appraisingly from Dymphna to Merab and back again. "Dymphna, you'll do as is."

Dymphna, whose beard had grown another two inches overnight, burst into tears.

"As for you, sweet Merab, you're far too comely for a midnight hag." Zipporah stuck her head into the wardrobe, rummaged about, and emerged in triumph a few moments later holding a tattered cloth of graying gauze. Holding it by the corners, she tossed it over Merab's head and watched as it settled lightly around her shoulders and hips, until its ragged edges just dusted the floor.

"You look like a plinth," Dymphna snuffled, dragging a frayed sleeve across her nose. "A cobweb-covered plinth."

Zipporah studied Merab's costume critically, the corners of her mouth turned down. "Don't just stand there, Merab. Wave your arms!"

Merab flapped her arms like a wounded stork.

"Now, moan."

The wounded stork keened and howled, as if near death.

Zipporah chortled. "That will have to do."

Merab dropped her weary arms and staggered about the room in a tight circle. "I can't see very well."

With a guiding hand on her back, Zipporah pushed Merab towards the door. "Never mind. You won't have to. Just follow my lead." She glanced over her shoulder at Dymphna, still sulking by the hearth. "Snap out of it, Dymphna! Come, now! It's show time!"

"Show?" Dymphna squeaked.

"Show!" cried her older sister.

"Show! Show! Show!" flapped the stork.

* * *

As the women had planned, Macbeth and his party stumbled upon the Weird Sisters on the banks of a rocky, babbling stream. Dymphna had coaxed some kindling and a pile of short logs into a hot fire and had set a small, three-legged cauldron, filled with water, over it to boil. When the steam began to rise, Zipporah tossed in a handful of greenish-yellow pellets. Singing "The Poor Soul Sat Sighing by a Sycamore Tree" in her reedy soprano, she circled the cauldron, round and round, until smoke boiled from it, spilled over the sides, and billowed across the brown furze thick as a winter's fog, licking hungrily at their ankles. The hunting party, with trumpets blaring and dogs braying, thundered to a halt a few hundred yards away, their banners fluttering in the mild breeze. While their steeds snorted and stamped, rattling their bridles, two men dismounted and approached warily.

"Banquo and Macbeth," Zipporah whispered. "I recognize them from the organized horse-battles last spring."

Dymphna pouted. "You'd think they'd be polite enough to remove their hats!" she complained.

Zipporah touched her sister's cheek. "Sweet Dymphna. Have you taken a good look at yourself?"

Dymphna's lower lip began to quiver dangerously under its new growth of beard. Zipporah held up a finger to silence her. "Shh. Here comes Banquo."

A tall man, wearing a rust-colored tunic with ties up the front and a cloak thrown over his broad shoulders, stopped twenty paces away, his left hand toying nervously with the hilt of his sword. "Who are you?" he demanded. His eyes narrowed. "At first I thought you were women, but then..." He squinted at Dymphna. "You are bearded!"

Dymphna stuck her chin out defiantly, but Merab could see that her sister's fingernails were digging deeply into her palms.

Merab felt Zipporah's elbow sharp against her ribs. "Whooo, whooo, whooo," she moaned.

Banquo staggered backward. "Are you not of this world?"

His companion raised a cautionary hand, then advanced with long, confident strides. Slightly shorter than his friend, Macbeth wore a Saxon tunic with a wide, embroidered hem and loose oversleeves. A belt, inlaid with precious stones, was buckled at his waist; he wore fine leather boots. "Speak!" Macbeth commanded.

Zipporah spread her arms wide. "All hail, Macbeth. Hail to you, Thane of Glamis!"

"All hail, Macbeth. Hail to you, Thane of Cawdor!" cried Dymphna, quickly catching on.

"All hail, Macbeth, who will be king hereafter!" finished Zipporah with another flourish of her arms.

Macbeth's eyes widened with astonishment. "But how can this be? The Thane of Cawdor still lives!"

"Eeyow, eeyow, eeyow!" Merab shrieked, completely ignoring the question.

"Wait a minute!" Banquo interjected, his face alight. "You've given my noble friend here a happy fortune. If you can really see into the future, what do you see in it for me?"

"Hail!" cried Merab.

"Hail!" croaked Dymphna.

"Hail!" shouted Zipporah. She leaned in Banquo's direction and whispered, "More is less and less is more."

Banquo's brow knit in puzzlement. "What is that supposed to mean?"

"Thou shall get kings though thou be none," chanted Zipporah.

Merab felt the sting of Zipporah's elbow again. She spun in a tight circle, arms pinwheeling. "Banquo and Macbeth, all hail!" she chanted. "Banquo and Macbeth, all hail!" until Zipporah touched her arm, signaling it was time for them to depart. The women turned their backs to the men and their faces toward the river.

"Wait a minute! Tell me more!" demanded Macbeth.

But Zipporah said nothing. With a theatrical gesture, she tossed another handful of pellets into the steaming cauldron. A choking mist arose, enveloping them all. "Come, sisters," she hissed into the fog. "Let us fly!"

Leaving the two men to stumble blindly back to their horses, the Weird Sisters scurried away, following the bank of the stream until they found themselves once again in the safety of the wood. "Why did we run?" panted Dymphna, doubled over with her hands resting on her knees.

Merab had stripped off her shroud and was leaning against a tree. "Yes, why?"

"Always," Zipporah grinned toothily, "leave them wanting more." She peeled a wart off her cheek and laughed.

* * *

Two days later, the rising sun found the sisters gathered once more around their table. "It's a message from Lady Macbeth," Zipporah said as she spread the parchment out on the table in front of her. "Do you want the good news first, sisters, or the bad news?"

Merab circled the table, ladling pease porridge into their trenchers. "What does the message say?"

"The Thane of Cawdor has been executed for treason."

The ladle clattered against the pot. "That means ..."

"Exactly," said Zipporah. "And King Duncan is coming to Castle Inverness *tonight.*"

"But we haven't had time to prepare the potion with the power of persuasion," worried Dymphna, her face once again clear and pink owing to the belated application of a paste made of lentils, blue-green algae, and flaxseed.

Zipporah shoved her porridge to one side. "I know. And the lady requires more of the sleeping potion, as well." She rose from her chair and crossed to the shelf, where she rummaged through the clutter of flasks, vials, and bottles assembled there. One by one, she lifted the stoppers and sniffed. "Ah, here it is." She set the flask aside. "Now," she said, "we've no time to lose! Quickly, Dymphna! Where did you put the recipe?"

In less time than it took to churn butter, the Weird Sisters stood, once again, around a bubbling cauldron. "Double Bubble, spoil the bubble..." Zipporah read from the parchment Dymphna had produced.

Merab peered cautiously into the cauldron. "It's pink," she said in a worried voice. She dipped in an experimental finger. "And sticky."

Zipporah shook her head. "That's not right. It should be brown." She squinted suspiciously at the parchment, its edges brown and curling, the writing dense and crabbed. She held the parchment close to her nose, then at arm's length before sending an accusing glance in Dymphna's direction. "Are you sure this is the potion with the power of persuasion, sister?"

Dymphna nodded. "Would you like *me* to read it?"

Zipporah blinked twice, shrugged, then thrust the parchment toward Dymphna. "Very well. You read. I'll stir." She grasped the wooden paddle with both hands and began stirring, her whole body swaying rhythmically with each turn of the paddle.

Double, double, toil and trouble,
Fire burn and cauldron bubble,
read Dymphna.
Fillet of a fenny snake, in the cauldron boil and bake.

Dymphna nodded at Merab, who selected a serpentine object from the ingredients laid out on the table in front of her and tossed it into the pot.

As the snake sank, Merab studied the pink mixture with rising panic. Surely it wouldn't make any difference? What could it matter that she'd collected that snake from the woods and not from the fen?

"Merab!" She was suddenly aware that Zipporah was shouting at her.

Merab returned her attention to her task. As Zipporah stirred and Dymphna chanted, Merab tossed the ingredients, as Dymphna called for them, one by one into the pot.

Eye of newt...

Merab's heart began to hammer against her ribs.

*And toe of frog. Wool of bat, And tongue of dog.*Merab was breathing so rapidly she felt light-headed. Tongue of dog. Oh ye gods and goddesses! She hadn't been able to bring herself to do it. The mongrel had been brown and white, its tail wagging joyously, its nose wet and black against her cheek. Merab reached for the shriveled strip of dried venison she'd substituted for the tongue and tossed it into the pot instead.

Zipporah stirred more vigorously, her heels rising in and out of her shoes. "Now!" she cried.

Double double, toil and trouble, Fire burn and cauldron bubble, the three sisters chanted in unison.
Scale of dragon, tooth of wolf, Dymphna continued.
Witches mummy, maw and gulf Of the ravin'd salt-sea shark, Root of hemlock digg'd i' the dark...

Swift as raindrops flying before the wind, the magic words tumbled from Dymphna's mouth, and just as quickly, Merab tossed the ingredients, one after the other, into the pot. The mixture boiled thick and slimy—bubbles formed, swelled, and erupted on the surface of the sludge like breakfast porridge. As Merab watched, the porridge in her own stomach churning, the mixture gradually changed from pink to lavender, from lavender to gray, from gray a dull brown. The storm raging in her stomach began to subside.

Zipporah blessed the mixture with a final anti-clockwise stir. A pale finger of bluish smoke drifted toward the ceiling and swirled around the tied bundles of herbs drying in the rafters. "There! That should do it."

Merab stepped back from the cauldron with relief. "I'm curious about something, Zipporah. Back there on the heath. Why did you talk in riddles? Why didn't you tell Macbeth straight out that he'd be king?"

Using a wooden spoon, Zipporah ladled the potion into an earthenware jar that the queen's messenger would soon take to the castle kitchens. "Men like conundrums," she explained. "It gives them something to puzzle over. If Lord Macbeth didn't have to figure some of it out for himself, no one could convince him we'd given him his money's worth."

* * *

It was quiet in the woodland cottage for the next several weeks. While Zipporah tended the garden—plucking weeds, loosening the dirt around the roots of the parsnips and carrots, picking bugs off the leaves of the lettuce plants—Merab brewed up a batch of comfrey for the butcher's bronchitis and a love potion for the tavern-keeper, whose wife had run away with the handsome, young ironmonger. Dymphna studiously copied recipes into her book.

On the second day of the third week, the sisters had just settled down for a dinner of roast capon and peas, when a sudden commotion on the roof of the cottage made them lay down their knives and look up at each other in alarm. A clatter like hail erupted from the hearth and smoke blew backwards down the chimney, scattering ashes in every direction.

Suddenly Hecate stood solid as a tree before them. From neck to ankles, the Mistress of the Moon was swathed in diaphanous silver robes; a cape spun of cobwebs shimmered from her shoulders. In contrast, her face was flushed with rage and her mouth worked up and down soundlessly.

Merab sprang to her feet, gingerly brushing a glowing cinder from her skirt.

"Hecate! Why do you look so angry?"

Hecate shrugged out of her cape, letting it drift to the floor, where it settled in a glistening pool at her feet. "Haven't I good reason, you brazen hussies?" she hissed.

Zipporah rose from her chair, elbowed Merab out of her way, and stood before the enraged goddess. "I'm sure we don't have the slightest idea what you're talking about, Madam."

Hecate leaned forward, sputtering hellfire. "How *dare* you work spells on behalf of that man without consulting me?" Her eyes, cold as winter ice, locked with Zipporah's. "Amateurs! Bumbling amateurs! Do you know what you've done?"

Merab shook her head, eyes downcast, as Hecate's icy gaze settled on her "Do you?" Hecate shouted at Dymphna.

Dymphna recoiled.

Hecate jabbed a long, crooked finger in the direction of Dymphna's upturned nose. "What on earth did you tell the man? What did you tell Mac—"

"Please, Madam. Sit." With the toe of her shoe, Zipporah pushed a stool cautiously in Hecate's direction. Hecate considered it for a moment, then reining in her temper like a team of wild horses, she swallowed her anger and sat down with a thump.

"We told him he'd be king," Zipporah confessed. "We thought we'd give him something to think about until we had time to prepare the potion that would actually make it happen."

Hecate's voice dripped with sarcasm. "Apparently the man and his lady wife were unwilling to wait."

"What?" Merab's hands flew to her cheeks, her mouth yawning wide.

Hecate nodded gravely. "Macbeth murdered King Duncan that very night."

Dymphna collapsed heavily on the hearth, her hands pressed between her knees. "Surely you're mistaken! Lord Macbeth a murderer? But he seemed so good-natured!"

"No mistake," said Hecate. "And they wasted little time moving their household from Inverness to the royal castle at Dunsinane."

"But what about King Duncan's bodyguards?" Merab wondered.

"Suspicion fell on them at first, of course," Hecate explained, "especially when they were found smeared with blood, sleeping with a bloody dagger between them."

"Sleeping?" Merab cried. "That makes no sense at all. Why wouldn't they have flown after committing so vile a deed?"

"They were locked—all unknowing—in Morpheus's arms." Hecate reached inside her purse and withdrew a familiar, pear-shaped object. "I discovered this flask near their cots."

Merab plucked the familiar flask from Hecate's hands, removed the cork, stared at the milky residue coating the bottom, and sniffed. She turned toward Zipporah, one eyebrow raised in surprise. "This is the sleeping draught prepared for Lady Macbeth!"

Hecate leaned forward. "I rather thought so."

"So the Lady drugged the guards and murdered the King while they slept?"

"Not the Lady. Lord Macbeth himself."

Dymphna sprang to her feet. She had found her tongue at last. "But what of the other portion we prepared for the Lady?"

Hecate's eyebrows knit in puzzlement. "What other potion?"

"Our plan was bloodless, Madam, and twofold. Lady Macbeth was to introduce the potion into the mussel broth to be served at the banquet. It would bewitch King Duncan with an overwhelming desire to join his son in England. Then the nobles, equally enchanted and twice as fickle, would declare Macbeth king."

Zipporah groaned. "We sent complete instructions! Oh, why didn't Lady Macbeth use the potion? Why didn't she give it a chance to work?"

Hecate's words were blunt. "Maybe she did. Perhaps the fault lay in the potion."

Thinking about her secret economies, Merab felt herself shrinking inside her skin. Soon she would be as tiny as the field mouse that sometimes winked at her from the darkened corner near the hearth. If only she hadn't been so selfish! If she had it to do all over again, she'd pay whatever it cost for the newt. Yes, she'd even sail to Constantinople and slice the nose off Sultan Ala-ud-din-Kaikobad himself.

"But we followed the formula," Dymphna protested. "Exactly."

Hecate's voice softened. "Yet something went quite wrong at the banquet, I fear. Lord Macbeth had a fever on the brain. He had visions of bloody heads. He saw Banquo's ghost. On and on he raved, until Lady Macbeth sent the guests home and hustled her husband, raving still, to his bedchamber."

"Perhaps he was drunk," Merab suggested.

"Besides," Zipporah added, "Banquo's not dead. We saw him ourselves not long ago. With Lord Macbeth. On the heath."

"Oh, Banquo's quite, quite dead." Hecate cast her eyes heavenward. "I passed his blameless soul as it soared over the moon, heading towards the stars."

"Who ... ?" Dymphna's eyes grew wide.

"Three thugs, his spirit told me. Hired by Macbeth."

Zipporah bowed her head. "Macbeth is obsessed, 'tis certain, twisted by ambition. Even now, with the kingship firmly in his grasp, he rages on." She looked up. "Oh, Hecate! Does his lust know no bounds?"

"I must lay that responsibility at your feet, Zipporah. What did you put into that potion? Insane root?"

Merab stepped between Hecate and her older sister. "No potion's to blame, Madam. We told Banquo he would beget kings."

"And for that, he died," Dymphna whimpered.

Zipporah straightened. "Where's Macbeth now?"

"Pursuing Macduff," Hecate informed them.

"But surely I heard that Macduff is safely away with Malcolm in England?"

Hecate looked grave. "No one, I fear, is safe from Macbeth's evil designs and enterprises. But rest easy," she continued. "I believe I've found the solution. Remember the old sow's blood charm?" She grinned. "I used it to conjure up some apparitions for our impatient king. First a talking head. Then a bloody child. 'None of woman born shall harm Macbeth,' I bid the child say." She cackled, her mouth wide, revealing black and pointed teeth. "I'm particularly proud of that riddle."

"*All* men are born of woman," Dymphna insisted.

Hecate looked amused. "So it would seem."

Dymphna stared at the rafters for a moment, then shrugged and pointed at her sister. "Zipporah's good at riddles."

Hecate considered this information with a satisfied expression on her face. "Try this one, then: 'Macbeth shall never vanquished be until Great Birnan wood to high Dunsinane hill shall come against him.'"

The furrows deepened in Dymphna's brow. "How could a wood remove to the top of a hill?"

Zipporah spoke at last. "It can't, of course. That's what makes it so brilliant! With Macbeth secure in his kingship, the carnage should cease."

Dymphna clapped her hands. "Moon and stars be praised! What you said about Macduff troubled me greatly for it's not only he who's endangered, but his wife and precious children, too." Hecate smiled modestly, then waved an impatient hand. "Speaking of danger, why didn't you answer my question? What *did* you put into that potion?"

Dymphna plucked the parchment from an earthenware pot where she had stored it, unrolled the document, and recited the ingredients, one by one, as her finger traced a path down the page. "Adder's fork, blind-worm's sting, lizard's leg, howlet's wing, goat gall, yew ..." When she had finished, she turned to Hecate. "Well?"

"It sounds right." Hecate sat in silence for a moment, thinking. "But in truth, I'm puzzled, because the insanity didn't stop with the king. Now it's Lady Macbeth who's gone stark-staring mad. Everybody's talking about it. The torches are always lit in the castle. She walks in her sleep. And lately I've heard reports of compulsive hand-washing." Hecate slid off the stool and hovered before them, her feet floating a hand's breadth above the floor. "I don't know what went wrong, but it's up to me, as usual, to set things right." Her eyes blazed. "Do you have any of that potion left?"

Zipporah nodded. "In the cupboard. In the large crock."

Hecate picked up the crock with both hands, crossed to the hearth, and emptied its contents into the cauldron. She glared at Merab. "Now, mistress, the rest of your stores!"

"Oh, no!" Merab wailed.

Hecate was firm. "It's the only way." While she stood to one side, heckling and prodding, the sisters reluctantly emptied all their potions, tonics, elixirs, tinctures, and physics, each bolus and pill, every ointment, syrup, and lotion, into the iron cauldron. Once, Hecate caught Dymphna's hand just as it disappeared into her pocket with a vial of syrup extracted from eastern poppies. "I said *everything*." and Dymphna watched, long-faced, as the precious pain remedy joined its brethren in the pot, soon swirling with a malignant, purplish-green sludge.

Zipporah's eyes lingered on her jars, flasks, flagons, bottles, boxes, and bowls, all empty, lined up on the tabletop. "I think your measures excessive, Madam."

Hecate gathered up her gossamer cloak and, with a flourish, settled the shimmering fabric over her shoulders. She floated toward the door. "Next time perhaps you'll consult me before going off with your bows half-strung. Now," she commanded, pointing to the cauldron, "dump it—*all* of it—into the loch."

"Loch Ashie?" The mixture stared up at Merab like a malevolent blob and she vowed she'd never bathe in the clear, cool waters of Loch Ashie again.

"No, fool. Loch Ness." And with a final stab of her finger, Hecate vanished.

"Come!" Zipporah ordered. "Let's get this over with before that wretched hag returns. Dymphna, you fetch the wheelbarrow."

Merab already had her arms around the belly of the cauldron at its widest part. "Umph!" she grunted. "I can't do this by myself."

Zipporah helped Merab inch the cauldron across the floor

of beaten earth toward the waiting wheelbarrow. "When I count to three, lift," Zipporah instructed. She adjusted her grip, took a deep breath—*One, two, three!*

"Oh!" shouted Merab, staggering under the sudden weight. She watched helplessly as the liquid swirled dangerously, reared over the lip of the cauldron with tentacle-like fingers, and sloshed, wet and slightly warm, all over her clothing. "Oh, dear," she exclaimed, but she was too busy to do anything but ignore it. Swearing and grunting, the women muscled the cauldron into the wheelbarrow, then stepped back, arms tingling with fatigue, to catch their breath.

Zipporah suddenly gasped. "Look, Merab! Look at your gown!"

Merab stared. Where once she had worn plain, gray homespun, scorched with pinholes and decorated with flecks of soil and food, her gown was now fine and white, spotless as a field of high mountain snow. "My spots!" she whooped. "They're gone!"

Dymphna smiled at Zipporah slyly. "I suppose you'll be wanting me to write this formula down, won't you, sister?" With her thumb and index finger, she penned an imaginary note against the cloudless blue sky. "Receipt for Spot Remover."

"What I want," Zipporah grumbled, "is to consign every drop of this loathsome liquid to the bottom of Loch Ness. Then, I plan to take up something safe, like midwifery, and forget we ever heard of the King and Queen of Dunsinane."

Merab's brow knit in puzzlement. "But I don't understand. If Macbeth..."

Zipporah pressed a finger, hard, against her sister's lips. "It's bad luck to say his name! I forbid it. From henceforth whenever we refer to that man, if we refer to him at all, it will be as 'that Scottish King.'"

She bent her knees, lifted the handles of the wheelbarrow, and with Dymphna straggling behind, rolled it down the path, through the garden, past the hives and into the wood. With the cat weaving about her ankles, Merab watched until Zipporah's silver head and Dymphna's copper one were lost among the shimmer of the early summer leaves. Merab gazed down in wonder at the pristine landscape of her gown. "Too bad it isn't blue," she said to the cat. And she went inside to consult the *Herbarium* to see what she could do about that.

Safety First

GEORGE STOOD ON the steps of Lakeland Public Library—*his* library—and studied his reflection in the tall glass doors. Intelligent gray eyes set in a pleasantly round face, a full head of auburn hair, all his own, thank you very much. All in all, a cheerful sort of guy. Squinting at his reflection, he smoothed back an unruly lock with the palm of his hand, straightened his tie, and wondered, for the fourth morning in a row, why such a friendly-looking fellow deserved such punishment.

Years ago, sitting at a solitary cataloger's desk deep in the bowels of Lakeland Public, aspiring to be head of it one day, he wished he had known then what he knew now. Management would be simple, he told himself, if it weren't for all the people.

These doors, for example. He winced as the plain glass panels whooshed open automatically before him, followed by a blast of heat that ruffled his carefully styled hair. At their weekly staff meetings the circulation librarian, Jean McBride, had gone on and on about the old revolving doors. "That's the second time this week a mother with a stroller's been caught in that door, not to mention the indignity of forcing our handicapped patrons to use the basement entrance!" Counter-arguments about the architectural significance of the doors—made of brass, glass, and ornately carved wood, part of the original building when Andrew Carnegie dedicated it at the turn of the century—not to mention the added cost of heating the lobby, had fallen on deaf ears. When the readers' services librarian and the head of cataloging had stood in solidarity with their colleagues, George had capitulated. Now, fully ten percent of his fuel oil budget was going to heat four parallel parking spaces on Cuyahoga Street and keep the blasted forsythia bushes warm throughout the winter. He had the bills to prove it.

"Morning, Dr. Hopkins."

"Morning, Jean." It annoyed him that no matter how early he arrived at work, that damned woman was there ahead of him. Already his stomach was in knots thinking about the staff meeting he'd scheduled for later that morning. He prayed they wouldn't gang up on him again.

Jean had been a particular challenge. When he'd first taken the directorship, Jean had been manning the circulation desk wearing tennis shoes, slacks, dumpy sweaters, and once, to his horror, a Mickey Mouse T-shirt. At his first staff meeting, he'd impressed on her, indeed on all "front office" staff, the importance of their appearance. "If we don't look professional," he had admonished, "how can we expect our customers (never patrons!) to treat us as such?"

Today he smiled at Jean, who wore, he was pleased to note, a frilly white blouse under a chic, navy blue suit. He pictured navy hose ending in black, patent-leather T-strap shoes, but could only imagine this without leaning very obviously over the counter.

George punched the Up button and waited, pacing, while the elevator made a slow, creaking ascent from the basement.

When the doors shuddered open, he climbed aboard and rode to the fifth floor, where his office was tucked into a corner with windows overlooking Lake Erie on two sides.

Lolly, his secretary, was already at her desk, head bent over her keyboard. When he pushed through the double doors, she popped up as if shot from a toaster. "Dr. Hopkins! Can I get you a cup of coffee?"

As he crossed the carpet to his office, Lolly orbited around her cubicle, keeping her body between her boss and whatever was displayed on her monitor screen. George's eyes narrowed. "Coffee will be fine, Miss Taylor." He took three steps toward his office, then suddenly turned, catching his secretary, already on her way to the coffee machine, off guard. "What's that on your monitor?"

Lolly smiled uncertainly. "Just a screen saver."

George squinted toward the monitor where manic dogs frolicked, gradually gobbling bits of the Word document Lolly had been working on. He scowled. "What's wrong with the one that came with the computer?" he demanded, thinking of the soothing, cloud-studded landscape that materialized on his screen whenever it had been idle for ten minutes.

Lolly's dark eyes bored into his, her lips forming a thin, hard line. She opened her mouth, then seemed to reconsider. "I'll change it back," she whispered.

George grunted. "What if a board member should come in

and see that? Very unprofessional!" He unlocked the door to his office and slipped in, thinking this was not an auspicious start to the day.

For the next two hours, sipping the hot coffee Lolly periodically provided, hoping, vainly, to feel the revitalizing effects of caffeine surging through his system, George proofed the final draft of his annual report. On page twenty-seven, he added a paragraph that had just occurred to him about estate planning and the Friends of the Library Foundation. Then, exuding self-confidence after a short, but productively persuasive telephone conversation with an elderly, chronically ill donor, George gathered up the annual report, slid it into his secretary's in-box, and headed toward the conference room, smiling.

His confidence evaporated the minute he entered the room. Arranged in a horseshoe around the table was his staff, presided over like a malevolent Buddha by Claudia Fairfield, head of readers' services, narrow-eyed and unsmiling. Instantly, he regretted appointing Claudia head of the facilities management committee. Before he had time to pull up his chair, she thrust her triangular chin over the table and announced, "We have our report."

George swallowed, the coffee he'd recently consumed making an unwelcome comeback. On his left sat Jean McBride, hands folded on the table in front of her, quietly studying her painted thumbnails. On Jean's left was Belinda D'Arcy, the archivist, leafing through some papers and refusing to meet his eyes, still fuming, no doubt, over George's refusal to grant her request for leave without pay to take care of her mother. Next to Belinda sat Miles Nichols, the head cataloger who, with his floppy hair, flattish nose, and lipless mouth, reminded George of a lizard. Miles had an elderly mother, too. If George were to grant Belinda's request, soon Miles would be asking for leave, and the next thing he knew, the whole staff would be expecting George to bend over backward for them. There'd be no end to it. Time off to attend classes. Write a thesis. Get married. Go on vacations even.

George had done his homework on Belinda, at least. She'd threatened to quit, but George had been through her personnel folder and knew that the threat was an empty one. Just two years short of retirement, Belinda could hardly risk losing her pension.

As Claudia droned on about the annual picnic, vending machines in the staff area (including one that dispensed cappuccino), and electrical outlets in the ladies' rest rooms to accommodate their damn hair dryers, George zoned out. He found himself wondering about the package he was expecting from L.L. Bean and whether he'd have time to eat before his evening karate class.

"Overtime." The word sliced through his reverie like a knife. George had replaced his predecessor's rather lackadaisical approach to payroll with a computerized system, well aware that the institution of time cards would make him about as popular as mosquitoes at a nudist colony. But it had to be done. Now, it appeared, he was being punished for his pains. "Because of the Friends' meeting, I worked forty-nine hours last week," Jean was whining. "How does the library plan to pay me for it?"

Controlling his exasperation, George explained, for what seemed like the hundredth time, that overtime hours had to be approved in *advance,* and referred her to the new staff manual.

"Nobody told me I had to ask in advance," Jean complained.

"It's in the cover memo I sent out to all staff," George reminded her. He hastily finessed by referring Jean to the personnel office all the while knowing, with fear's cold fingers squeezing his gut, that before long he'd be summoned by the Brunhilde in charge of *that* office and forced to attend another session of "sensitivity training."

"And now," Claudia continued with relentless momentum, "we want to discuss some new concerns about library safety. As you know, Lakeland is an *elderly* library, and because of budgetary constraints, needed repairs have been shamefully neglected."

George knew all about budgetary restraints. He'd met with the Board of Governors just last week, and although he'd pleaded for more money, none had been forthcoming. Indeed, the bond issue in November had failed; the librarywould simply have to make do with funding at last year's level. George doubted he merited the confidence the Board had placed in him. With automatic cost-of-living salary increases and the price of magazines and newspapers spiraling out of control, George was at his wit's end. Even if he fired that good-for-nothing gaggle of Madonna wannabees who shelved the books with all the speed of molasses in January, he'd save only enough to buy a one-year subscription to *Science Citation Index.* It was discouraging.

"Nevertheless," Claudia forged on, "we must address some safety issues."

"Which are?" George inquired.

Claudia raised an index finger. "One. The dumb waiter. It doesn't work half the time. Yesterday I looked up the shaft to see what was holding it up and nearly got decapitated when it suddenly decided to come down."

George suppressed a smile. If *that* happened, Claudia's mouth would go on flapping a full ten minutes after her head had parted company with her body. He nodded sagely, his fingers tented over his lips.

"Two. The compact shelving. The hand cranks are stiff and difficult for our older staff to manage." Claudia braved a sideways glance at Belinda. "Nowadays, they're *electric*" she added, as if George had just emerged, dazed and blinking from a time machine sent from the seventeenth century.

"With automatic shutoff controls. I shudder to think what would happen if someone was reaching for the Bryant Papers when somebody else decided to check out the World War Two correspondence."

Miles, who had until this point been mindlessly tracing the lifeline on his palm with a ballpoint pen, raised both hands in front of his face and brought them sharply together.

"Splat!"

Belinda glared at him from across the table. "Not funny, Miles." Miles shrugged and returned to his doodling.

"Three." Claudia soldiered on, like a suffragette on a mission. "We've got to get rid of the halon."

"Why?" George inquired. "It's the most effective fire retardant ever invented. And since it's a gas, it doesn't ruin the manuscripts as water would."

"True," Claudia admitted, "But it does deplete the ozone layer."

"Like freon," Jean added.

All around the table, George's staff nodded sagely. Good God almighty! He was captaining a Greenpeace vessel. "But surely..." he began, until Claudia raised a caterpillar-like eyebrow.

"No choice, I'm afraid. Halon gas hasn't been manufactured since 1994, and in 2003 it will be banned altogether."

With fat, ringless fingers, she started a three-page Internet printout on a circuit around the table. When it reached George, everybody waited silently while he scanned the document. Indeed, halon was being phased out in favor of an alphabet of substances like FM200 and ETEC Agent A, but it was the price tag that caught his eye. If he handed over his entire salary for a year, it would just about cover the cost of a retrofit.

"Besides, it sucks all the oxygen out of the air," Jean commented. "What if there was a fire and Belinda was working in the vault when the halon went off?"

Miles threw his head back, eyelids fluttering grotesquely over the whites of his eyes and gurgled like a clogged drain.

"Nonsense!" George scoffed. "There are safeguards." Although he didn't have the vaguest idea what they might be. "Let me study the issue and get back to you. Anything else?" His question met a wall of silence. "Good. Back to work, then."

George stood, shook the kinks out of his calves, and concentrated on shoving papers back into his folder. When he glanced up again, everyone had gone except Belinda. "Dr. Hopkins?"

"Yes, Belinda?"

"I was wondering if you'd reconsider your decision about my request for leave without pay."

George stared. "I thought we'd settled that."

"Well, I consulted the city employees' manual, like you suggested just now, and it clearly states that leave without pay may be granted under certain circumstances." A button dangled from her cardigan by a thin thread and she twisted it round and round. "I met a clerk at the court house yesterday who's on three months' leave just to study for her bar exam!"

George tucked his folder under his arm. "If you had read those regulations carefully, Miss D'Arcy, you'd have seen that such leave is granted at supervisor discretion. If I let you go for so long a time, it's as good as announcing to the Board of Governors that I don't really *need* an archivist."

A tear slid down Belinda D'Arcy's cheek and made a dark splotch on her lime green blouse. "My mother has Alzheimer's, Dr. Hopkins."

"So you said." George leaned against the doorframe. "Look, I don't wish to appear uncompromising and hardhearted, but I have a library to run, Miss D'Arcy. Surely there are, uh, arrangements you can make. Adult day care? Hospice? A nursing home? We certainly pay you enough."

Belinda turned and fled.

George stooped to pick up the button that had fallen from the archivist's sweater. "Wait! You've lost your button!" But the door to the corridor slammed, and Belinda was gone.

George spent the next week glued to the chair in front of his computer, plugging new figures into his Excel spreadsheet, moving them about from column to column like some elaborate chess game. If he put off the new photocopier acquisition until next year, he discovered, the dumb waiter could be fixed, but replacing the compact shelving and the halon system that protected the manuscript vault was simply out of the question, either now or in the foreseeable future.

Late one afternoon, with the cleaning staff busily emptying trash baskets nearby, George determined that the cranks on the compact shelving units did work a bit stiffly, but nothing that a little WD-40 couldn't fix. He worked the lubricant well into the crank mechanisms at the end of each row of shelves, then, beginning with the section where the atlases were kept, he knelt and began spraying WD-40 on the tracks that ran along the floor. He was so intent on his task that it took him a while to notice that the shelves were closing in on him. "Hey!" he shouted over the drone of the vacuum cleaner. "Someone's in here!" But the gap continued to narrow.

George scrambled to his feet and braced his arms, Samson-like, against the shelves. "Hey!" he shouted again, feeling the flab on his upper arms quiver ineffectually beneath his sleeves. "Hey! Hey!"

It was an oversize *Atlas of the World: 1750, Volume IV* that saved him when he managed to wedge it into the narrowing gap between the shelves. Underarms ringed with sweat, he stepped over the blessed book and peeked out into the room. "Who's there?"

But he saw no one. Even the cleaning crew had vanished.

Later, relaxing at home with a cold glass of Chablis, his blood pressure and heart rate returned to normal, George almost succeeded in convincing himself that it was one of the cleaning crew who had moved the shelves but was simply too frightened to admit it. Yet a feeling of uneasiness hung about him like a cloud, and for the next couple of days, he rarely left his office.

Until Belinda D'Arcy called. "Please come down to the manuscript vault. Dr. Hopkins. I have something to show you."

George laid aside his *Publishers Weekly* and sighed. It had been a fine, sunny day. He had eaten lunch at a picnic table in the park. Later, his mother had telephoned to say that she was *not* coming for Christmas this year. Yes, a near perfect day. The last thing in the world George wanted to do was spoil it by talking to Belinda D'Arcy. "Can't it wait until tomorrow?"

"No."

"What is it, then?"

"I'll have to show you."

George checked his watch. "Okay. If it's that important, I'll try to stop by on my way home."

In the next few minutes while George packed up his briefcase, locked his office door, and caught the elevator to the archives on Sublevel A, he wondered what was bothering the archivist this time. A dead rat, probably. Or a bit of condensation on the pipes. He found Belinda waiting for him in the spacious vault, standing behind one of two long, narrow study tables, her plain face unflatteringly sallow under the bright fluorescent lights. "What did you decide about the halon?" she asked.

"We'll need new cylinders, pipework, and nozzles," George explained. "I'm putting them into the five-year plan."

"But it's dangerous *now*," Belinda complained, moving between George and the door.

"Look," George snapped. "I've studied the installation carefully. I've read the manual. Even if halon should suddenly fill this room, it would last only ten seconds." He pointed to a gridded opening near the floor. "After that, those big exhaust fans kick in and suck it all out. Nobody's in danger."

"Really." It was a statement, not a question. "I've left a report on the table," she said. "I suggest you read it."

Before he could reply, Belinda slipped out the door and slammed it shut behind her.

At first, George wasn't alarmed. It wasn't the first time Belinda had stormed out of a meeting; for someone in her sixties, she was surprisingly immature. The room was scrupulously neat so it didn't take him long to find the folder where she had left it for him, on the table farthest from the door. He skimmed over the report—something with an official-looking logo from a firm called Foggo, Inc.—but it didn't seem to contain anything he didn't already know. He put the report down and went to the door, but the damned woman had slammed it so hard that it was jammed. "Belinda?" Feeling foolish, he pounded against the door with his fist. "Belinda!"

Her voice was soft, and surprisingly close, just on the other side of the door. "I suggest you read the small print, Dr. Hopkins."

The woman had lost her marbles! George was caught up in some sort of macabre game, and if he wanted to get home tonight in time to feed the cat, the only thing he could do was play along. He grabbed the report and flipped through it again, noticing for the first time where someone—probably Belinda—had highlighted a footnote with yellow marker.

> *Caution. Do not place boxes, papers, or other objects on shelves or tables near the nozzles as they will be blown off by the extremely high velocities created by the gas shooting from the tanks. To minimize this potential hazard, install pegboard sheets at the ends of shelving units near the nozzles in order to allow penetration, but deflect the blast. Ceiling panels must be secured...*

George felt his face grow hot; blood pounded in his ears. He glanced quickly around the room. No pegboard sheets. Boxes all over the shelves. And how the hell was he supposed to know how the ceiling panels were secured?

"And by the way, *George,*" he heard Belinda say. "I think I smell smoke!"

George's stomach lurched. "Belinda! Open the door!"

"Fire, fire, fire!" she singsonged.

George knew the klaxon would be loud, but he was totally unprepared for the ear-splitting sound of the halon being discharged. It exploded from vents all around him, knocking the boxes off their shelves, sending their contents—manuscripts and letters and antique photographs— swirling about the room in a furious hurricane. Floor tiles erupted from their framework grid, narrowly missing his head as they shot toward the ceiling. All around him, the air shimmered as halon mixed with the oxygen in it.

Ten seconds? It seemed to George like ten years.

A tile flew up, striking a shelf, which tilted. A bronze bust of Commodore Oliver Hazard Perry teetered on the edge, then toppled, falling on an aquatint of the barge *Seneca Chief,* dated 1825, shattering the glass. A glistening shard spun through the air, sliced through his collar, and severed his jugular.

By the time the exhaust fans kicked in, George was already dead.

Vital Signs

IT WAS WRONG. All wrong.

The helmet of bandages, the tubes and the wires, the machines that whirred and sighed and bleeped. I closed my eyes against the glare of the lights and the harsh reality of what lay beneath that thin, white blanket in intensive care. Lucy. *My* Aunt Lucy.

Behind my eyelids it was summertime. The honk of a car horn, the slap of a screen door and Aunt Lucy—all flowered aprons, broad smiles and damp, cinnamon-ginger hugs—waiting for me on the stoop. After Mother married Kyle the year I turned ten, she would park me at Aunt Lucy's farm the minute school let out in June. Kyle didn't take much to kids.

Those blissful summer days are gone now, and so are Mother and Kyle. When Uncle Chet died of Parkinson's a few years back, he left just me, Aunt Lucy and Roy Allen, their son. Soon it would be just me and Roy. I didn't want to think about it.

The doctor laid a hand on my shoulder and guided me toward a chair. "Your aunt suffered massive head injuries, I'm afraid. The surgery helped alleviate the pressure on her brain, but..." He shrugged. "That tube in her windpipe is hooked up to a ventilator. It's breathing for her. We're monitoring her heart and her blood pressure, and she's being fed through that other tube you see in her nose. It's the best we can do." As he spoke, the ventilator cycled on and off, making a sound like air being released from a tire.

"I wish you had known her when..."*when she was alive,* I had started to say.

"She's the kindest woman I've ever known, Doctor. Always taking in strays." I swallowed hard, wondering if one of Aunt Lucy's strays had turned on her. "Back home, when Harry Emerson lost his job at the bank? She invited him to move into the old tenant house with his three disabled sons. Harry'd do odd jobs for her, but she refused to let him pay rent. Then there was this deaf kid, Sheila Sue. When she was sixteen, my aunt hired her as a part-time housekeeper; even paid to send her to a special school in Washington, D.C. And Peg!" I smiled at the memory of my aunt's semi-reluctant, one-legged farmhand. "She even rescued the town hobo..."

I rattled on and on.

The doctor probably thought it'd be therapeutic because he nodded sympathetically, patted my hand once or twice and otherwise showed no signs of being in a hurry to leave.

"She'll make it." I was reassuring myself as much as him. "She's a tough lady. She used to say that if she could make it through the Depression, she could make it through anything."

"Are you her next of kin?" he asked.

"That'd be her son, my cousin, Roy." I gathered up my sweater and my handbag and we walked out the door together. "I've already called him. He's flying in from Tennessee tomorrow."

Roy came, but he didn't stay for long. "There's nothing I can do here, B.R.," he told me after only one day. "Besides, I gotta get back to work." He made it sound so reasonable. He had important clients to take care of, surely I could understand that, and some hot real estate deal on the front burner. If that fell through, he explained, there wouldn't be any money to pay the hospital bills.

"You check in with Mother and let me know if there's any change. Call me right away. You will, won't you?" He was standing half in the hall, holding the door open with one hand. His brown suit was rumpled, as if he had slept in it, and the blue eyes behind his glasses were rimmed with red. "If there's anything she needs..."

"Sure, Roy, sure," I said. But I was thinking very un-Christian thoughts. "You S.O.B.!" I wanted to shout. "Running out on her again. Always expecting me to pick up the pieces. As if I didn't have a life. And a parish to take care of."

My cousin stepped back into the room and gave me a one-armed hug, his chin resting for a moment on the top of my head. "Thanks, B.R." I had just opened my mouth to remind him that my name is Bailey Rose, if you please, but he had already gone.

I came to visit Aunt Lucy every day after that, although they wouldn't let me stay for long. I'd sit by her bed and reminisce, retelling family stories that used to make us laugh. Often as I talked I'd pick up one of her hands where it lay limply on the blanket, hold it and stroke it, the flesh thin and smooth and loose, moving easily, too easily over her bones. Skin so delicate that I thought it might tear. Stroking gently and wondering *who would do such a thing?*

It had happened so fast. A neighbor at Holiday Hills had

dialed 911 within seconds of finding my aunt and as soon as the ambulance screamed out of the parking lot, had telephoned me at St. Stephen's where I was putting the finishing touches on my sermon for Sunday. The police were still there, the woman reported, complaining about the way the paramedics had messed up the crime scene while trying to save my aunt's life.

At the hospital, a detective came to see me because I'm listed on the form at the retirement home. He was hoping she'd come out of the coma. He wanted to get a statement. "Detective Martinez." He extended a hand. "Fa...? Reverend? Ma'am?"

There was an uncomfortable silence while he took in my black suit, gray shirt and white dog collar. It's a reaction I'm used to by now. "Ms. Lawrence will do just fine." I smiled.

"Sorry about your mother," he said, tucking his hat under his arm.

"She's my aunt."

"Oh." He shifted his weight from one leg to the other, as if his feet hurt. "Well, ma'am, we think your aunt interrupted a burglary in progress. Looks like she'd just come in with the groceries. We found a torn paper bag. Food scattered all over the floor. And her pocketbook was missing. Place was a mess. They really tossed it." He glanced over his shoulder at Aunt Lucy and shook his head. "Bastards didn't have to kill her."

"She's not dead yet," I reminded him.

He had the decency, at least, to look embarrassed. When he spoke again, his voice was softer, with the edge knocked off. "We've dusted for prints, Ms. Lawrence, but we really don't expect to find anything. Whoever did it probably wore gloves." He handed me his card. "Please call me if she comes to." He paused. "Or if anything changes."

He expected her to die. They all did, even the paramedics who were first on the scene. Shortly after surgery, when the nurse first hooked Aunt Lucy up to the IVs and the monitors, one of the EMTs stopped by. He stood just inside the door for a few moments, heavy work gloves clutched in one hand. When he turned to go, he noticed me for the first time. "Oh, sorry! I just wanted to see how she's doing." He looked toward the bed. "You know, we thought she was dead. Her head was all..." He touched his temple. "Well, there was an awful lot of blood and she wasn't breathing. My partner said, 'She's gone, man' but me, what do I know? First week on the job. It coulda been my grandma lying there! I had to do something!" He confessed that he had never performed CPR on a real patient before, just practiced on a dummy. Though nearly exhausted, he and his partner had kept it up all the way to the hospital.

He smiled. "I guess I saved her life, huh?"

"Yes, you did," I said. "And I'm very grateful."

He glanced sideways at my aunt, taking in the motionless cocoon of bandages. "I'm wondering now if it was worth it."

"I don't know," I told him truthfully.

I was feeling responsible, too. If it hadn't been for me, she wouldn't have been here at all. Aunt Lucy had been thinking about leaving the farm, moving to one of those life-care communities. She came here because of the weather. Thought she'd give Tampa a try. "But I don't like it," she'd told me after her third month. "It's so relentlessly... pleasant. I miss the mountains and the smell of new-mown hay and the way the mist lies on the fields in the morning. God help me, I even miss the damn frogs. When the lease is up, Rosie, I'm going home."

Seven days after they brought her in, I thought her wish might come true—Aunt Lucy opened her eyes. The doctor called me at church with the good news. "She's out of the coma, Ms. Lawrence." But then he socked me with the bad. "But, she's suffering from aphasia, I'm afraid. She can't talk. She may sometimes appear to be awake and alert, she may even look at you, but she doesn't seem to be able to transform her thoughts into speech."

I hurried to the hospital to see for myself. As I passed the nurse's station on my way to Aunt Lucy's room, I asked for details. "How's she doing?"

"I think you'll be pleased." Nurse Jacobs looked up from a chart, while her pen still scribbled away. "All those prayers must be working. Several times this morning I caught her following me with her eyes, and I've noticed that she's shifted around a bit in the bed. But she seems to be having spasms in her hands and feet. Not surprising, though, considering the extent of her injuries." She slipped the pen into the pocket of her uniform and smiled at me sympathetically. "I keep thinking how hard it must be for you, Ms. Lawrence, coming here day after day, seeing your aunt in this condition. All those hours you've spent with her! If you don't mind my asking, what do you find to talk about?"

"I apologize, mostly. For being such a pigheaded kid." I smiled, remembering. There was always plenty of work to do on the farm but I was usually off in a world of my own, climbing trees or chasing fireflies, or with my nose stuck in a book. I never managed to clean my room or do my assigned chores on time. But even if she had to remind me over and over, Aunt Lucy never lost her patience.

I was expecting a miracle, of course, so I was disappointed when I saw her—Aunt Lucy appeared to be sleeping. I stooped to kiss her forehead and to tuck away a wisp of silver hair that had escaped from the bandage. When her eyes suddenly opened, I was so startled that my heart thudded hard against my ribs and my stomach lurched and I wanted to shout, *Hooray!* But I grabbed the cold metal frame of the bed instead, squeezed tight and said, as calmly as I could, "Hi, Aunt Lucy. Welcome back." I caressed her cheek. "I knew you were in there somewhere, just waiting to get out."

"Do you mind?" Detective Martinez materialized out of nowhere, almost as if he had been lurking behind the door, scaring the bejezzus out of me. "The doc said this might work." Against my objections, he held a smooth, white writing tablet up in front of my aunt. "Who did this to you?"

Aunt Lucy kept dropping the Magic Marker he gave her to write with so Nurse Jacobs brought in a board with the alphabet painted on it. With an unsteady finger, Aunt Lucy pointed out "Q,P,M,X" before I made Martinez stop. "Go away," I pleaded. "Can't you see she's not up to this?" and I had to go around to the other side of the privacy curtain so Aunt Lucy wouldn't see me cry.

After Martinez packed up and left, promising to return the next day, I dragged the only chair in the room over to the bed, fell back into it and started talking. About anything. About nothing. About how wonderful it would be when she got better. About books we'd read, shows we'd see, trips we'd take with Roy and his wife.

Suddenly, tears began to gather in Aunt Lucy's eyes, filling them, spilling over, rolling sideways down her cheeks and onto the pillow. Her right hand, the one not connected to the IV, began to move spasmodically as if picking lint off the blanket.

"It's okay," I told her, trying my best to sound convincing. "You're going to be fine."

Aunt Lucy struggled to raise her hand from the blanket, her frail body trembling with the effort. She crossed her fingers as if making a wish. Then she made a tight fist. Crossed her fingers again. Made a fist. Her eyes remained locked on mine. She did not blink.

"Sweet Jesus God," I whispered. "Sweet God almighty!" I grabbed her hand and pressed it to my lips. "I'll be back in a minute, Auntie."

In seconds, I was out the door. I interrupted the nurse who was talking on the telephone. "Nurse!" I shouted, "Nurse Jacobs! I fumbled for the business card that was still in the pocket of my sweater. "Here!" I plopped the card down on the counter in front of her and jabbed at it with my finger. "Call that police officer right away. Tell him to get over here, and tell him to bring someone who understands sign language. Those weren't muscle spasms you saw. My aunt is finger spelling and she wants to tell us something!"

"She must have learned sign language from Sheila Sue, her deaf housekeeper," I told Detective Martinez before the interpreter arrived. "I know the alphabet, is all. It's R-A, officer. Over and over. She's asking for R.A."

"What's R.A?" he asked.

"It's a who," I told him. "Her son, Roy Allen. We called him R.A. as a kid. She's making other signs now, but I don't know what they are."

Neither of us was aware that the interpreter had entered the room behind us until she spoke. "She's saying, 'R.A. was angry. He hit me again and again. I begged him...'"

Unexpectedly, Aunt Lucy's hands fell to her sides, the fingers relaxed and I saw that her eyes had closed. I rushed to the bed and rattled the safety rail. "No!" I shouted. "Aunt Lucy! Don't die!"

Nurse Jacobs glanced at the monitors and touched my arm. "Don't worry. She's just fallen asleep. The effort's exhausted her, poor thing."

That evening, they arrested Roy Allen at his home in Nashville. He would be extradited to Florida and charged with the attempted murder of his mother, Lucille Norton Lawrence. Roy Allen hadn't been very bright. He had argued over the fare with the cabby who'd driven him from the airport to his mother's apartment. The cabby remembered him particularly because he didn't carry any luggage, not even a briefcase, and he hadn't left a tip. When confronted with an American Airlines passenger list with his name printed on it plain as day, Roy confessed. He couldn't have his mother moving back to the farm, he told Detective Martinez, because there wasn't any farm to move back to. When his father was first diagnosed with Parkinson's disease, Roy had persuaded his parents to put the farm into a trust in order to protect his mother's assets. They made Roy sole trustee. Then Roy had some half-baked scheme to build a shopping center and he'd put up the farm as collateral; when the shopping center failed and he couldn't make the payments, the bank had foreclosed.

Roy goes to trial sometime next month and he says he'll plead guilty, but that doesn't make it any easier on his wife and the kids, or on me.

As for my aunt, she seemed drained after that, as if every ounce of strength, every reserve had been expended in the effort to wake up and tell us what happened. She relapsed. She faded away, like the stars in a dawn sky.

Yesterday, I visited Aunt Lucy for the last time. I was reading to her from the Sunday section of the *Tampa Tribune* when those fragile, expressive hands which hadn't stirred for days suddenly began to move. One hand, palm down, made repeated circles— *Please, please*—on her chest. With the fingers of her right hand she formed a crooked "V" and plucked at her left, then, with obvious effort, laced the fingers of both hands together and wiggled them up and down.

The interpreter, summoned from the hospital cafeteria where she had been having lunch, watched for a few minutes, waiting patiently while my aunt shakily unlaced her fingers and extended her hands, turning the right palm up and the left palm down. The interpreter leaned forward and her own hands began to move, in a slow, fluid ballet. "I'm telling your aunt that I understand."

"Yes, yes," I pressed. "But what's she *saying?*" Aunt Lucy turned toward me with wet and pleading eyes as the interpreter translated, "'I love you, Rosie. Now, please, unplug the machine and let me die.'"

Many tearful prayers later, for once in my life, I did exactly what Aunt Lucy wanted me to do the very first time she asked.

Miss Havisham Regrets

IT WAS JOHN Forster who, in his *Life of Charles Dickens* (1874) first revealed that Dickens had written a different ending to *Great Expectations* at the urging of his friend, the novelist Edward Bulwer Lytton. A proof of an earlier version and part of the manuscript have since been discovered. It wasn't until 2002 that an American scholar, researching the life of Anthony Trollope among the papers of the Ternan family at the University of London, uncovered yet a third ending to Dickens's classic tale. Experts have identified the handwriting as that of Ellen Lawless Ternan, who met Dickens in 1857 while she, her mother, and sister were acting in a charity production of *The Frozen Deep*. Ternan was Dickens's mistress until his death in 1879 and almost certainly served as the model for the heroines of his last three novels: Estella *(Great Expectations)*, Bella *(Our Mutual Friend)*, and Helena Landless *(The Mystery of Edwin Drood)*. Whether this third ending was written at the suggestion of Miss Ternan or by Miss Ternan herself is a matter open to debate.

As an aid to the scholar, text matching the 1861 edition of *Great Expectations* is printed in *italics*.

—Editor.

"Tell me as an old, old friend. Have you quite forgotten her?"

"My dear Biddy, I have forgotten nothing in my life that ever had a foremost place there, and little that ever had any place there. But that poor dream, as I once used to call it, has all gone by, Biddy, all gone by!"

Nevertheless, I knew while I said those words, that I secretly intended to revisit the site of the old house that evening, alone, for her sake. Yes even so. For Estella's sake. I had heard of her as leading a most unhappy life, and as being separated from her husband, a pompous lout named Bentley Drummle, *who had used her with great cruelty, and who had become quite renowned as a compound of pride, avarice, brutality, and meanness. And I had heard of the death of* Drummle, *from an accident consequent on his ill-treatment of a horse. This release had befallen her some two years before; for any-thing I knew, she was married again.*

The early dinner-hour at Joe's left me an abundance of time, with-out hurrying my talk with Biddy, to walk over to the old spot before dark. But, what with loitering on the way, to look at old objects and to think of old times, the day had quite declined when I came to the place.

There was no house now, and the cleared space it had once occupied had been enclosed with a rough fence. *Looking over it, I saw that some of the old ivy had struck root anew, and was grow-ing green on low quiet mounds of ruin. A gate in the fence standing ajar, I pushed it open and went in.*

A cold silvery mist had veiled the afternoon, and the moon was not yet up to scatter it. But, the stars were shining beyond the mist, and the moon was coming, and the evening was not dark. I could trace out where every part of the old house had been. "Its name is Satis House," Estella had told me once. Greek or Latin or Hebrew—she didn't care which—for "enough."

Enough. Sufficient. Adequate. No, hardly adequate, for it had been a sad and deserted place even then. I recalled an over-grown garden tangled with weeds; an empty pigeon-house in the brewery yard, blown crooked on its pole by the wind; unoc-cupied stables; a vacant sty; a wilderness of empty casks upon which Estella and I had once, as children, played, watched from an upstairs window by Estella's adoptive mother, Miss Havisham, who had, over the years, grown ever more eccentric and reclusive.

All were gone, long gone, and even the courtyard, which had once been paved, had disappeared under a sea of mud, potholed and rutted by the constant to and fro of the removal carts.

At the far end of the lane, a wooden gate in the high enclosing wall stood open. I picked my way carefully along a furrow—for little else was left to mark where the lane had been—and was astonished to discover, when I passed into the old brewery yard, that the latch on the gate was new and the brewery had not been pulled down.

Where once the odor of malt and hops had lingered on damp and molding wood, the premises now fairly gleamed with prom-ise. Bright paint lacquered the doors, the sills, and the window casements; even the mullions had been decorated in the same cheerful blue, as if word had been received that the queen, in her golden coach, might at any moment be passing by. Gaps in the brewery's foundation had been repaired with new stone, its brick and stone-faced walls had been repointed, and a roof, part gabled and part gently arched, led onto a new four-sided chimney nearly forty feet high, its sides neatly tapered and faced with brickwork fluting. The grime-encrusted windows through which I had once fancied a ghostly vision of Miss Havisham hanging from a wooden beam and beckoning to me—an apparition from which I, then a common labouring boy, had fled in terror—had been cleaned and glazed anew. As I stood there, entranced, a skylark began its cheerful song and I thought, as it sang, that all might be well.

Who in the village, I wondered, had the resources to revive the old enterprise? As I drew closer, I spied a sign, newly painted, propped against an open door and girded round with rope, ready for the workmen who would hoist it into position on the iron scrollwork that crowned the archway. The sign bore a picture of a sheaf of wheat, and beneath the sheaf, black letters spelling out the words "Wm. Pumblechook, Ltd."

So, I chuckled, Joe's Uncle Pumblechook, that pompous old seed merchant, he who had taken shameless credit for every happy rise in my social condition—even though he had nothing whatever to do with it—had invested in the old brewery. Perhaps Pumblechook had tired of his hot gin and water, or he had grown weary of having his ale sent round from the Boar. I resolved to call at the Blue Boar on my way back to Biddy and Joe's to quiz Squires, the landlord, on the particulars of the matter.

Twilight was closing in as I left the brewery behind and passed back through the gate. I was strolling *along the desolate garden walk, when I beheld a solitary figure in it.*

The figure showed itself aware of me, as I advanced. It had been moving toward me, but it stood still. As I drew nearer, I saw it to be the figure of a woman. As I drew nearer yet, it was about to turn away, when it stopped, and let me come up with it. Then, it faltered as if much surprised, and uttered my name, and I cried out:

"Estella!"

"I am greatly changed. I wonder you know me, Boy."

"I should always know you, miss," said I. *The freshness of her beauty was indeed gone, but its indescribable majesty and its indescribable charm remained. Those attractions in it, I had seen before; what I had never seen before was the saddened softened light of the once proud eyes; what I had never felt before was the friendly touch of the once insensible hand.*

We sat down on a bench that was near, and I said, "After so many years, it is strange that we should thus meet again, Estella, here where our first meeting was! Do you often come back?"

"I have never been here since. "

"Nor I."

"I have very often hoped and intended to come back, but have been prevented by many circumstances. Poor, poor old place!"

The silvery mist was touched with the first rays of the moonlight, and the same rays touched the tears that dropped from her eyes. Not knowing that I saw them, and setting herself to get the better of them, she said quietly:"Were you wondering, as you walked along, how it came to be left in this condition?"

"Yes, Estella."

"The ground belongs to me. It is the only possession I have not relinquished. Everything else has gone from me, little by little. "

"Indeed. My Uncle Pumblechook, it appears, has acquired the brewery."

"He has," said she, a frown unaccountably darkening her face. "He made me a generous offer. Restoration is well underway, as I'm sure you noticed, although how that silly man can make a success of it when none has done before, is a mystery to me."

"But I have kept this. " She tapped her foot upon the ground. *"It was the subject of the only determined resistance I made in all those wretched years. "*

"Is it to be built on?"

"It was, but..." She paused, and a tear fell, unchecked, upon her cloak. "Oh, Pip, Pip, whatever shall I do?"

"Estella, dearest!" A frenzy of unhappiness welled up within me. I clasped her hand to my breast and cried, "What is wrong? You must tell me!"

"Just when I thought myself to be free"—and by that I presumed she referred to the untimely death of her boorish husband—"that horrid man, Compeyson, long the author of my family's misfortune, has encroached again upon my happiness."

My heart began to hammer like a drum within my chest. Compeyson! The scoundrel who seduced Miss Havisham, played upon her affection, and by vile trickery joined with her wastrel brother, Arthur, to cheat her of her inheritance, and more. *The marriage day* had been *fixed, the wedding dresses were bought, the*

wedding tour was planned out, the wedding guests were invited. The
day came, but not the bridegroom. He wrote her a letter, which she
received at twenty minutes to nine, when she was dressing for her
marriage, the very hour and minute at which she afterward stopped
all the clocks. Compeyson! The betrayer responsible for the death
of Abel Magwitch, my friend and benefactor and whose hated
name I believed to have been struck for ever from my lexicon
as I watched him sink into the muddy waters of the Thames.

"But that's impossible!" I cried, taking but little time to consider the matter. "Compeyson is dead! He fell overboard with
Magwitch and both were sucked under the keel of a steamer."

"Alas, he survived," wept Estella.

"But his body washed ashore," I forged on, despite the
hopelessness that was invading my brain, "and was identified
by certain papers in his pocket, still quire legible, despite having been weeks in the water."

"The papers may have been Compeyson's, but the body was
someone else," Estella sobbed. "That wretched man called at my
home in London—for I live in Chelsea now—and threatened
to reveal the awful truth about... about..." Her terrified tears fell
fast upon my hand.

Estella's sobs tore at my heart. "There, there," I soothed in
a gentler voice. "This will pass. Even if he lives, Compeyson is
a fugitive and can hardly afford to make his presence known."

Estella turned her red and tear-filled eyes toward me. "He
intends to flee to New South Wales, and for that he requires
assistance," she said. "I'm to give him five hundred pounds or he
threatens to publish the truth about my mother!"

I had long ago extracted, as one would a tooth, the truth about
that delicate matter from Jaggers, our mutual lawyer and friend.
I almost smiled, but recomposed my features when I sensed that
a smile on my face, at that moment, would do nothing to miti-
gate the abject misery that contorted hers.

When I had pressed Jaggers for information about Estella's
mother, he had spoken in parables and endless put-the-case-that's,
all the while exchanging odd looks with his clerk, Wemmick, until
I'd guessed the truth of Estella's parentage and we'd ended our
conversation by touching our lips gravely with our forefingers.

And so, "I know about your mother," I confided to Estella,
and before she could object, I touched my hand to her damp
cheek to silence her.

Her dark, luminous eyes searched my face. "You know?" she exclaimed at last. "But how?"

"I discovered it of an evening while dining with Jaggers," said I. Longing to erase all doubt from her mind about the specific knowledge that I held, and in hope of bringing a smile to her lips once again, I said, "I know that you are the daughter of Molly, Jagger's maid."

"Molly!" Estella's hands flew to her face. "Molly isn't my mother, dear fool! Miss Havisham is!"

I felt my face flush with surprise and shame. I had been so *hot on tracing out and proving Estella's parentage,* that in my haste, I had jumped to unwarranted conclusions. How could I have been persuaded when Molly served us at dinner that Molly's hands were Estella's hands, and her eyes Estella's eyes?

Once, I had detected in Estella's looks and gestures a tinge of resemblance to Miss Havisham which I dismissed as being acquired as a child from a guardian with whom she had been much associated and secluded. But, as I studied Estella now, I realized how wrong I had been. In the moonlight, and with the patina of age soft upon her features, she resembled her mother, Miss Havisham, without any doubt. Whatever child Molly had borne to Magwitch, it had not been Estella.

"Then who ...?" I began, before swallowing my words, as the answer came as clearly as a bolt of lightning in the night sky. "Compeyson is your father."

Estella nodded. "He used my mother most cruelly. First he robbed her of her maidenhood, then her money, then, for all intents and purposes, her very life."

I recalled Miss Havisham as I had last seen her, lying upon the banqueting table under a loose, white sheet, her grievous burns covered from foot to throat with white cotton wool. All around her had lain the ruins of that ancient banquet, dominated by the rotten bride cake, shrouded in cobwebs.

"At first," Estella continued, "Miss Havisham stayed within the house to hide the undeniable fact of her condition. Jaggers sent a maid trained as a midwife to attend her, and after I was born, I was removed and placed, with great secrecy, in a convent to be raised with other well-to-do orphans. On my third birthday Jaggers brought me back to Satis House and introduced me as Miss Havisham's ward.

Where once she had been Miss Havisham in name only, Estella was now Miss Havisham by right of birth.

"But why do Compeyson's threats trouble you so?" I inquired. "Surely, it's preferable to be Miss Estella Havisham, daughter of the late Miss Havisham of Satis House in Kent, than of Molly, a maid in service, who has stood trial for murder?"

"I can hardly find the words," Estella replied. "Compeyson, though married, was a deceiver. He sowed seeds of his deceit everywhere."

"Please, Estella. We are old and dear friends. Kindly speak to me plainly."

"Compeyson taunted me." She lowered her head, and even in the early December light, I thought I saw a flush upon her face. "I am not his only love child, he told me. Love child! As if what passed between that villain and my mother could be dignified by the gentle name of love!"

My *involuntary start occasioned her to lay her hand upon my arm. "No!" she cried, imperiously stopping me as I opened my lips.* "You must hear all."

"Do you recollect my late husband, Bentley Drummle, who fancied himself next in line to a baronetcy . . .?" She laughed derisively. "Bentley, too, was conceived on the wrong side of the blanket, to Katherine Drummle and her secret lover, Compeyson.

"I dropped my face into my hands, but was able to control myself better than I could have expected, considering the agony it gave me to hear her say those words. When I raised my face again, there was such a ghastly look upon Estella's countenance that it impressed upon me the awful truth of what she had just revealed to me.

Estella leapt to her feet and began pacing in front of the bench, her handsome dress trailing upon the ground. "For all I know, I may have tens of brothers and sisters in the shire. Hundreds! Thousands!" She leaned forward and placed a hand on each of my shoulders, then peered deeply into my eyes. "You know what this means, don't you, Pip? It means that I married my brother!"

I drew a ragged breath, fearful that I'd need to thump my chest with a fist to start my heart beating again. Married to her half brother! Thank God there had been no children of the union. I struggled to find some comforting words for my darling Estella, but none at all came.

Estella was the next to break the silence that ensued between us.

"To settle this matter, I've arranged to meet Compeyson at

the Blue Boar, where I'm lodging, on Tuesday. He's traveling under the name of Gerrard."

My mind was racing furiously. Something had to be done to stop him!

After several minutes I found my voice, and a plan. "I'm lodging nearby, at Joe and Biddy's." I took Estella's hand and pulled her down onto the bench next to me. "You'll prepare a note to 'Gerrard.' In the note you'll instruct 'Gerrard' to meet you here, at the brewery, at eight-forty."

The significance of the time was not lost on Estella. She nodded.

"I'll post the note to 'Gerrard' in care of the innkeeper. On the appointed day you will slip quietly out of the inn and meet me at the forge. You will arrive at the forge no later than eight o'clock."

Again, she nodded. I stood, drew Estella up to stand before me, and with my mouth close to her ear, told her what I planned to do.

* * *

But for his shock of black curls, I should not have recognized him. From a window I watched Compeyson stride, with confidence, along the muddy path that led to Pumblechook's brewery, inside which I had concealed myself. Compeyson's body was the same height and girth of my recollection, but the clothes he wore were brown and rough, like those of a farmer. His face was disfigured. A red welt bisected an eyebrow and meandered in a jagged path down his cheek, and his nose was flattened like a pug. Compeyson disappeared from my view for a moment, and then the door yawned wide, and he entered.

"Miss Havisham?" he called.

It was not Miss Havisham, but I, who stepped from the shadows.

The wretch staggered back, startled. "Pip! I didn't expect to see you here."

"No, I don't imagine you did, Compeyson." I wrapped my fingers more tightly around the hammer I had borrowed from my brother-in-law's forge and ventured closer, with a confidence buoyed only by the weight of the weapon clutched in my hand. "So tell me," said I. "How is it that the dead can walk?"

"Your friend Magwitch is responsible for this," said he, indicating the scar that marred his once handsome cheek. "Although gravely wounded, I managed to swim ashore." He laughed, an ugly sound that rang harsh and hollow in the vastmess of the deserted brewery. "A kindly farmer's widow nursed me back to health." Then he leered. "Shocking, isn't it, when a gentleman can't travel the queen's highway on legitimate business without being set upon by vagabonds?"

Never had I hated another human being as much as I hated Compeyson at that moment.

He indicated his jacket, which upon closer inspection proved to be a faded tattersall. "Her husband didn't need it anymore."

I gasped, a dread suspicion seizing hold of my brain. "You didn't...?"

"Murder her husband for his clothing? No." He sneered. "Just let us say that the poor sod who washed ashore wearing the jacket that bore my papers didn't have much need for his body anymore."

While we were talking, Compeyson had circled round until he stood between me and a copper boiling vat. I controlled an almost irresistible urge to erase the smirk of self-satisfaction from his face with a single blow of Joe's hammer, but I wasn't done with Compeyson yet, and neither was my clever Estella.

"What's that?" I inquired suddenly, tilting my head at an angle like a spaniel who'd sensed a rabbit in the underbrush.

Compeyson shrugged, stared at me silently for a moment, then pulled a watch out of his ragged pocket and flipped the case open. "What do you want, old chap? I haven't got all day."

"I'm certain I heard something," said I.

From far above, in the rafters of Pumblechook's deserted brewery, came a peal of laughter so crystalline, that even Compeyson could not fail to hear. He glanced upward, his eyes traveling from the copper vats on the wooden floor before him to the mash tuns on the level above, up yet again to the water tanks on the upper floor, and across to the iron stairway that led to a storage room and a high, open-worked gallery upon which Estella—Miss Havisham—now stood.

She was dressed all in white, and she had bridal flowers in her hair, from which a long white veil depended. Jewels sparkled at her throat and upon her fingers. A bridal slipper was on one foot, but the other foot was unshod.

"Who is that?" cried Compeyson.

"I must have been mistaken. It's nothing but the wind," said I, as if my life's love were not standing fifty feet above my head wearing a wedding dress that had once belonged to my deceased sister, Mrs. Joe.

The laughter pealed out again, and Compeyson's jaw grew slack. Comprehension dawned on his startled face, and I said a silent prayer to Magwitch who had been the unwitting author of my plan.

As Magwitch told the tale, Arthur Havisham, Estella's uncle, had been Compeyson's willing partner in forgery and swindling; yet when Arthur lay raving in Compeyson's house, driven to insanity by visions of his dead sister in her wedding clothes—Compeyson spoke hardy, but never came nigh himself.

Now Miss Havisham's ghost had come again, and this time, Compeyson would have to face her.

Yet, to my great surprise, it was not fear that seemed to drive him now. Eyes glued to the vision in the gallery, Compeyson, his voice choked with emotion, croaked, "Mirabella!"

Now it was my jaw that dropped, as I had never heard Miss Havisham called by her Christian name.

"Mirabella?" Compeyson cried again. "I must explain!" He turned and bolted up the stairs, his rude farmer's boots clattering on the iron treads. I followed close behind.

As Compeyson neared the gallery, Estella extended an arm, as I had instructed, and shook out a shroud. "I'll put it on you at five in the morning," she sang, in a clear, high soprano.

Compeyson covered his head with his arms, pleading, "Take it away from her, take it away!" But instead of lifting himself up hard and dying, as Arthur had done, Compeyson screamed, "There's blood, blood!" and staggered backward against a water tank, stumbled over a bag of malt, tumbled over the railing, and fell into a mash tun, where he lay, twitched thrice, then once again, until he moved no more.

Estella sank to the floor, sobbing, Mrs. Joe's wedding gown pooled in a silken puddle around her. I gathered her into my arms and stroked her hair, as Miss Havisham had once done when Estella was a child crooning — *I wanted a little girl to rear and love, and save from my fate.*

"It's finished," I said. The circle is closed. Her revenge is complete—for poor, mad Arthur, for you, for Magwitch, and, yes, perhaps even for me.

"Let me take you back to the Boar," I urged. "A hot toddy is just what the doctor ordered."

"I'll be arrested!" She shuddered.

"For murdering Compeyson? How can you have murdered Compeyson?" I asked reasonably. "He's already dead. Drowned in the Thames before witnesses, including a boatload of constables." Besides, I added gently, "Any inquest would rule it an accident."

My eyes shifted, on their own volition, to the motionless form in the mash tun below. Compeyson would lie there until spring, at least, when farmers would fill Pumblechook's till with money for seed. Longer, perhaps for all eternity—food for vermin, like Miss Havisham's bride cake—if Pumblechook's investors couldn't raise the funds he needed to continue construction of the brewery.

I assisted Estella down the stairs, wrapped her in her cloak, which had been hanging in the room that was to be Pumblechook's office—if the oversize desk and chair were any indication—and we walked, arm in arm, back to the Boar.

Although it was early in the day for hot toddies, Squires fixed her an ample one, adding an extra bit of lemon to ward against a chill. "Here 'tis, miss. Good for what ails you!"

I sat with Estella by the fire until her mug was empty, then saw her to her chamber and urged her to rest. I promised to join her for lunch the following day, after which we'd catch the afternoon coach to London.

* * *

The day dawned crisp and clear and the sun shone warm upon my head as I walked briskly to the Boar, carrying my satchel and dressed in my traveling coat. As Estella had not yet come down, I shook off the chill, poked up the fire, and ordered an ale.

"You here to see the young lady, Mr. Pip?" asked Squires as he drew me a pint.

"Yes, Squires, I am."

"Why, she left on the morning coach," said he, "but asked me to say if you called"—and here he cast his eyes upward as if reading Estella's instructions off the wooden beams—"'I'm to say: 'Miss Havisham regrets she's unable to lunch today.'" Squires reached into the pocket of his grimy apron and withdrew an envelope. "And here's a note, sir." *It was addressed to*

Phillip Pirrip, Esq. and on top of the subscription were the words: To Be Read at Satis House.

I took the note from his hand and, with a heavy heart, returned to the ruined place where Satis House had once stood, the scene of my greatest happiness and greatest sadness. Once again I took the garden path that lead to the bench we had so recently shared, sat down upon it, and opened Estella's letter.

"I have often thought of you," wrote *Estella. "Of late, very often. There was a long hard time when I kept far from me the remembrance of what I had thrown away when I was quite ignorant of its worth. But, now I have given it a place in my heart. I little thought,"* the note continued, *"that I should take leave of you in taking leave of this spot.* Yet, when the innkeeper inquired this morning if "Mr. Gerrard" had found me well, I thought it best to leave. When Compeyson's body is found, as surely it must be found, I will be far away, beyond reach of the law.

"You once *said to me, 'God bless you, God forgive you!' And if you could say that to me then, you will not hesitate to say that to me now—now, when suffering has been stronger than all other teaching, and has taught me to understand what your heart used to be. I have been bent and broken, but—I hope—into a better shape. Be as considerate and good to me as you were, and tell me we are friends. And will continue friends apart."*

Disconsolate, I remained on the bench for several hours, the stone hard and cold beneath me, rereading Estella's words, as if by study, or rearrangement, they might contain some secret clue to as to where she might be found. Then I folded the letter and slipped it into my pocket, next to my heart, and with new determination, walked *out of the ruined place.*

And, as the morning mists had risen long ago when I first left the forge, so, the evening mists were rising now, and in all the broad expanse of tranquil light they showed to me, I knew I would countenance *no shadow of another parting from her.*

Driven to Distraction

WHEN HARRISON KEELED over and died I didn't think I'd marry again, but Mama said, "Life goes on, Marjorie Ann. When you fall off a horse, you have to climb right back on."

Given a chance, Mama would have matched me up with one of Harrison's law partners, right there at South River Country Club as they converged on the roast beef carving station after the funeral. But I have my pride. I waited a respectable year before marrying Stephen, who swept me off my feet with the lean, rawboned, good looks of a Montana rancher, a laid-back wrangler who spoke fluent U.S. Tax Code. The way Stephen handled Harrison's estate was nothing short of dazzling.

Stephen was clever with gadgets, too. In his office at home, he had a desktop computer, a laptop, a scanner, three monitors—one as big as an over-the-sofa painting of the Last Supper—two cameras that scanned the room like disembodied eyeballs, and wires that snaked kudzu-like around the table legs. I pretty much kept out until cleaning day when I'd have to run the vacuum and dust his office myself. Theresa refused. The blinking and beeping unnerved her. She was convinced the machines would steal her thoughts, and to tell the truth, I half agreed with her.

The last thing Stephen needed was another piece of electronics, so for his fortieth birthday I gave him a fabulous five-course dinner at Northwoods Restaurant and a gift card from American Express. He reached across his crème caramel, gathered up my hand and pressed it to his lips, his green eyes flashing "thank you" in the candlelight. By the way he glanced at his watch, I suspected he wanted to skip the after-dinner glass of Remy Martin and rush straight off to the mall to cash it in, but, fortunately, the mall had already closed.

I hoped he'd use the card at Nordstrom or Eddie Bauer, but the next morning Stephen left the house early and was probably waiting at Circuit City when the doors slid open. He came home lugging a box labeled MapMasterIV and spent the rest of Saturday morning holed up in his office, reading the manual. After lunch, he plopped his new toy onto the dashboard of his pickup and drove off, happy as a clam.

Sunday morning when I eased into the passenger seat of the BMW, I found Stephen balancing the MapMasterIV on his knees. He plugged its cord into the cigarette lighter socket and jiggled what I took to be an aerial up and down. He leaned sideways, so close I could smell his Akthar Noir aftershave, adjusted the MapMaster on its bean bag base, positioned the whole shebang on the dashboard, and punched a few buttons. Then he backed carefully out of the driveway, grinning.

"Just listen," he said.

Drive point two miles west and turn right.

The MapMaster was female and she spoke in a calm, non-judgmental voice, like the 411 information lady.

Obediently, Stephen turned right onto Dogwood Lane. "It'll direct us to church."

"You know how to get to church."

"Of course I know how to get to church, Marjorie Ann, but it's interesting to see how the MapMaster will route us."

Drive one point seven miles south and turn right.

Stephen tilted the MapMaster slightly in my direction so I could see the bright yellow display. He tapped the screen with his index finger. "Here's our route in pink. That's the interstate over there, in red," he explained, as if I were a particularly slow and difficult child.

Continue point five miles and take ramp right.

Stephen flipped on his turn signal and eased the car onto the interstate. "It's fantastic technology." He beamed. "Uses the global positioning system. It gloms onto satellites, figures out where you are, then gives you driving directions." He waved a hand. "It comes preprogrammed with hotels and restaurants, or you can put in a street address..." His voice trailed off. "I've got it programmed for St. Margarets."

Drive four point one miles and exit right.

I watched as Allen Parkway, our usual turnoff, receded in my side view mirror. "Why didn't you turn back there, Stephen?"

Stephen stared straight ahead, one hand resting lightly on top of the steering wheel. "I wanted to see where Marilyn would route us."

"Marilyn?"

"MapMaster. M. M. Get it?"

I rolled my eyes toward heaven. Where in the marriage vows did I promise to cherish a guy who names his toys after dead movie stars? I sighed. "Well, I can understand why, uh, Marilyn might be helpful if you're living in a strange city and don't know where you're going," I grumbled. "But if you already know the way, why waste time fooling around?" I swiveled the screen toward me and studied the buttons: Find, Route, Menu.

"Don't mess with it, Marjorie Ann! You'll screw up the settings."

"Okay, okay." I raised both hands in self-defense. "I won't touch your precious whatzit." I folded my arms across my chest and settled into my seat, wishing I could turn on the radio, but I knew better. Stephen wouldn't be able to hear MM over the sound of NPR.

A few minutes later, MM chirped, *In four hundred feet turn right.*

Stephen pulled off the expressway and, following MM's instructions, wound through a public housing project and an industrial neighborhood until at last, by some miracle, we turned onto a street I recognized and I could see St. Margaret's steeple directly ahead.

Arriving at destination on right.

"Well I'll be darned," I said.

Stephen eased into the parking lot, switched off the ignition and grinned like a schoolboy. "Ain't technology grand?"

Even Reverend Nelson's interminable sermon on life lessons to be learned from the parable of the Prodigal Son didn't dampen Stephen's enthusiasm for his new toy. After the benediction, he hustled me out to the car, not even pausing on the chapel steps to shake the good Reverend's meaty hand.

"We need to stop at the store for toilet paper," I reminded my husband somewhat breathlessly. "And milk."

Stephen drove the few blocks to our Whole Foods market and waited while I went into the store. When I returned to the parking lot carrying my purchases, Stephen demonstrated how to set a waypoint.

"You just drive where you want to go, Marjorie Ann, and press the Mark button." A number popped up on the screen. "Now you use this rocker pad to rename the waypoint. W...H...O... There. Whole Foods." Looking over his shoulder, I noticed that Stephen had already set up waypoints for his office, Home Depot, Golds Gym, B&B Yachts, and our home, of course. He punched the waypoint labeled "Home" and peeled out of the parking lot, tires squealing.

Between Whole Foods and Home, the bypass around the construction site on Truman Street threw MM for a loop.

Off route. Recalculating.

"Why did it do that?" I asked.

"It's a new road, Marjorie Ann. Marilyn doesn't know about it."

MM dutifully recalculated and wanted us to go up Route 2 and take the Route 100 bypass, but Stephen decided not to.

Off route. Recalculating.

The woman was far more patient with my husband than I was.

As soon as possible, make a U-turn, she recommended politely.

"You could make money" I mused, "designing special voices for this thing."

"What do you mean?"

"You can already select a language," I said. "So why not come up with some alternate voice chips like the nagging wife. Instead of saying 'Off route, recalculating,' she'd say, 'You missed the turn, you idiot! But do you ever listen to me? Nooooh.'"

The corner of Stephen's mouth twitched upward.

"Or," I continued, warming to my invention, "you could punch in a waypoint for your mother. Then every time you bypassed her house it's 'So, Mr. Bigshot. How come you never visit your mother? Make a U-turn. Now!'"

Stephen joined in, dredging up a *Beavis and Butthead* voice from somewhere in his reckless youth. "Whoa, dude, like there's a fork in the road. Huh huh huh. Fork. Get it?" He chuckled, a rare event, and turned to study me over the rims of his sunglasses. "You patent that, Marjorie Ann, and we can both retire to the south of France."

Truth is, Stephen made excellent money as the head of his own firm. We could retire to the south of France like, any minute, if he wanted, but Stephen preferred to spend his money and his spare time on boating or golfing or offroading in the Arizona desert. The previous weekend he'd dragged me to the GM dealership to check out a Humvee. As if.

I squirmed in my seat. MM had selected a route home that didn't involve a freeway. If she didn't hurry up, the milk would spoil. "I think you should just go straight up 32," I said, feeling testy.

Stephen ignored me.

"I'll bet this route is ten minutes longer."

"Than?"

"Than going straight up 32."

"Where's your sense of adventure, Marjorie Ann?"

"I don't know, Stephen. I think I lost it back in 1998."

MM was feeling testy, too. *Off route. Recalculating.*

Stephen slapped his palm against the steering wheel. "Damn!"

I flinched. "Why'd she say that?"

"I missed the exit. I was listening to you, Marjorie Ann. Can't you keep quiet even for a minute?"

I turned my head and glared out the passenger-side window, my eyes shooting darts into the trees, my mouth clamped shut, feeling glad that Stephen was leaving town the next day for the annual AICPA tech conference in Las Vegas. He was giving a talk on the paperless office. Paperless, ha! Good thing nobody at the AICPA had to empty Stephen's wastepaper basket or they'd ask for their money back.

I would have gone along—the Venetian Hotel has lagoons with gondolas floating through it, et mind-blowing cetera—but Mama was having an eyelift and I felt obliged to stay home and hold her hand. So, while Stephen spent his days holed up in frigid conference rooms and his nights playing blackjack on the Strip, I spent mine fetching and toting for Mama. I bundled up her newspapers for recycling, cleaned out her refrigerator, and scoured the shelves at Blockbuster for Russell Crowe DVDs. She invited me to the film fest, but I think it was because she wanted me to make the popcorn.

Midweek, I was taking a break from Mama and getting a pedicure when she rang through on my cell phone.

"Can you pick up Elroy in Shady Side?"

Elroy was Mama's handyman. His truck had "broke down" and Mama was too hopped up on pain killers to drive down there herself.

I didn't feel like going anywhere and told her so.

"Do *you* want to pick dead leaves out of my swimming pool, Marjorie Ann? Or mow the lawn?" Without waiting for an answer, Mama started rattling off directions to Elroy's, but I tuned out about halfway through. I had Elroy's address. I had Stephen's MapMaster. Piece of cake.

Stephen had left the MapMaster locked up in his truck, so when I got home from the beauty parlor, I moved it into the BMW. When I plugged it in, MM politely informed me she was acquiring her satellites, then waited for me to press FIND, then ADDRESSES. I used the rocker key to spell out, number by number and letter by letter, Elroy's address, then pressed Go To.

MM, bless her little batteries and computer chip heart, got me to Elroy's and back to Mama's without a hitch.

I was backing down her driveway, mere seconds from a clean getaway, when Mama popped out her front door, waving her arms. "Trash bags, Marjorie Ann! I need heavy-duty trash bags. And bug spray!" I waggled my fingers so she'd know I'd heard her, then punched Home Depot into the MapMasterlV.

I hardly ever go to Home Depot, especially from Mama's house, so it didn't particularly surprise me when MM directed me off the freeway and onto a quiet street in Morningside Heights. I was surprised when she advised me to turn right into a cul-de-sac and absolutely astonished when MM announced that I was arriving at destination, smack dab in front of a cute little Dutch Colonial.

I recognized the house. It belonged to Cheryl, from church. She sang in the choir with Stephen. At the Ferguson wedding they'd sung a duet, "One Hand, One Heart," and there hadn't been a dry eye in the house.

Why had Stephen set a waypoint for Cheryl? I felt dizzy, wondering if all the hours they'd spent practicing "One Hand, One Heart" had escalated into Two Hands, Big Breasts.

Deeply suspicious, I selected the waypoint Stephen had set up for Gold's Gym and pushed Go To. MM directed me out of the cul-de-sac, back onto the freeway and through the center of town. Gold's Gym had long disappeared from my rear view mirror when MM instructed me to turn into Foxcroft Acres, a new development on the south side of town.

Arriving at destination on right.

I eased my foot onto the brake and stared at the name on the mailbox: J. BARTON. I recognized that name, too. The "J" stood for Julie and she was Stephen's personal trainer.

So, Julie had set up private practice in her home? Helping my husband with his pushups perhaps? If Stephen hadn't been in Las Vegas, I would have beaned him with one of his own five-pound, handheld dumbbells.

I slammed the accelerator to the floor and peeled out of there. Mama's trash bags and bug spray would just have to wait.

The waypoints labeled T&E and RUSSELL turned out to be

just that, the Art Deco building housing the city's most prominent accounting firm and the office of Russell Herman, Stephen's
attorney, respectively. But when I followed MM's directions for
B&B Yachts, she took me miles out of town, down Route 214
and onto a narrow country road that ended in a long wooden pier.
Arriving at destination.

The BMW's tires crunched on the gravel as I eased onto
the shoulder and cut the engine. Just ahead, at the water's edge,
stood a cluster of summer cottages that had been converted
into year-around homes. A child of perhaps three or four rode
a tricycle around and around on the blacktopped driveway of a
white clapboard rancher adjacent to the pier. I scrunched down
in the driver's seat and watched the kid pop wheelies, my head
swimming. What the hell was going on?

Almost immediately, the garage door yawned open and a
woman appeared, her hair a nimbus of gold against the dark interior behind her. I scrunched down even further. When I dared
to peek again, she had hustled the kid into a car seat and was
backing her PT Cruiser out of the garage and down the drive.

B&B Yachts? Hah! I knew what was going on. Stephen was
leading a double life. He probably had mistresses, maybe even
wives and children, scattered all across the city. The county. The
state of Maryland. Maybe even the world!

After all I'd done for the SOB! I watched the dust kicked
up by his girlfriend's tires swirl down the road behind me and
remembered a moment just before our wedding, at the rehearsal
dinner. I had been leaning over the sink in the ladies room, touching up my lip liner, when Mama took me aside and in one of
those priceless mother-daughter moments, came the closest she
ever came to discussing sex with me. "Remember, Marjorie Ann,
give a man steak at home and he won't go out for hamburger."
Well, I'd been giving Stephen filet mignon twice a week since our
honeymoon, so what the hell was he going out for? Tenderloin?

When the dust had settled, I climbed out of the car, hoping
that a walk in the spring sunshine might clear the sick visions
out of my head. I strolled to the end of the road and stepped
onto the pier. To my left, three sailboats bobbed quietly, water
chuckling softly along their sleek fiberglass hulls. To my right, a
half dozen kayaks were lined up on a narrow strip of sand, each
stern bearing a TWHA stencil to show that they belonged to

the Truxton Woods Homeowners' Association. If I took one out for a paddle, probably nobody would notice or care.

I reached the end of the pier and sat down on the rough boards, dangling my feet over the water. A soft breeze lifted my hair and cooled the hot tears that streamed down my cheeks. I turned my face toward the afternoon sun. As far as I was concerned, Stephen could take a long walk off a short pier.

I sat up straight. Where had that come from? Perhaps the snowy egret elegantly fishing in the shallows had whispered the suggestion into my ear. *A long walk off a short pier.* I scrambled to my feet, brushed off the seat of my slacks and hurried back to the car to fetch MM.

With the MapMaster tucked under one arm, I returned to the beach and selected what appeared to be the most seaworthy kayak. I switched MM to battery power, then laid her carefully on the bottom of the boat. I plopped down on the sand, rolled up my pant legs, removed my shoes, and set them next to MM. When I was confident nobody was looking, I eased the kayak into the water, climbed aboard, and paddled to a spot about fifty feet off the end of the pier where I figured the water would be nice and deep. I balanced the paddle across the gunwales and lifted MM onto my lap, my thumbs hovering over her array of buttons.

I had been half listening when Stephen showed me how to set a waypoint; I hoped I wouldn't foul it up. Following his instructions as I remembered them, I punched the Mark button to capture my present location, somewhere in the middle of Calvert Creek. When MM asked me to, I used the rocker pad to scroll through the letters, carefully relabeling my new waypoint, B&B YACHTS, and obliterating the old one.

When Stephen came home from Vegas on Friday it was all I could do to remain civil, wondering with whom he'd shared his king-sized bed at the Venetian, wondering who had been his lucky charm at the blackjack tables, wondering who had been his partner for the two-for-the- price-of-one buffet dinner special at the Mirage. I could hardly bear for Stephen to touch me, wondering as his fingers caressed my cheek exactly where those hands had been lately.

Monday night, no surprise, Stephen called on his cell phone to say he wouldn't be home for dinner. "Where are you now?" I asked.

"Just leaving the gym and heading back to the office."

In the background, MM chimed in. *In point three miles take ramp right.*

I paused, doing my own recalculation. Ramp right. From his gym to the office was a straight shot down Fairmont. No right ramps anywhere in that scenario. "I see," I said, each word a frozen shard.

"It's tax season, Marjorie Ann. Need I remind you? I'm working late. I have a lot to do."

Drive one point three miles then exit left.

Where had I seen an exit left recently? Ah, yes. On the way to whoever lived at B&B YACHTS.

Inside me, something snapped. "Lies, Stephen. All lies."

"What are you talking about, Marjorie Ann?"

I held the receiver to my ear, silently seething, listening to Stephen pile excuse upon sorry excuse while in the background, turn by turn, MM was confirming what I already knew. In a few minutes, Stephen would be heading down a dark, dusty country road, where a beautiful blonde awaited him in a white clapboard rancher adjacent to a pier.

"Marjorie Ann? You still there?"

"As far as I'm concerned, Stephen, you can go straight to hell!"

"You can't..." Stephen began, followed by, "What the—?" and seconds later by the nearly simultaneous explosions of shattered glass and deploying airbags.

And MM's voice, softly reassuring. *Arriving at destination.*

The Queen Is Dead,
Long Live the Queen

And Cain talked with Abel his brother: and it came to pass, when they were in the field, that Cain rose up against Abel his brother, and slew him. And the LORD said unto Cain, Where is Abel thy brother? And he said, I know not: Am I my brothers keeper?... And the LORD set a mark upon Cain.... And Cain went out from the presence of the LORD and dwelt in the land of Nod.

Genesis 4, v. 8—9; 15—16

IT WAS BAD. Too bad for words.

Clutching the pages, Claire squeezed her eyes shut and shook her head, wondering if even a single sentence could be salvaged from the chapter her sister had written. *Heather smiled up into Chad's carefully capped teeth, wondering, not for the first time, because she'd seen his photograph many times before in* Vanity Fair *and* Country Living, *what brand of toothpaste he used.*

Oh. My. God.

In the late morning sun, sweat beaded like fine mist on Claire's forehead. Her reading glasses began an inexorable slide to the tip of her nose, fell, until brought up short at the end of a beaded chain, a gift to Arabella, handmade by one of her fans. Ignoring the glasses, Claire held a page at arms length to read: *"I've been waiting for you," she enthused, before plunging on with all the subtlety of the neckline of the ribbed-knit cerulean sweater that strained over her voluptuous, surgically enhanced breasts.*

Claire's fingers itched for her blue pencil, but even if she had brought one with her to poolside, the only improvement she could make to that hash of a sentence was a great big swooping delete. The next sentence was almost as bad: *"Shall we get right down to business?" Heather queried anxiously. Chad dropped her hand and strode past her to the bar, where he ordered a dry martini with three olives, all on the same toothpick.*

Claire read the sentence aloud, hoping it would improve upon hearing, but if anything, it sounded worse. She rested her head against the back of the recliner and screamed, "Arabella Latham-Smith, how could you *do* this to me?"

"What now?" The answer came from across the patio where,

seated at a table shaded by an umbrella, Arabella was alternately munching Fritos and applying autographs with a black felt-tipped pen to a stack of eight-by-ten glossies: *Warmest wishes, Arabella Latham-Smith (and Flaubert, too!)*. Although one couldn't actually read it, Claire grumped, the so-called signature being one long squiggly line with a loop at the beginning. Lazy, like everything else her sister did. Even Flaubert's pawprint would be added later, using a rubber stamp, when Ricky, their personal assistant, reported for work later that afternoon.

"This is terrible!" Claire wailed, waving the offending pages at her sister. "Just awful!"

Arabella laid down her pen. "You don't have to shout."

"Chad's a recovering alcoholic, you idiot. He would never order a martini."

"How am I supposed to know that?" Arabella shouted back.

Exasperated, thinking *Good riddance to bad rubbish,* Claire tossed the manuscript into the air where, one by one, the wind lifted the pages and tumbled them like dry leaves into the herbaceous border which was ablaze with asters, hollyhocks, salvias, rudbeckia, and clematis. "If you'd actually read any of the books you're supposed to have written," Claire snarled, "you'd know that Chad went on the wagon after he lost his driver's license in *Death Takes a Walk.*"

"Make it a Diet Coke, then."

"He drinks Sprite"

"Who cares?"

"Your readers care."

Arabella stood, removed the scrunchie that had been securing her hair into a ponytail at the nape of her neck, shook out her coppery curls and strolled to the edge of the swimming pool. "If you think you're so smart, Claire, just do it yourself!"

"You know I can't do that, Arabella. It's your picture on the back of the book jacket, not mine."

Arabella sent her a withering glance. "Try plastic surgery, then." And she dived into the clear blue water.

Claire sat in silence, seething, watching a fly buzz around the remains of the cantaloupe on the fresh fruit plate Juanita had fixed her for lunch. Eight years ago, there'd been no cook, no housekeeper, no chauffeur, and certainly no cottage in the Hamptons with a gardener to manicure the grounds. Claire had been living in a fifth-floor walkup in Queens, flogging her manuscript unsuccessfully around New York City, garnering rejection after rejection until some well-meaning agent had sent her a photocopy of an article from *The New York Times* about age discrimination in publishing. It was the first time she'd heard the term "mediagenic." Claire had taken the advice to heart, and two weeks later, Arabella—twelve years younger and undeniably prettier— had sold *Doggone Dead* to Simon & Schuster in a three-book deal. That was seven books and two publishers ago.

An errant page fluttered into view. Idly, Claire picked it up. *Her hot pink stiletto's clicked on the tiles as she scampered after him.* Earlier, her grammatically challenged sister had written about *pealing potato's.* Hard to believe she'd spent four years attending Sweet Briar College, but no doubt her sister had had other priorities.

"You said you wanted me more involved." Water cascaded off Arabella's hair as she bobbed to the surface at Claire's end of the pool.

"What I meant was you should *read* the books, Arabella. That Q and A at the National Press Club was a disaster."

Arabella waved a languid hand. "Oh, *that.*"

"Flaubert is a bichon frise, you moron, not a freaking poodle!"

With a graceful one-armed thrust, Arabella eased out of the pool, grabbed a towel, and strolled back to her chair, toweling her hair. Unflappable. "So, you're not going to use my chapters?"

Claire shook her head. "Not if we want people to buy the book."

"I was going for the crossover market," Arabella explained. "Romance *and* mystery. Our fans will eat it up."

"We write dog mysteries," Claire reminded her sister. "Not romantic trash."

"But romance is huge!" she complained. *"PW* says so."

"Her breasts protruded like the Alps?" Claire quoted. "Give me a break!"

Arabella scowled. She plopped down in her chair, picked up the felt-tipped pen, but instead of autographing photos, she glared darkly at Claire and absent-mindedly clicked the cap on, and off, and on, and off.

Somewhere deep within the house, a telephone trilled, but Claire ignored it. She scrambled after the scattered pages, hoping to salvage something out of the mess. She'd have to, after all, or they'd never make their deadline.

Seconds later, the glass door to the patio slid open and Juanita appeared carrying a portable phone. "It's for you, Miss Arabella. Your agent."

Our agent, thought Claire sourly as she rescued several pages from the birdbath and patted them dry against her jeans.

"Hey, Lou, what's up?" chirped Arabella into the receiver. "No, I'm not going to do it." She paused. "I don't care what you tell them! Make something up."

Claire began to collate pages.

"I don't care if it's in the freaking south of France," Arabella insisted. "I'm toured out. In fact," she added, with a sideways-through-the-lashes glance at her sister, "I'm thinking of retiring."

Claire stifled a gasp. Bent over the rescued manuscript, she steadied her breathing, watching Arabella out of the corner of her eye.

"Tell them I'm on vacation!" Arabella snapped. She held the phone away from her ear as Lou sputtered at the other end, his curses reduced to a Munchkin-like crackle. "Be nice," Arabella said after he'd wound down. "Remember who's paying your salary."

* * *

Over the next month, Claire repaired the damage that had been done to *Murder Unleashed* by returning to an earlier version she'd backed up on her PC, while Arabella, true to her threats, stayed home and sulked, feeding a ravenous appetite that included her fingernails. As Arabella's nails grew shorter, her cheeks plumper and her hips broader, Claire worried. More than once, she tried to draw her sister out of her funk.

"What's Laurie wearing when Bradley offs her at the charity ball?" Claire asked one dreary afternoon after Arabella had ignored both her appointment with Jean-Louis and her emerging black roots in favor of vegging out in front of the TV. "Emeralds or pearls?"

Arabella aimed the remote and pressed the mute button. "How the hell should I know?"

"You'll need to know eventually," Claire said brightly.

"I'll read it when you're done," Arabella replied, reaching for one of Juanita's gooey chocolate brownies.

"C'mon, Arabella. Help me out here. Pick something. Emeralds or pearls.

Arabella polished off the brownie in two bites. "She's a bitch, right?"

Claire nodded.

"A homewrecker?"

"Uh-huh."

"Rubies, I think," Arabella suggested, licking her fingers.

As Claire would point out later, it was like pulling teeth.

Three days before deadline, and ten thousand words short, Arabella— on a sugar high—giggled uncontrollably and suggested checking Flaubert into a kennel so Heather could sleuth on her own. "That's it!" Claire snapped. "You need fresh air. C'mon."

Before it was too late, before the horse might buckle under the extra weight of her, Claire persuaded her sister to squeeze into her jodhpurs and go riding. Side by side they rode, then single file as the bridle path narrowed. With each echoing *ka-clop, ka-clop* of hooves on the forest floor, Claire strategized. Their recent effort, *Dog Days of Summer,* would be out in a month, and Arabella would have to hit the ground running. But she'd fired her trainer. And her hair screamed out for the hands, the sheer magic hands, of Jean-Louis.

They reached a scenic overlook, and dismounted. Far below, fields of gladioli bloomed, shimmering red and yellow in the summer heat. As their mounts, reins dragging, grazed contentedly nearby, Claire summoned her courage. "Lou called about *Dog Days*," she said at last. "It's the *Today Show,* and Leno. A twelve-city tour."

Arabella stared, eyes dark as currants in a plump cinnamon bun. "What is it about 'retired' that you don't understand, Claire?"

"You can't be serious." Claire swallowed hard, tasting the sausage she'd had for breakfast a second time.

"Oh, I'm deadly serious."

In a flash Claire saw it all—plummeting sales, the shortest shelf life in Barnes & Noble history, *Dog Days of Summer* remaindered in three weeks, languishing on sidewalk tables in front of the store, still unsold at $2.95 until they practically had to give the books away. Something snapped. Claire's arms shot out like pistons, slamming her sister in the chest, propelling her over the cliff—down, down, down—strangely, eerily quiet. The little bitch was too lazy even to scream.

Leaving her sister's horse to graze, Claire climbed into the saddle and loped home, her thoughts churning, turning to novels she'd stored away, literary novels that might one day make her famous under her own name.

"Where's Arabella?" Ricky wanted to know as Claire slipped in through the mud room door. "I have fan mail for her to sign."

"Am I my sister's keeper?"

Ricky raised both hands, palm out. "No big deal."

"Sorry," she said, peeling off her gloves. "I didn't mean to snap. We had a little tiff, and Arabella rode off on her own. She'll be back shortly, I imagine."

The horse came back, of course. Alone. Two days later, they found Arabella's body and the headlines screamed: QUEEN OF MYSTERY DIES IN TRAGIC FALL. At checkout aisles in grocery stores from Maine to California, tabloids pictured the helicopter, the paramedics, the black body bag, with an inset of Arabella in happier times, smiling, dressed in white silk and sequins at the Edgar Awards, when she was dating that actor from the fourth season of *Law and Order*.

"She was so depressed," Claire had sobbed when the police chief came to tell her. "Surely it wasn't—"

"Suicide?" He patted her hand. "Thrown from her horse. A tragic accident, nothing more."

The funeral, at Madison Avenue Presbyterian, was mobbed. New York's Finest erected barriers to keep the fans at bay while inside, Claire dabbed at her eyes with a ragged tissue, and one mourner after another eulogized her sister, recalling Arabella's beauty, her generosity, her enormous talent. A literary voice silenced too young and too soon.

The publisher scrambled. *Dog Days of Summer* debuted at number one on the *New York Times* best-seller list. It was joined three weeks later by an omnibus edition of the first three Latham-Smiths with a spectacular cover (tastefully edged in black) and a memorial introduction hastily penned by her sister.

After a decent interval—the books had dipped to number nine and ten, respectively—the publisher came knocking. Who knew Arabella best? Would Claire consider completing the novel left unfinished at her sister's death?

At first Claire demurred.

They upped the ante.

She was tempted.

They upped it again.

When she (reluctantly!) agreed to give it a try, *Publishers*

Lunch crowed, hailing it as a "major deal." The *New York Times Magazine* carried a feature story, "Stepping into Her Sister's Shoes." Sixty thousand people visited Flaubert's blog—*Paws to Reflect*—on that single day alone.

Claire Latham-Smith—the new queen of mystery—was finally on her way.

Ten thousand words later, Claire typed "The End" and asked Juanita to uncork the wine. *Murder Unleashed* was a winner; she knew it. Florida setting, tight plot, characters so real they practically leaped off the page. Topical, too, she thought with pride, as Flaubert busted CopyCats, a crooked cat cloning operation preying on the affluent elderly.

Her editor beamed. "Absolutely seamless. You can't tell where Arabella left off and you begin."

The art director loved it. "Dogs *and* cats," he crowed, rubbing his ink-stained hands together. "We'll add a teapot to the cover and sell millions."

Marketing went ape, too, predicting a *Today Show* Book Club selection in her future.

Depending on the reviews.

But Claire wasn't worried about the reviews. Elaine Viets, that hardnosed reviewer from the *Times* who'd cut her teeth at *Kirkus,* who hated almost everything, had always been a Latham-Smith fan. And wasn't *Murder Unleashed* the best thing "Arabella" had ever written?

Claire packed her bags and took a Caribbean cruise.

The Friday after her return, her agent called. "I've got an advance copy of the *Times* review. Are you sitting down?"

Claire topped off her coffee and sat. "That good, huh?" she said, thinking that up in heaven—or wherever it was that Arabella'd gone— she'd be looking down, mad as hell and pea-green with envy.

"Not good," said her agent.

Claire thought she'd misheard. *"Not* good? What's the matter? Didn't they give it to Elaine Viets?"

"Oh, they gave it to Viets, all right. But I think it's fair to say she hated it."

Lou was prone to exaggeration. "It can't be that bad," she said. "Read it to me, Lou."

I don't dare."

"Well, fax it to me then, coward!"

Claire dropped the receiver into place, carried the coffee to her office and paced, waiting for the fax machine to spit out the review like a malevolent tongue. She snatched it, still warm, from the tray:

> *As a rule, I never read franchised or as-told-to books, but there has been such a buzz about the mystery novel completed by Claire Latham-Smith for her late sister, Arabella, that I just had to dig in.*
> *I have two words for you. Why bother? Claire stumbles badly in this less than spectacular effort. After the first few pages it is apparent she has none of her sister's talent. The flat characters, convoluted plot and pedestrian prose were excruciating, serving only to tarnish her sister's literary legacy. Nice try, Claire, but do the mystery world a favor, and hang up your pen.*

So she did.

Home Movies

Little Italy

Parents: Please do not allow your children to sit, stand, or lean on the railing surrounding the seal pool.

ANGIE WASN'T COUNTING, but she must have heard the announcement fifty times since she arrived more than two hours ago. The recording was grating on her nerves.

The sun had clocked around to the west, too, so her bench no longer sat in the shade of the National Aquarium, its hulk—all glass and Mondrian-style triangles—looming like the Matterhorn behind her. Sweat beaded uncomfortably along her hairline; it ran in rivulets between her breasts, soaking through the fabric of her Victoria's Secret T-shirt bra.

Damn! Baltimore was hot in July.

Squinting through her Ray-Bans, Angie scanned the bustling Inner Harbor, searching for the sailboat, a Sabre 402 named *Windwalker.* To her right rose the honey-beige tower of Baltimore's World Trade Center, and if she turned her head to the left—past the raked-back masts of the *USS Constellation,* past the red brick walls of the Maryland Science Center—the crimson neon of the Domino Sugars sign, five stories high, glowed like a beacon. Blue-canopied water taxis ferried visitors from the two pavilions that housed the shops and restaurants of Harbor Place across the water to dine at the Rusty Scupper, or to points beyond, like the tourist-magnet neighborhoods of Little Italy and Fell's Point.

But there was no sign of Jack or his boat.

Angie had visited the Sabre website, so she knew that a 402 cost almost a half a million dollars. Even a used model could set you back two hundred thou. But it wasn't the price that impressed her; it was the fact that the boat had two separate cabins with doors. That locked. With any luck, though, she wouldn't have to use them.

Angie yanked her cell phone out of its holster and checked

to make sure she had her brother Johnny on quick dial, in case things turned sour. Then she punched in the number Jack had given her, but voicemail kicked in right away. Damn! Maybe he was out of signal range, or talking to someone else. She scowled at the phone.

Jack. Jack freaking Daniels!

Angie imagined her mother's disapproving voice. "With a name like that, Ange," she would have warned, shaking a finger, "he's gotta be an axe murderer."

Angie'd argue she found it hard to believe that anybody'd make up a name like Jack Daniels.

"You don't know anything about the man!" her mother would say. "Safer to stay home."

Once, Angie had hitchhiked from Baltimore to San Francisco and back, and lived to tell the tale. "Pure dumb luck," her mother had scoffed, with emphasis on the dumb.

Angie's mother had never approved of blind dates, either, so the idea that her only daughter planned to sail off with a guy after meeting him for the first time on the Internet would have sent her into cardiac arrest.

So Angie hadn't told her.

"I'm taking a vacation, Mama," she'd said. "Got a great rate out of Providence to BWI. I'll visit Johnny in Baltimore, see how he's doing at Hopkins, then who knows? Florida, maybe."

The Florida part was practically true. After Baltimore, Jack said he was planning to sail down the Intracoastal Waterway to Fort Lauderdale, then across the Gulf Stream to the Bahamas.

On the bench next to her, Angie had a canvas tote with *Cruising World* stenciled on the side in blue letters. She rummaged inside and pulled out the ad that had been clipped and sent to her post office box in Providence, Rhode Island.

> Energetic, forty-eight year old Italian American engineer with a comfortable, well-equipped two-cabin, two-head 40' sloop needs an adventurous, athletic female partner to island hop in the Bahamas, year round if possible. Safe sailor, good navigator, I dive, fish, cook, and clean. Healthy, intelligent, 5'11", 185, lots of salt-and-pepper hair. Previous female mate references available.

Angie had responded that she was an adventurous, free-spirited young lady who wanted to sail where the weather is warm, the wind is steady, and the islands are beautiful. After a flurry of e-mails, they'd agreed to meet.

She hadn't called his references.

* * *

Angie lived life on the edge.

Parents: Please do not allow your chil—

Someone pulled the plug on the recording, thank God. Angie joined the crowd around the outdoor pool as aquarium staff prepared to feed Ike and Lady, the gray seals who lived there. She rested her forearms against the railing and watched Ike flounder onto a rock, snap up the fish tossed his way, and honk appreciatively for the crowd.

When feeding time was over, Angie strolled along the seawall, past the grinning black hulk of the USS *Torsk* permanently tied up there, wondering where the hell Jack Daniels had gotten to. He was coming from Annapolis, he said, so she'd timed their meeting carefully, taking the crowds into consideration. Maybe Jack was already on island time.

So she wouldn't mess up her cutoffs, Angie selected a relatively clean spot and sat down on the granite wall, her legs dangling over the water. Her feet ended in Docksiders. No one could say she didn't dress like a sailor.

The water taxi came and went, its canopy flapping as it chugged through the still, humid air. Motorboats flitted about the harbor, weaving around the fleet of paddleboats that puttered around like ducklings. Sailboats bobbed quietly at anchor, suddenly swinging wide, facing into a puff of wind that rippled a path along the water.

"Stevie! Stay away from the water!" A woman's voice, screeching. When Angie turned her head to check out the kid, she saw it: a Sabre motoring in under bare poles, its blue hull bright against the greenish-brown mound of Federal Hill. It would be ten, twenty minutes maybe, before the captain found a spot to anchor amid the sea of tethered vessels.

Angie extracted a digital camcorder, smaller than a paperback, from a plastic bag in her tote. She flipped it open and centered the sailboat in the viewfinder. She zoomed in, waited for the cam to focus. No mistake. *Windwalker* was stenciled in gold letters on its hull; an inflatable dinghy bounced along in its wake.

She panned aft to where the captain, his features indistinct in the shadow of a baseball cap, manned the helm, then forward along the life lines. *Well, that's a surprise.* Jack Daniels had crew. A young man in chinos and a blue polo shirt stood on the bow, his foot resting lightly on the anchor chain as it screamed over the windlass and snaked into the water, pulled along by the weight of the anchor as it sank into the muck at the bottom of the Patapsco.

When the anchor was secure, the two men piled into the dinghy, cranked the outboard to life, and motored to the dock where they jostled for a spot, bouncing off the other inflatables like oversized inner tubes.

Through the viewfinder Angie watched the men disembark, watched the young guy shake Jack's hand, watched as he seemed to be saying goodbye. Good, she thought. One less Y chromosome to worry about.

From behind the camera, Angie stared, comparing the man coming toward her to the photo from the e-mail attachment. The man in the photo had darker hair, a wider nose, a less prominent chin. Angie sat on the seawall, puzzled, her knees pulled up, hugging them, studying the man with the salt-and-pepper hair who *had* to be Jack from under the brim of her hat. Son of a bitch knew he was late, too, hustling along the pier, glancing at every female face, probably wondering if she'd given up on him. Let him sweat. Angie had the advantage, after all. She hadn't sent Jack a picture—only a description. One couldn't be too careful.

Jack reached the end of the pier and stopped to gaze out over the water, big hands hanging at his sides. She stuffed the videocam into her tote bag, stood, and followed.

"Jack?" she called, settling the strap of the tote comfortably against her shoulder.

He turned. His sunfrosted eyebrows lifted. "Mandy?"

"That's me." She smiled ruefully. The name sounded strange pinned on her, rather than on the drugged-out cousin to whom it actually belonged. Angie extended her hand, and he took two steps forward to take it. "Shall we go somewhere to talk?" she asked, eager to get on with it.

Walking side-by-side, chatting casually, they crossed the brick-paved causeway to Barnes & Noble, the ho-hum of its chaindom somewhat mitigated by being sandwiched between its trendier cousins, the ESPN Zone and Hard Rock Cafe. Once inside, they wound through smokestacks tattooed with rivets, rode up the industrial-style escalators to Starbucks.

"My treat," Jack said, and bought them each a mocha frappuccino.

"Do you want to see the boat now, before you make up your mind?" he asked, sitting down at the table opposite her.

"How about the other guy?" She jammed a straw into her drink.

"What other guy?"

"The guy I saw riding in on the dinghy."

Jack actually blushed. "You must mean Tim. He works for the yacht broker."

"Tim, then."

"He installed a self-steerer in the Sabre. Wanted to make sure it worked."

"Self-steering will come in handy on the ocean," Angie commented, taking a sip from her mocha frappe. "So, tell me about the trip."

While Jack extracted a map from his fanny pack and smoothed it out on the table, Angie studied his face. The eyes were right, and so were the ears, but the nose and chin bothered her. Plastic surgery? If so, the scars were hidden in the tiny creases of his well-tanned skin.

Jack anchored a corner of the map with his drink. His finger traced a line from the Abacos to Eleuthera, down the long Exumas chain to Great Exuma. Angie smiled and nodded and asked all the right questions—about sending and receiving mail, about satellite phones and how they'd divide up the duties and the costs—but knew it was time to move on.

She leaned over the map. "I'd like to see the boat now, Jack."

His eyes, dark as cinnamon, locked on hers, and something went *ka-plump* in her chest. Goddamn. She hoped that wouldn't be a problem.

Minutes later, opposite the aquarium, Angie held back. "Wait a minute!" she said, grabbing Jack by the arm and dragging him along. "You have to see the seals!" She led him to the seal pool, where they stood side-by-side, leaning against the railing, the crowds pressing in around them.

Ike and Lady eeled soundlessly through the water in their idyllic, 70,000-gallon world. Mounted on the railing was a sign—

CAUTION: THROWING COINS OR OBJECTS IN THE POOL CAN KILL
THE SEALS.

Well, not so idyllic, maybe.

They watched in companionable silence for a while, then
Jack turned to face her.

"Mandy," he said. His eyes seemed to drink her down. "This'll
probably not sit too well, but you could be the figurehead on
my ship of life."

"That's bullshit," she said, smiling.

"No," he said. "Gilbert and Sullivan."

"About the figurehead. I don't think so ... Bill." Her voice
dropped an octave on his name, like a late night DJ. Her smile
evaporated and she waited, giving him time to let the significance of her words sink in.

"Shitfuckdamn." He blinked slowly. "How the hell did you
find me?"

"We're betrayed by our buying habits, Jack. Take me, for example." She plucked at the collar of her gauzy shirt. "If I wanted to
disappear, I'd have to stop shopping at Chicos."

Jack relaxed against the railing. Perhaps he was relieved. "So
what gave *me* away?"

"The West Marine catalog."

"No way." He actually grinned.

She slipped a hand into her tote, easing it down deep along
the side. "I called their 800-number to complain that we hadn't
received our catalog since we moved, and were they still sending it to the Providence address." She shrugged. "'Oh, no,' the
woman told me, 'it's going to your new address in North Car-
olina.'" Angie smiled. "Of course she confirmed that for me."

Jack laid a hand on her shoulder, and again she felt it, like a
jolt of electricity straight to her heart. "But why you?" he asked.

"Not me," she said, leaning closer, so close that her nose was
filled with the Tide-washed freshness of his shirt. "It's Michael
Cirelli who's looking for you. He wasn't amused when you rat-
ted. When your testimony sent his son to jail." She paused. "It
irks him that Danny's cooling his heels at Lewisburg while you
are ..." Angie waved a hand in the direction of *Windwalker*, bobbing quietly at anchor in the harbor behind them. "Sailing off
into the proverbial sunset."

"I'd like to be sailing off with you," Jack whispered.

She stood on tiptoe, her lips warm against his cheek. "I'm really sorry, Jack."

The knife cool in her hand. Its blade, long and thin, penetrated his shirt and the skin of his chest, slipping cleanly between his ribs, piercing the left ventricle of his heart. Still leaning against the railing, Jack only looked surprised as she withdrew the knife and dropped it back into her tote. Jack slumped against her—another amorous couple enjoying the summer evening. Her lips brushed his ear as she whispered, "But if I'd sailed off with anybody, it would have been with you."

With a fluid, practiced move, she lifted and pushed, gently tumbling him over the railing, onto the concrete skirt that surrounded the seal pool, where he lay still, one hand trailing in the water, his eyes wide, locked on hers. It would take several minutes for his heart to bleed out, flooding his chest cavity. Plenty of time for Jack to call out—*Help! Murder!* or even her name. But he lay quietly along the skirting, defeated, dying.

Lady surfaced, the water sleeking off her mottled fur. She snorted, her whiskers twitching curiously next to Jack's hand. Bobbing, she studied the dying man with dark, sorrowful eyes.

"Sorry, Lady," Angie whispered, thinking about the warning sign. Then, "Call 911!" she screamed. "He's having a heart attack!"

In the subsequent confusion, she slipped away, weaving quietly through the crowd, moving confidently against the grain.

Near the causeway between the Power Plant and Baltimore's Public Works Museum, the wig came off with the hat, in one quick swoop. By the time she crossed President Street, Angie had fluffed up her flyaway copper curls, and the disguise was tucked safely into the plastic bag that had once held her videocam.

She strolled down Fawn Street, almost to Gough, before finding a Dumpster where she ditched the bag. She doubled back to Exeter. Angie wasn't worried. Two thousand people were crowded in Little Italy tonight, out to enjoy the film festival. *Cinema al fresco* would generate tons of garbage. Nobody was going to be pawing through the Dumpsters in the morning.

On Stiles, at the far end of the bocce court tucked between High and Exeter, she found her brother and his team, all duded up and slicked back, their asses being whipped by *paisanos* on Social Security, wearing team shirts, Bermudas, and tube socks. She perched on a park bench painted red, white, and green to watch the massacre, wondering, not for the first time, how Johnny could bet serious money on a game that was a cross between lawn bowling and horseshoes. After a while, she wandered off and bought herself a meatball sub and ate it at the corner of High and Stiles, where Johnny found her later, just as it was growing dark. He carried a couple of lawn chairs.

"Sorry I'm late, sis."

She presented her cheek for a kiss.

He unfolded a chair, placed it on the sidewalk, and held it steady while she sat down. "Glad you stopped by."

"I'm starving," she said. "What's in the box?"

"Dessert," he said.

"From Vaccaro's, I trust," she said, holding out her hand for the box.

"How's Mom?"

"Just fine," Angie replied, liberating a chocolate-dipped cannoli from a square of wax paper. "She thinks I should get a life."

"And Providence?"

"Not so good as when Buddy Cianci was mayor, but thriving." She took a bite of the cannoli, savoring the sweetness of it on her tongue, feeling giddy. "You should visit sometime, Johnny."

"Maybe I will," he said, "if I'm not on call over Thanksgiving."

From the third floor bedroom of John Pente's apartment directly over their heads, a blue stream of light projected the opening scenes of *Moonstruck* onto a blank white billboard across a parking lot crammed with people: a street festival meets the drive-in, but without all the cars.

"They always start with *Moonstruck*," her brother explained, "and end with *Cinema Paradiso*."

"All Italian?"

He nodded, chewing, his mouth full of amaretto tiramisu. "Mostly." He fished in his pocket and pulled out a printed schedule.

"So if it's mostly Italian, how come they're showing *A Fish Called Wanda* next Friday and not *The Godfather*?" Angie asked after reading it over.

Johnny licked whipped cream off his fingers. "The neighborhood would never go for *The Godfather*," he said.

"Why not? It's classic."

"You know." He tucked his hands in his armpits and tipped his chair back to rest against the formstone.

"What?" Angie said, comprehension dawning. "Too much like home movies?"

Johnny snorted. "Yeah. Everybody thinks we hang out on street corners with stupid meatheads named Vito saying 'fahgedaboutit' all day."

Angie laughed out loud. "Does any rational person *seriously* believe that every Italian-American family has a mobster or a hit man somewhere on their family tree?"

"Stereotypes," said her brother.

"Cultural bias," said his sister, settling back to enjoy the movie. "Fahgedaboutit."

Author's note: When the seal pool at the National Aquarium in Baltimore closed for renovation in early 2002, Ike and Lady were sent to live at the Albuquerque Biological Park. Ike died several years ago, at the ripe old age of thirty-two, but Lady, now thirty, thrives in New Mexico.

Two Sisters

The elegant Marlborough Apartments (1700 Eutaw Place), erected in 1904 on the location of the nineteenth-century Popelein mansion, closed in 1970. Claribel and Etta Cone, friends of Matisse, Picasso, and Gertrude and Leo Stein, once housed their collection of twentieth century art there. The Marlborough re-opened in 1977, with rehabilitated living units for the elderly, funded by Federal grants.
— Chesapeake Bay Magazine, November 1997

TRUDY PLUNKED A tea bag into a mug and covered it with boiling water. Holding the string, she plunged the bag up and down in the hot liquid, amusing herself by imagining it was her son's head. True, it was Stephen who had provided her with the laptop computer that was her main connection to the outside world these days, but she wouldn't have needed the laptop in the first place if she were still living in her own home instead of a retirement unit in the Marlborough Apartments. Still scowling, Trudy tossed the teabag into the sink. The laptop was probably a hand-me-down anyway, she grumbled, a reject from that fancy-pants insurance agency Stephen ran out of a glass and steel skyscraper overlooking Baltimore's Inner Harbor.

Trudy shuffled to the bedroom of her apartment and powered up the computer. She waited, quietly sipping her tea, as the Windows logo gave way to a blue screen, then to her desktop theme, a family photograph. It featured Trudy surrounded by three of her grandchildren, taken by Goofy at Disney World last fall. She smiled, remembering, as the landscape framing her grandchildren became populated with the familiar icons labeled My Computer, Explorer and WordPerfect, and by others she didn't know anything about but Stephen sometimes used. Whenever Mr. Bigshot wasn't too busy to visit, that is.

With some effort, Trudy banished Stephen from her thoughts. She was expecting an e-mail from home. (Former home, she corrected.) Victoria always wrote late Sunday night; her e-mail was the first thing Trudy looked forward to reading on Monday morning.

Trudy double-clicked the Explorer button that would bring up her Comcast Webpage, access to her e-mail account, and news from her best friend. She watched while the screen filled, not with the display she expected, but with a colorful Webpage associated with the Baltimore Museum of Art.

What on earth?

Trudy clicked the back button as Stephen had instructed, but nothing changed. She remained stuck at www.artbma.org, on a page that shouted in uppercase letters: THE CONE COLLECTION. What the heck was the Cone Collection? A collection of cones and, if so, what kind? Ice cream cones? Traffic cones? Pine cones? Volcanic cones? Rods and cones of the human eye? How very odd.

She scanned the unfamiliar display looking for a button that would lead to her e-mail, but nothing seemed appropriate, so she clicked HOME. The screen cleared, then slowly refreshed itself: She was back at the Baltimore Museum of Art.

Trudy was caught in a death loop.

Not that Trudy had anything against art. Oh no. She'd heard that Baltimore, Maryland had many fine museums and as soon as she got settled in, she intended to visit some of them, but at that particular moment, all she wanted was her e-mail. Back home the Second Baptists had told Brother Bill to knock- off-your-affair-or-else with Janelle Owens, the Sunday school director, and Victoria had promised Trudy an update. Being kept in limbo about hometown gossip was maddening.

When in doubt, reboot, Stephen always said. Trudy tried rebooting, with equal lack of success. When the monitor came to life, there were those damn cones again, cluttering up her screen. A computer glitch. Hell's bells! She'd have to call Stephen after all. Serve him right if he had to come and fix it for her; he hadn't been to visit in weeks.

Trudy reached for the phone, punched in Stephen's number, but got his answering machine. After the beep Trudy swallowed her pride and purred into the telephone. "Stephen, this is your mother. If you're there, please pick up." She paused a fraction of a second before continuing. "I think I've got a computer virus. Can you come help me out? Thank you!" she caroled, then slammed the receiver into its cradle.

At least Stephen's daughter, Alison, paid attention to her. Her granddaughter's weekly visits were the highlight of her life. Trudy glared at the screen from the Baltimore Museum of Art that refused to disappear, no matter what she clicked on.

She sighed with exasperation. With Stephen not immediately available, she'd have to go to Plan B.

Trudy padded to her closet, slipped out of her nightgown and into a gray fleece jogging suit. In front of the mirror, she adjusted the backs on the diamond-stud earrings Carlton had given her on their fortieth wedding anniversary, then added a strand of Barbara Bush pearls. Still wearing her slippers, she shuffled next door to the apartment Monty shared with his marmalade cat, Fangdango. Monty often joined Trudy's table in the Marlborough's community dining room, and she seemed to remember him babbling about working with computers.

Monty's door had a brass knocker shaped like an anchor. In celebration of Halloween, he'd decorated the knocker with a witch doll made of straw and patchwork fabric, fastened securely with plaid ribbon and raffia. Trudy grabbed the witch around the waist and rapped smartly. On the other side of the door, she heard applause alternating with *dings* as Vanna White (she presumed) turned the letters. Trudy knocked again, Pat Sajak was silenced in mid-sentence, and Monty opened the door wearing khaki pants and a blue Oxford cloth button-down shirt under a brown V-neck sweater. Monty had a prize-winning comb-over that defied the laws of gravity. It began an inch above the nape of his neck and swept upward, a comb-over so elaborate that even Donald Trump's hairdresser would have taken three steps backward and fallen to his knees in awe of it.

"I hate to bother you," Trudy began, still smiling over Monty's remarkable hair-do, "but I'm having a problem with my computer. I'm afraid I've got some sort of virus. Can you take a look?"

Monty grinned broadly, revealing a row of perfectly even, perfectly white teeth that probably rested comfortably in a glass on his bedside table each night. "Been years since I did any troubleshooting," he said, "but let me see what I can do."

It wasn't until Monty was inside her apartment that Trudy remembered the way he had eyeballed her cleavage at dinner the previous Friday, and that her laptop was inextricably hooked up to printers, modems, power strips, and such in the bedroom. She certainly didn't want to give the old man ideas! Trudy backed up against the door frame and pointed her neighbor in the right direction. "In there."

She observed from the hallway while Monty sat down in the swivel chair, adjusted his eyeglasses, leaned forward, and peered at her monitor. A few clicks of the mouse later he announced,

"You don't have a virus, Trudy, you just changed where HOME is. See ..." He flapped a hand, motioning her into the room. Trudy approached cautiously, until she was squinting at the screen over his shoulder. Monty pointed to an icon shaped like a house on the menu bar of her Explorer page. "From what you told me, HOME should be set to Comcast.net. Look, you have it set for www.artbma.org."

Trudy stared in disbelief. "I didn't change anything, Monty. When it comes to computers, I'm a complete moron. I turn the computer on. I turn the computer off. I click on the little envelope to read my e-mail. That's all I know how to do."

"Well, these things happen," he said, clearly not buying a word of it. "I'll change it back for you."

Several clicks and a flurry of keystrokes later the BMA's Cone Collection Webpage morphed into the Comcast screen she recognized. "Oh, thank you!" Trudy gushed, truly and enormously grateful.

"No problem. Anytime." Monty stood, hitched up his pants and grinned toothily.

"Would you like some tea?" she asked. Trudy wanted to dig immediately into her e-mail, but felt she owed her neighbor a little something for his efforts. "The water's still hot."

"Don't mind if I do."

"That was so strange," Trudy said to Monty over her shoulder as he trailed after her down the hall. "What's the Cone Collection, anyway? Do you know?"

"Everyone knows about..." Then he paused, blushed. "Sorry. I forgot you're new to Baltimore. Claribel and Etta Cone were spinster sisters who started buying Matisse and Picasso back at the turn of the century, back when they were starving artists. Those two old birds amassed the largest collection of Matisses in the world.... and right here in the Marlborough Apartments! When Etta died, she left it all to the Baltimore Museum of Art. They've got it over there now, in a special wing."

"Goodness!"

"The Cones were personal friends of Gertrude Stein and Alice B. Toklas, too," he added.

Trudy pressed a hand to her chest. "Gertrude Stein? And Toklas? Were the Cone sisters ... ?" She took a deep breath.

Monty raised an eyebrow, then helpfully filled in the blank. "Lesbians?" He shook his head so vigorously that his comb-over started sliding down the back of his skull like an oversized cinnamon bun. "Hard to say. I've got a book about them somewhere. Be happy to loan it to you."

"Thank you, Monty," she said, warming to her neighbor. "Why don't you go look for it while I put the kettle back on."

Within five minutes, Monty was back. With the book tucked under his arm, he drifted toward the kitchen table, which Trudy had set for tea: a teapot under a rooster-shaped tea cozy, two colorful mugs, her best sterling silver spoons, milk and sugar, and a plate of Milano cookies.

While Monty stirred two heaping spoonfuls of sugar into his tea, Trudy leafed through the pages of the book, *Dr. Claribel and Miss Etta.*

"I see what you mean about the Marlborough Apartments," Trudy said, turning a page. "Oh my goodness! It says here that Etta lived in Eight A. That's my apartment!"

Monty nodded. "And Claribel lived in Eight B. The living and dining room of Claribel's apartment is now my studio."

Trudy ran her fingers gently over a glossy plate of *Woman in Turban.* "It must have been marvelous to see." She sighed wistfully. "All those glorious paintings! And right where we're living, too."

Monty held up a finger. "Hold that thought! Let's go back to the computer."

"What for?" Trudy squinted suspiciously at his departing back, but she was curious, so she set her mug on the table next to Monty's abandoned one, grabbed the book, and followed.

At the end of the hallway Monty turned, stepped aside, and allowed Trudy to enter the bedroom ahead of him. "I just remembered something about the BMA Webpage," he told her. "They've got a virtual tour of the Cones' apartments with all the artwork in place, just as it was when they lived here." He pulled out her chair. "Here. Sit." He pushed the mouse toward Trudy's hand.

Trudy sat, and following Monty's instructions, guided the cursor across the screen to a door, clicked, and watched as it slowly opened to reveal a bedroom stacked high with old-fashioned trunks; paintings covered the walls. She clicked on a painted chest, and a drawer slid open revealing beautiful lace collars and fabric samples. "Oh, my."

"What's over there?" Monty touched the screen with a long finger.

Obligingly, Trudy clicked on another door and found herself floating like a disembodied spirit down a long, narrow corridor lined with paintings. At the end of the corridor, she clicked on another door that swung open to reveal a dining room. To her surprise, a man sporting a trim beard and mustache stood there, one hand thrust casually into the pocket of his three-piece, double-breasted suit, the other resting lightly on a buffet. Trudy stared at the screen. "Who the heck is that?" The image stared back at her through round, black-framed eyeglasses.

Monty snorted. "Looks like Sigmund Freud."

"Don't be silly. What would Sigmund Freud be doing in Etta Cone's dining room?" Trudy reached for Monty's book and flipped to the index, then thumbed through the volume to the page she wanted. "Just as I thought. It's Henri Matisse." She smiled, comparing the photograph in the book with the image on her computer monitor. "He doesn't look much like an artist, does he?"

"It says here that Matisse came to visit Etta in Baltimore on ..." Monty squinted through a pair of half glasses at the page Trudy had pointed out to him. "... on December 17 and 18, 1930." He glanced up at Trudy and winked. "Spent the night, too. I guess that lays to rest your lesbian theory!"

Trudy scowled at Monty's joke, then continued to cruise around the virtual apartment, examining the paintings. "My gosh!" she exclaimed as she opened a door and found herself (virtually, at least) in a bathroom. "Etta's got oil paintings hanging in the john!"

Monty stole a glance at his watch. "Speaking of johns, I've got to ..." he winked broadly, "... freshen up. Bridge game downstairs in ten. You play?" His eyebrows shot up in anticipation.

"No, but thanks."

"Well, if you have any more trouble getting to your e-mail, you just call me, hear?" He flashed a crooked grin and hurried away.

Trudy washed and put away the tea dishes, then returned to the computer to check on the e-mail she'd neglected. She clicked around the screen the way Monty had shown her, but no matter what she did, she could only return to the Baltimore Museum of Art Webpage and the virtual tour of the Marlborough Apartments. She sat back in her chair. Perhaps she didn't have a virus at all. Maybe her computer was haunted. Maybe she needed an exorcist. Trudy hated to bother Monty again, but if she telephoned her son, he'd think she was a senile old bag. She turned the computer off at the power strip, counted to ten, then turned it back on.

This time, when the monitor came to life, Henri Matisse was standing in a sitting room of some kind, between a piano and an old-fashioned radio. Over the radio hung a portrait of a woman in a yellow dress, seated before an open window. Trudy lingered over the portrait, imagining how it would look hanging on the wall of *her* sitting room, noting with satisfaction how the vibrant colors — the yellow of the woman's dress, the red of the tiles — matched the fabric on her sofa. Then the rumbling of her stomach reminded her that half a Milano cookie hardly constituted a meal and she'd better put on some proper shoes and get downstairs to the dining room.

After lunch — a particularly satisfying grilled tuna and cheese — Trudy kept her appointment with the hairdresser, then hurried back upstairs to her computer. When she logged on this time, Matisse had moved into a hallway, his head partially blocking Trudy's view of a wonderful painting of a dog asleep beneath a table. She clicked her mouse on the painting: *Interior with Dog*. Everything about the painting made her smile: the magnolia branches springing from the blue and white Chinese vase, the colorful wall hanging, the dog's checkered blanket. It burst with life!

Over the course of the afternoon, with each click of her mouse, Trudy found herself falling in love with the paintings that had once, long ago, hung on her walls.- *Standing Odalisque Reflected in a Mirror* — a little plump around the middle to be wearing pantaloons and going topless, Trudy thought, but who am I to talk about plump? The exquisite *Anemones and Chinese Vase,* and, her favorite of all, *Interior with Flowers and Parakeets.* She felt like she could reach right into the painting, feel the texture of the embroidered curtain, drink from the tea cup, talk nonsense to the lime-green parakeets. Trudy decided that the next time her granddaughter came to visit, they'd go to the Baltimore Museum of Art and see the paintings in person.

The next morning, all thought of e-mail abandoned, Trudy discovered that Matisse had wandered into a room crammed with dressers and tables. Picasso's famous portrait of Gertrude Stein dominated the room, but it was the smaller portraits flanking the author that interested Trudy the most: charcoal drawings of Etta and Claribel Cone. She zoomed in for a closer examination.

Suddenly, the cursor took on a life of its own, flitting around the screen like a Ouija planchette, taking Trudy into another room and depositing her in front of a portrait of two women sitting on a balcony, watching a parade. She clicked on the painting and a label popped up: *Festival of Flowers*. Two women. Etta and Claribel?

Trudy stared at the winking cursor, thinking hard. Was Henri Matisse reaching back through time, trying to tell her something? Claribel Cone, she remembered, had died some twenty years before her sister. Maybe she'd been murdered!

Trudy laughed out loud. Better not mention *that* hypothesis to Stephen. She imagined his patronizing smile, his sarcastic, "You've been reading too many mystery magazines, Mother."

To test her theory, Trudy once again referred to the book Monty had given her. No, she read, Claribel had died of pneumonia in 1929 while living in Lausanne, Switzerland. How about Etta, then? She flipped pages until she reached the end of the book. It told her that Etta died of heart failure in 1949. Nothing unusual about that. The old girl must have been almost eighty.

Trudy's tired eyes returned to her monitor where Matisse stared out at her, unblinking. "Henri," she told his image, "you are beginning to creep me out." Maybe she needed a break.

When Trudy returned to her computer following the Tuesday night after-dinner Oldies But Goodies Songfest, Henri Matisse had migrated to another sitting room. Behind Monsieur Matisse, outside his window, it was fall, the leaves on the trees a palette of reds, golds, and greens.

Trudy nearly fell out of her chair. "Holy cow!" she exclaimed aloud. "I recognize that view! That's the window in *my* living room!" Index finger furiously working her mouse, Trudy zoomed in to study the drawings and paintings to the right and left of the artist — a vase of peonies, a landscape by Cézanne. Still, whatever message Matisse was trying to send remained elusive. She adjusted the cushion at the small of her back and leaned into it, thinking. Except for the view of the trees, everything had changed about Etta Cone's apartment over the course of fifty years and two major renovations. Nothing remained on the walls except, except... Trudy took a deep, steadying breath. Everything, that is, except the solid oak paneling!

Trudy dashed to the kitchen and scrabbled through a drawer,

looking for her sturdiest carving knife. Without even pausing to close the drawer, she scurried back to the living room where she sat cross-legged on the floor in front of the window, and began digging at the edges of the paneling. She forced the blade between the paneling and the window sill, twisted the handle. With a screech of nails, the paneling began to separate from the wall. When the opening was large enough, Trudy peeked inside. Nothing but a narrow, dark space. Cautiously, she stuck her hand into the opening and, holding her breath, felt around. A few minutes later, a rusty can of Tab, a handful of nails, two pennies, and a short length of pipe, greasy and dusty with age, littered the floor around her.

Trudy held the pipe to her eye like a telescope. Something was inside. She slid two fingers into the opening and eased out another tube, this one wrapped in oil cloth and tied with two pieces of rough string. With her heart pounding, Trudy carried the tube into her kitchen, untied the strings, and unrolled its contents carefully on the table, weighting the edges down with ceramic teapots from her collection.

She stared, open-mouthed, hardly daring to breathe. On the table before her lay a painting of a woman dressed in oriental robes, lounging in a green and yellow striped armchair. As if the red tile floor hadn't been a dead giveaway, she recognized the chair — Matisse had featured it in *Seated Odalisque, Left Leg Bent*. And the delicate lace curtains in the window were from another painting, *Nude with Spanish Comb*. The artist was unmistakably Henri Matisse. If that wasn't enough to take Trudy's breath away, it was the subject of the portrait that also made her gasp: Etta Cone.

Trudy leaned back against her stove, reeling. A genuine Matisse! With her index finger, she caressed a corner of the lost masterpiece. It must be worth millions! She could sell it, buy a house in the south of France, hire round-the-clock help — now that was assisted living! — and thumb her nose at her stuffy, good-for-nothing son.

But, how on earth had the painting gotten inside the wall? Trudy remembered reading that after Etta died, security guards had been posted at the door while the collection was inventoried prior to moving it to the BMA. Perhaps one of the workers had planned to steal the painting, stashing it there, hoping to come back for it later? A museum employee? Trudy wondered. One of Etta's own staff?

But no, that couldn't be it. During Claribel and Etta's lifetimes, the collection had been extensively catalogued. There were account books, inventories, customs declarations. Just to be sure, Trudy pored over the Cone inventory in Monty's book, reading it over several times, Nothing remotely resembling this masterpiece was listed among the hundred and forty-nine paintings, ninety-seven drawings, fifty-four sculptures, one hundred and fourteen prints, and three illustrated books that had been among the sisters' Matisse collection at the time of Etta's death.

As far as Trudy was concerned, there could be only one explanation: Matisse must have brought the painting with him when he visited Baltimore in 1930. It had been a gift for Etta, one she'd not wanted to share. Trudy knew with absolute certainty that Etta herself had hidden it.

For the next few days, Trudy did little else but worry about what to do with the painting. Rather than join the other residents for dinner, she ate yogurt topped with Raisin Bran alone in her apartment. Monty knocked on her door several times; the social director called to check on her, too, but she'd sent them both away, pleading a migraine.

Not that she was lying, exactly. Henri Matisse had turned into a major headache. Every time she went for her e-mail, he'd materialize over her inbox, standing by the virtual front door to Apartment 8-A. And, was it her imagination, or did he appear to be frowning?

In self-defense, Trudy would shut off the computer, watching as Matisse's image faded away. But morning after morning, when she powered up, the artist would be back, loitering by the front door. She figured he'd stand there forever unless she did what she had to do.

Trudy picked up the phone and punched the buttons. "Alison, sweetie," she purred when her granddaughter answered, "How would you like to visit the art museum?"

Before long, Trudy's e-mail returned to normal: no-cost mortgages, cheap Canadian prescriptions, offers of untold wealth from exiled Nigerian princes, and miracle concoctions guaranteed to enlarge body parts she didn't possess, but perhaps the Nigerian princes did. Sam's Club wanted her to renew her membership, and Victoria was annoyed that she hadn't stayed in touch. Brother

Bill had ditched Janelle, Victoria announced triumphantly, but his wife had kicked him out of the house anyway.

In the virtual world on the other side of her computer screen, Matisse would show up in the dining room from time to time, but for the most part, he was gone, back to Nice, Trudy supposed. She almost missed him.

But week in and week out, Alison, her reliable (and clever!) granddaughter would meet her at Gertrude's (ten percent discount to BMA members!) where they would lunch on crab cakes, and visit Etta Cone, hanging happily on the north wall in the Cone Collection, next to her favorite painting, *Interior with Flowers and Parakeets.*

Lunch was Trudy's treat. It was Alison, after all, who first uttered the magic words — finders keepers; the third-year-law student who said with some authority, "You own the condo, Granny. What's inside its walls belongs to you."

Stephen had sputtered and blustered, of course, but it was Alison who brokered the deal with the Baltimore Museum of Art, resulting in a fat check funded by a National Endowment for the Arts Purchase Grant and a generous gift from the Rory L. and Carol A. Chase Foundation.

Sitting at her computer in recent days, Trudy enjoyed pulling her bank account balance up on the screen, tracing her finger over all the numbers to the left of the decimal point. A cottage in the South of France — near Nice? — was not entirely out of the question.

"We'll case the joint, Granny," Alison had laughed the day they logged on to www.cunard.com to see about booking passage on the Queen Mary 2.

Trudy guided her cursor over the screen and clicked BOOK NOW.

"Assisted living at its finest, my dear."

She was certain both Henri and Etta would approve.

Can You Hear Me Now?

"WHEN YOU TAKE public transportation, sit next to a serviceman. You hear me, Marjorie Ann?"

Of course I heard, and the hundred times before that too, but I suppressed a sigh, and tried not to roll my eyes.

"Memorize his rank and insignia," Mama added. "If he tries any funny business, Uncle Sam will know where to find him. That's what Papa always said."

The only thing Mama ever got from following her father's advice was knocked up, but she married the guy, and the result was me, so I guess it'd be small of me to complain.

Actually, I hadn't taken the kind of transportation Mama was talking about—bus or train—for quite some time. My late husband had had many faults, but dying penniless wasn't one of them. Since Stephen, I usually fly first class, particularly after Delta sent my luggage to Chicago and me to Las Vegas, where I ended up crying on the shoulder of an oilman from Houston who . . . well, never mind.

I go first class by train too, but old habits die hard, so when I boarded the *Acela* in D.C., bound for New York, with the specter of Mama practically perched on my shoulder, what could I do but wander down the aisle, scanning the rows, looking oh-so-casually for a serviceman to sit next to. Halfway through the car I had one of those head-smacking moments like, duh, Marjorie Ann, whose army is going to pay a per diem for a soldier to ride first class on the *Acela*? So I picked a seat next to a long-legged businessman with a profile chiseled out of marble and a laptop perched on the fold-down table in front of him.

"Is this seat taken?"

He glanced up with a languid, "Be my guest," blinked twice with eyes the color of the Mediterranean flecked with gold, and grinned. I often have that effect on people. It's my hair, Mama says, quoting Sylvia Plath: *Out of the ash, I rise with my red hair / And I eat men like air.*

I was in a relationship, as they say, so this guy was in no danger of being eaten alive by me. I also wasn't in the mood to encourage him, so I sat down, melted into the plush blue upholstery, and dug around in my bag for a book. I'd brought two along: a thriller that had just hit number three on the *New York Times* best-seller list, and a copy of Agatha Christie's *Mort sur le Nil*. In French, *bien sûr*. Another one of Mama's tricks. If you're stuck next to a busybody who wants to talk until your ear melts down about her grandchildren or her hysterectomy, you can look up from your *roman policier*, flash a sweet, slightly puzzled smile and say, *Je ne parle pas l'Anglais*, even if that's the only bit of French you know. I'd done that once, but trust me, thumbing dumbly for hours through pages of gibberish is *très* dull.

Thankfully, my seatmate already had his nose glued to his laptop, where a Gantt chart he'd created in Excel pulsed across the screen in a rainbow of living color. He frowned, studying it—a serious, silent type—so I picked up the best-seller and began reading where I'd left off.

The guy might have been serious, but I was way wrong about the silent. From the confines of a tooled leather holster attached to his belt, a cell phone launched into Papageno's theme from *The Magic Flute*. I got a gentle elbow in my arm as he dug it out. "Brad here."

I don't know about you, but listening to anyone rattle on for—I checked my watch—ten minutes about rearranging plane reservations had me wishing I'd sat in the quiet car. Brad was giving some travel agent a hard time about switching tickets from San Francisco to Belize, poor guy, adding an excursion to the Altun Ha Mayan ruin. Honestly, it just about broke my heart.

Eventually Brad got things sorted out, and I returned to my book. Ness, Joel, and Toby had just been dumped on their aunt's London doorstep, when Brad's cell phone rang again. Clearly he'd taken the time to personalize his contacts with customized ring tones, because this time, instead of Mozart, the phone began buzzing like a demented insect. *Psszt psszt psszt* it rang, like bugs being fried by an ultraviolet zapper on a hot August night. I shuddered.

"This is Dave," Brad answered, sweet and smooth as chocolate-cream pie.

Dave?

"The market was up yesterday," he drawled. "Let's sell a hundred thousand of the index fund."

I kept my eyes on my book and my curious ears cocked while "Dave" dumped Time Warner and picked up Kraft, sold pounds and bought francs, bought December coffee at one ten, and liquidated his position in Futurepharm based on a phone call from a friend at the FDA. Why anyone'd risk being jailed for insider trading in order to save a lousy twenty-four thousand bucks was beyond me.

Make laws for the needy, not the greedy. Shades of Mama again, pontificating in my ear, misquoting Roosevelt.

Need can make men desperate, but greed, in my experience, makes men stupid. I needed twelve forms of ID to cash a check at Wal-Mart, but anyone could move millions on the telephone. Four phone calls later, I knew Dave's bank account number and pass code, his VISA card number (and expiration date!), and his passwords to Schwab and Ameritrade. Math had never been my strong point, but give me a string of numbers—TU 9-1997 (my grandmother's phone number); 25 left, 35 right, 21 left (the combination to my gym locker in junior high); 766-42-1057 (my first husband's Social Security number)—and my mind was a steel trap. I could be dangerous.

Good thing for "Dave" that I'm an honest kind of girl.

As I listened, pretending to read, Brad gave his cell phone a workout, didn't even let it cool down before calling home. "Melissa, sweetheart, it's me. I'll be late for dinner."

I'm sure Melissa knew what a hero she was married to, and how grateful she should be that his long hours and almost supernatural genius kept champagne in the fridge, Escada on her back, and a Mercedes-Benz in the driveway, but apparently Brad felt obliged to remind her of it anyway. In a déjà-vu haze—Harrison, my first husband, thought he was God almighty too—I found myself rooting for Melissa. I prayed for a dead zone, a tunnel, a weak battery, anything that would shut the arrogant S.O.B up. I was hopeful when the train rumbled out of Baltimore and into rural Harford County, but alas, not even crappy one-bar reception discouraged the man. Brad simply twisted in his seat, pressed the phone between his ear and the window, and barked, "Can you hear me now?" every few minutes before bidding his long-suffering wife a desultory good-bye.

I was sipping in silence, enjoying a glass of chilled tomato juice delivered to my seat by a uniformed attendant, anticipating the imminent arrival of a Greek salad with lamb, and appreciating the view as the train sped across the Susquehanna between Perryville and Havre de Grace, when Brad really harshed on my mellow. His blasted phone rang again, a jazzy piano tune this time, kind of classy, so I thought it might be Melissa calling him back.

"Hello. This is Phil."

I nearly swallowed my straw. Phil? What happened to Brad? Or Dave, for that matter? Oh, Annie, Phil cooed, slipping into his new identity as slickly as an undercover operative for the CIA. "Have I got a surprise for you."

I stole a sideways glance over the rim of my glass to see him pause, smiling, thoroughly appreciating (I imagined) the ooh-ing and aah-ing going on at the other end of the line. "How'd you like to spend a week in Belize, babe?"

Annie liked it, and was already packing her tankini, if the tinny shrieks of joy leaking out of the receiver were any indication. The way Phil practically drooled into the cell phone, I felt like handing him my napkin. From some hidden corner of my brain a phrase leaped out, an escapee from a poem I'd been forced to memorize in high school:

And her well-tanned arms
held hidden charms
For the greedy, the sinful and lewd.

Something like that, anyway.

While Phil made kissy-face with Annie, I tried to remember the title of the poem. Something about Alaska. I closed my eyes and pondered, as if the answer might be written on the inside of my eyelids. I was still teasing it out—"The Yukon," maybe?— when Phil said, "Well, hot *damn*" and my eyes flew open.

After a few sentences, I deduced that he was in touch with a banker, discussing hedge funds, AAA-rated Eurobonds, and bearer shares in Panama. And I couldn't help overhearing when "Phil"— sounding veddy veddy British—arranged a private off-shore bank account, set the password to his wife's birth date, and began redirecting his assets into it, with no more effort than applying for a rental card at Blockbuster. You had to like that in a banker. Last time I opened a bank account, they gave me a travel alarm.

When everything was arranged to his satisfaction, the guy made another call. I hoped he was going to share news of his good fortune, whatever it was, with his wife. But, no.

"Melissa, it's me again," my seatmate purred, wearing his Brad voice. "I'm sorry, but I won't be home tonight after all. They're flying me out of JFK on the red-eye. Hong Kong this time."

Liar, liar.

Did Melissa believe one word of the bullshit Brad was shoveling? Hard to tell from my end, what with Brad listening thoughtfully and nodding agreeably—yes, dear; no, darling; whatever you say, sweetheart—all the way to Wilmington. Barf. I felt like putting a muzzle on the guy, maybe a straitjacket too. Poor Melissa!

When the train stopped for passengers in Philadelphia, I closed my eyes and crossed my fingers, praying he'd get off and leave me to my book in peace, but it simply wasn't my lucky day. *Yada yada yada* for the hour it took to streak north at 120 miles per hour through the backyards of suburban New Jersey. *Blah blah blah* past the belching smokestacks and steaming garbage hills that spoiled my view of the Empire State Building, five miles in the distance, across the Hudson. As the train slowed to rumble through Newark Airport station without stopping, I remembered the nail file in my purse, a serious, old-fashioned metal one that TSA would have confiscated in an instant. I could put it to use! I could insert it neatly between Brad's ribs, and thrust, and twist, hard. I didn't know Melissa, but somehow I knew she'd be grateful.

Fortunately for Brad, I missed my chance. In no time at all, the conductor informed us we were arriving at New York's Penn Station, and it was time to gather up our belongings and leave the train and have a nice day. By that time, Brad had apparently smoothed things over with Melissa and was fussing over Annie again as he hurried out of the train and along the platform, his cell phone mashed between his palm and his ear, his laptop case swinging wildly from a strap looped over one shoulder.

I fell several passengers behind as we merged into single file to ride the up escalator, which spit everyone out into a vast concourse among the huddled masses, flanked by their luggage and the roaming homeless. Overhead, a prehistoric departures board whirred to life, informing everyone, letter by letter and number by number—- snick-snick-snick—that the Regional 171 would be departing, twenty minutes late, from gate 11.

After surviving the stampede, I caught sight of Brad again as he passed Houlihan's pub. I was headed in the same general direction myself, but by the time I trundled past the new-books display at Book Corner, Brad was some distance ahead. I watched as he finished his call, and slipped the phone into his belt.

Or so he thought.

Instead of nesting neatly in its holster, the cell phone slid down his pants leg, did a somersault on the polished marble floor, and spun away in the direction of Kabooz's Bar and Grill. Surprisingly, Brad didn't notice.

A kid toting a backpack sent the instrument skidding another two feet with the toe of his Birkenstock, and a woman pushing a stroller drove right over it before I was able to scoop it up.

"Wait!" I yelled, rushing after Brad ... Dave... Phil... whoever ... as fast as anyone could while dragging a wheelie bag behind. I followed him up the escalator at Madison Square Garden and out to Seventh Avenue, but Brad was unencumbered and well ahead of me by the time I emerged, dazed and blinking, into the bright sunshine.

"Hey!" I yelled. "Hey, you dropped your cell phone!"

Brad plunged on, oblivious, elbowing his way through the line of people waiting for a cab. I nearly caught up with him then, but he veered left, and crossed with the light at Thirty-third and Seventh, leaving me standing stupidly on the curb.

If I could just get his attention! But, what name should I use?

Brad, the family man?

Dave, the biz whiz?

Phil, the international playboy?

Who *is* this guy when he talks to his mother?

"Brad!" I shouted.

Across the busy street, Brad turned his head, puzzled, scanning the faces of the pedestrians snaking around him.

I waved the cell phone in the air. "You dropped this!"

Brad paused under the WALK / DON'T WALK sign, cupped his ear with his hand, stared at me, and shrugged.

"Your cell phone!" I screamed over the roar of noonday traffic.

Brad patted his empty holster, waved in cheerful acknowledgment, smiled, and stepped toward me from the curb. That was when it happened.

It wasn't my fault. Honest. The cab had the right of way when it sideswiped the jerk and sent him sprawling in the crosswalk, where a bus barreling down Seventh applied its brakes but...

My God, it was awful!

Tires squealed and passersby screamed as I turned away from the gruesome residue and stared at the cell phone in my hand, at the four-bar signal, at the tiny screen with its AT&T logo superimposed over a movie poster of Michael Douglas in *Wall Street* saying, "Greed is good."

That figured.

Naturally, I used Brad's phone to call 911.

Then, just as naturally, I thumbed through his directory, looking for Melissa. She deserved to be the first to know.

HOME popped up before MELISSA, so I highlighted the entry and punched SEND.

"Melissa," I said, when she came on the line. "You don't know me, but I'm a friend of Brad's. Do you have a pencil?" I waited for her to find one, and then said, "Write down this number. It may come in handy."

"Thanks," she said, "I guess."

"It's a bank account," I explained. "And the password is your birthday."

"How did . . . ," she began, but I mashed my thumb down on the red button, cutting her off.

I was booked into the Marriott on Times Square, so I waited until the cab dropped me off before turning Brad's phone off, wiping it clean on the hem of my jacket, and dropping it into one of the green trash cans in the median at Forty-sixth and Broadway. As Brad's phone sank like a stone amid a sea of newspapers, fast-food wrappers, and crushed soda cans, I noticed a billboard overhead, a kinetic light sculpture that proclaimed in flashing blue and yellow, THANK YOU FOR USING AT&T.

I'd been married to a cheating worm like Brad once myself. So I saluted the billboard. "You're very welcome," I said.

Night and Fog

MARGARET PRICE COULD keep a secret, no doubt about that. When Susan announced to the Methodist Women's Bible Study Group that she was pregnant with twins, Meg was the only person in town—other than Susan's husband and her gynecologist—who wasn't surprised. Meg had known about the pregnancy for months, ever since her friend's home pregnancy test had popped up positive, but she had agreed to keep it secret in case the *in vitro* had failed again. Joyfully, it hadn't.

I figure Meg would have taken her own amazing secret to the grave, too, had an editor at the *Washington Gazette* not been noshing on a chicken wrap at his desk while perusing a "This Day in History" calendar.

"Madison!" he called out.

He meant me.

"Do you realize," Zack Bailey said when I appeared outside his cubicle, a can of Diet Coke still sweating in my hand, "that August twenty-fifth is the seventieth anniversary of the liberation of Paris?"

I had been born during the post-Vietnam era, but thanks to an AP European History course in high school, my background was pretty solid. "When the Allies sent the Germans packing?"

"*Exactement.*" He planted both feet on the floor, sat up straight. "I'm thinking we need some sort of human interest story for the Sunday edition. Liberation Day from the viewpoint of the man on the street. Or woman," he added quickly. "Any ideas?"

My first thought was that ninety-nine percent of the Parisians who had welcomed the Allies with cheers, flowers, and kisses on that historic day were either long dead or confined to nursing homes playing bingo for M&Ms. But the book in progress on my bedside table was a Billy Boyle World War Two mystery, so after a moment I said, "How 'bout the S.O.E.?"

"Es oh what?" History wasn't Zack's strong point.

"S.O.E.F. to be specific," I said. "Britain's Special Operations Executive. The F stands for France." I paused while he took that in. "They were spies."

Zack's left eyebrow quirked. He was a James Bond fan. I'd sparked his interest.

"They worked undercover during the occupation," I continued. "One out of five never made it home."

Zack tapped his nose and made a clicking noise with his tongue. In Zack-speak, that meant "Go for it, Madison."

I spent the rest of the day in my cubicle mining the Internet. Then I made a few phone calls. By close of business, I'd tracked down the author of a recently published history of the S.O.E. to his flat in London. The following morning, in exchange for the promise of an Amazon link to his book in my article, he graciously agreed to share the names of his contacts. Which explains why two days later I was on American Eagle flight 3809 en route to Margaret Price's modest home near Scugog on the outskirts of Toronto.

Margaret—"please call me Meg"—had turned ninety-three on her last birthday but she didn't look a day over eighty. The former S.O.E. operative greeted me at the door wearing slim-cut blue jeans and a loose white t-shirt that said, OOT & ABOOT. Neatly-pedicured toes, lacquered bold red to match her fingernails, peeked out from a pair of flat-heeled, open-toed sandals.

Between her front door and her living room, I learned that Meg was a widow and that until his death, she and her husband, a retired Canadian Army colonel, had owned a Christmas tree farm.

We settled into matching chairs, upholstered in red damask, flanking a gas log fireplace. On the coffee table between us lay a staggering display of medals, ribbons, and assorted military insignia. "You asked to see these," she said as I leaned over the table for a closer look. "It's a little embarrassing, really."

Attached to a red ribbon, taking pride of place in a white silk- lined box labeled Toye, Kenning and Spencer Ltd, lay a gold cross engraved with *God and Empire*. "Wow," I said.

"That's an MBE," Meg explained, confirming my guess.

"I recognize this one," I said after a moment of awed silence. "May I?"

When she nodded, I picked up the Croix de Guerre, holding it carefully by the red and green-striped ribbon from which it hung. "The French don't give these out willy-nilly," I said. "You're a true heroine."

Her face flushed. "I'm not the heroine you're looking for," she whispered. "Veronique. She's the woman you should be talking to, not me." Meg pressed a hand to her chest, caught her breath. "Sadly, she passed away over ten years ago."

I laid the medal down, fingered an embroidered paratrooper patch. "I don't remember running across anyone named Veronique during my research," I said, glancing up.

She smiled. "You wouldn't."

"Can you tell me about her?"

Meg laced her fingers together and placed them in her lap. "Unlike most S.O.E. operatives who used aliases, Veronique Barbier was her real name," she began. "When the war broke out, Veronique was reading History at Somerville College in Oxford..."

I held up a hand, interrupting her story. "Do you mind if I take notes?" I was already pulling my notebook out of my bag.

"We trained together," Meg continued once I'd opened it to a fresh page and uncapped my pen. "First at Beaulieu down in Hampshire. As wireless operators." A corner of her mouth turned up wistfully at the memory. "My goodness, she was fast! Twenty-six words a minute. Most of us could manage only half that."

She placed her hands on her knees and leaned forward. "Speed was important, you see, or the Nazis would D.F. you."

"D.F.?"

Meg twirled a finger in the air. "Nazis crawled the streets in trucks with radio direction finders spinning around on top. The Germans could triangulate a radio signal in thirty minutes, so you had to get your messages out quickly."

"Did you work together, then?" I asked.

"Not really. Veronique made her way back to Paris via Spain. After I parachuted into the Mayenne in the spring of 1944 I didn't see her again until ..." She paused. "Would you like some coffee?"

The cheddar cheese bagel I'd snagged at a Tim Horton's in Port Perry seemed like days in the past. I worried about the interruption—would Meg lose her train of thought?—but my empty stomach won out. "Yes, please."

Meg rose and motioned for me to follow her into the kitchen. Over the hiss and sputter of a Keurig coffee machine she told me, "Winston Churchill authorized the S.O.E. to set Europe ablaze, so there I was, running around the countryside pretending to be a simple French schoolgirl. Laughable when you think about it, really."

She handed me the mug. "Milk and sugar?"

When I nodded, she wagged a finger in my face. "*That* could get you killed, young lady."

"I beg your pardon?"

"Veronique liked her coffee white, too, but you not only had to *think* French, you had to *be* French, and the French drank their coffee black."

I took a sip of the dark, bitter brew and winced. Clearly, I'd have made a rotten spy.

Meg opened the nearby fridge, reached in, then handed me a container of half and half. "But we're not in hiding from the Nazis here, thank God." She pointed toward a sugar bowl on the counter. "Help yourself."

As I stirred a teaspoon of sugar into my cup, she added, "You had to totally immerse yourself in French life, Madison. We lost one agent when a German patrol caught him riding his bicycle on the wrong side of the road."

Maybe it was the jolt of caffeine, but something she had said earlier finally registered. "You said Veronique made her way *back* to Paris?"

Meg slotted another coffee pod into the brewer. "She did. Her mother had an apartment there. She was English, married to a French banker, but he died in 1939. Good thing, too. The sight of a swastika flying from the Arc de Triomphe would have killed him."

After her own cup of coffee had gurgled through the machine, Meg handed me a package of maple cream cookies and we returned to the living room.

"As I was saying earlier," Meg continued after we'd settled back into our chairs, "Veronique Barbier was much braver than I. While I was lodging with farmers, eating boiled rabbit and turnips, moving my wireless from barn to barn to avoid detection, she went undercover in Paris which was, quite literally, swarming with Nazis." She paused to nibble on a cookie. "Her mission got off to a rocky start."

"How so?" I asked.

"Veronique went to the address she'd been given, planning to meet her contact, code named Nicole, but minutes before she got there, the Germans raided. Her contact was arrested and the wireless seized.

"Veronique knew where Nicole had been taken, of course, almost everyone did. 84 Avenue Foch, the headquarters of the *Sicherheitsdienst*, the Nazi counter-intelligence service."

I scribbled and nodded, encouraging her to go on. I'd figure out how to spell *Sicherheitsdienst* later.

"They built cells on the fifth floor where prisoners were 'held for questioning.'" She drew quote marks in the air.

I winced. "I hate to imagine."

Something passed over Meg's face like a dark cloud, impossible to read. "Today, Veronique would have pulled out her cell phone and texted an S.O.S. back to headquarters, but in those days . . ," She let the thought die. "Figuring that her contact had been betrayed—she was right, as it turned out—she did the only thing she knew how to do. She went back to her mother's flat to lie low, waiting for London to miss Nicole's scheduled transmission.

"Have you ever been to Paris?" she asked suddenly.

"Never," I said, "but a gal can dream."

"Avenue Foch has a wide, park-like median," she explained, "so it was fairly easy for Veronique to keep an eye on the SS building from there. Sometimes she would walk her mother's dog, a little Bichon Frise named Mozart. Sometimes she'd simply sit on a park bench reading a novel, something uncontroversial, a Simenon mystery would be my guess. The Nazis shut down all the newspapers in 1940.

"It didn't take long for Veronique to observe that every day around mid-morning, German officers would begin to trickle out of the building. They liked to frequent *Le Poisson d'Or,* a café on Avenue Bugeaud near the Place du Marechal. So, Veronique started turning up at the cafe, too. Every day, regular as clockwork." Meg closed her eyes, as if the memory were a video spooling past inside. "She always wore a plain cotton dress, loosely belted. A short jacket, bought second-hand, a bit frayed at the cuffs. Smart, but well-worn shoes. Rayon hose, bagging slightly at the knees. Even the little red cloche she always wore soon became a familiar sight at *Le Poisson d'Or,* fading into the background like the waiters in their crisp, white jackets or the nouveau tulip wallpaper that decorated the vestibule."

Her eyes flew open. "Have a cookie, or don't you like them?"

I'd never had a maple leaf cream before, but I took one bite and rolled my eyes with pleasure.

Apparently satisfied that the cookie exceeded expectations, Meg continued her story. "Every day, out on the sidewalk if the weather was nice, she'd sit in a wicker chair at a little round table and order *une tasse d'espresso* and sip it slowly, making it last. Sometimes she'd bring little Mozart along, sometimes not. A book, perhaps. Her knitting, too. Always her knitting.

"They tested her, of course, the Nazis. *'Entschuldigen Sie bitte, haben Sie den zehn-Franc-Schein fallen lassen, der unter Ihrem Stuhlliegt?'*"

I paused in mid-scribble. "French major," I said. "Help me out here?"

Meg chuckled. "He was asking if she dropped a ten franc note under her chair. Veronique was fluent in German, of course, but she didn't move a muscle when she heard that. She simply sat, knitting calmly as if she hadn't heard the officer. Veronique was way too clever to fall for it, even though she was certain there must actually *be* a ten-franc note under her chair. Eventually, the officer tapped her on the shoulder and called her attention to the money, speaking in fractured French." Meg sighed. "No reason for any of them to learn to speak the language. France was disappearing. All the street signs had been repainted. Buildings were being renamed. *Zentral Ersatzteillager. Wehrmachts-gottesdienst. Deutsches Rotes Kreuzt.* " She sniffed, wrinkling her nose. "Certain books were banned, art was stolen, and as time went on, people began vanishing, too."

"*Nacht-und-Nebel,*" I said, recalling my research. "Night and fog. Hitler's top secret order."

"Yes. They were to be *vernebelt,* " she added. "Vanished. Transformed into mist. Nobody was ever to know what happened to them."

In spite of the warmth of the room, a chill ran along my spine.

"What was she knitting?" I asked in an attempt to lighten the mood.

Meg's eyebrows disappeared under her steel-gray bangs. "That's exactly what Major Kieffer asked her."

Kieffer. I searched my memory bank for the connection.

"Waffen SS Sturmbannführer Hans Josef Kieffer," Meg supplied, pronouncing each word with clear distaste, as if eager to get it off her tongue. "He was the senior officer in charge of the place."

I scribbled down the name so I could Google it later.

"Like so many things, wool was rationed. Sensing another trick question, Veronique explained that she'd unraveled a sweater that had once belonged to her father and was knitting a winter scarf. 'It's for my brother,' she told Major Kieffer. 'He's stationed in Berlin with the 33 Waffen Grenadiers.'"

Meg sniggered. "If Kieffer had decided to check, it wouldn't have been a lie. Not that Henri had wanted to go, you understand. Like so many French lads, her brother had been drafted by the Nazis and forced into service for the Reich."

"Did Henri survive the war?" I asked.

"Sadly, no. He died in the Soviet assault on Berlin." She sat quietly for a moment, then indicated the package of maple creams. "Have another cookie.

"After that, Kieffer left her in peace," Meg said, smiling with satisfaction as I reached into the bag. "Veronique was knitting from memory, you know. Printed patterns were not allowed."

"Why not?" I asked, munching greedily. Maple creams, as it turns out, are addictive.

"Messages could be concealed within the instructions," Meg explained. "Crossword puzzles were suspect, too. The clues might be used to pass intelligence to the enemy."

I felt the conversation drifting, so I said, "How long did it take for London to figure out that Nicole had been captured?"

"Ah, right. Well, there's the difficulty. On the second floor of Avenue Foch, the SS had set up a wireless room where operators sent bogus coded messages back to England. It took weeks before someone on our end realized that it wasn't Nicole's fist."

I thought I'd misheard. "Fist?"

"Sorry." She grinned at my confusion. "Every wireless operator has a distinct style of transmission. Maybe they use slightly longer dashes, or put shorter gaps between words. That's called their fist. Nicole had what's known as a good fist. Whoever was impersonating her was sloppy, harder to read. London should have twigged to it immediately, of course, especially when her messages didn't end with the prearranged code word that indicated everything was okay. But they were blooming idiots! What can I say?"

She pressed her hands together, fingertips touching as if in prayer. "Finally, after several weeks, London became suspicious and got word to me. They sent me to make contact with Veronique. Now that they knew Nicole must have been arrested, everyone was afraid that Veronique's cover might have been blown, especially if Nicole had broken under torture."

"And had she?" I asked.

Meg held up a hand, palm out. "I'm coming to that. Times were risky, Madison. There were Gestapo in plain clothes everywhere. Once I got into the city, I kept checking my reflection in the shop windows to make sure I wasn't being followed. And I didn't dare knock on the door of Veronique's apartment.

"One day, I followed her to *Le Poisson d'Or*. It was a mild, gloriously sunny day, the kind that Paris is famous for, so the café was busy. I waited for a table, keeping one eye on Veronique while chatting up a young couple and fussing over their baby who was napping in his pushchair. Eventually, Veronique noticed me and her face lit up. I'd taken a step in her direction when her eyes darted right, then left, then right again, warning me away. Hard to say exactly why, the place was so crowded. But I took the hint, stepped back and cooed over the baby some more. Eventually, two old codgers got up to leave, and I sat down at the table they'd vacated, ordered a beer and pretended to read the *Pariser Zeitung* one of them had left behind.

"When the waiter brought my beer, a dark, malty Doppelbock, I got distracted. Because of food shortages, we'd been starving in the country. I'd lost at least fifteen pounds." Again, she closed her eyes. "I can still taste that beer, Madison. Chocolaty, almost fruit- like." After a moment, her eyes flew open. "I practically inhaled it. Lord knows I needed the calories. Next thing I knew, Veronique was gone! Did she expect me to follow her? Honestly, I didn't know what to do. And then I saw that she'd left her knitting behind."

Meg paused, inhaled deeply.

I did, too. I was so engrossed by her story that I'd almost forgotten to breathe. "And you picked it up."

"That scarf made all the difference," she said after a moment. "Would you like to see it?"

"You still have it?" I asked, feeling stupid the minute the words left my mouth.

Without answering me directly, she pattered away, her sandals slapping the hardwood floor. When she returned a few minutes later, she carried a white Hudson's Bay department store box. After she removed the top, I could see it was lined with tissue paper.

"Do you knit?" she asked as she began peeling the tissue paper aside.

"Back in college, but I wasn't very good at it," I confessed. "I kept dropping stitches."

"So you know the basics."

I nodded. No matter how complicated the pattern, knitting involves only two simple stitches: knit and purl. Knits resemble tiny arrowheads while purls turn into bumps. The sweater I'd knitted for my father had been a disaster by any measure, but the crooked ribbing and the cabling that snaked erratically up the front had been a combination of just those two stitches, however amateurishly rendered.

Meg lifted the scarf out of its box. She held it in front of her chest and allowed it to unroll like a scroll, a scroll so long that one end puddled at her feet. "What do you see?" she asked.

Meg had mentioned Veronique couldn't use a pattern. Perhaps that explained the eccentric, almost schizophrenic design. "Looks like she took knitting lessons from me," I joked, stepping closer. I squinted, trying to sort the random knits and purls into some coherent pattern.

"Oh my gosh," I said after a moment, feeling like I'd stepped into a novel by John Le Carré. "It's a code!"

Meg beamed as if I were a prize student. If she hadn't been holding the scarf, she might have patted me on the head. "Every day as Veronique sat, she listened. She recorded—here— everything important the Nazis said." Meg ran her hand along the length of the scarf, caressing it. "It's in Morse code, as you guessed. Knit, purl, knit, purl—dash, dot, dash, dot. That's Morse code for N.N."

My heart flopped in my chest. *Nacht und Nebel.*

She nodded. "And here," she said, fingering a section of the scarf about halfway down. "Purl, knit; knit, purl; knit, knit, knit, purl. R-A-V and so on. Ravensbrück. Followed by a list of names."

She looked up, her eyes glistening with unshed tears. "As the Allies advanced, rather than release their captives, the Nazis pushed their prisoners deeper into Germany. Ravensbrück was one of the places they sent the women. Many of them died, some quite horribly.

"Veronique recorded troop movements, too, but . . ." She

paused, began to refold the scarf, perhaps as a distraction while she regained her composure. "Other camps are listed here, as well: Dachau, Pforzheim, Natzweiler. Other names. If it hadn't been for Veronique, they might have vanished into mist, just as Hitler intended."

"And Nicole?" I asked.

Meg dredged up a smile from somewhere. "She survived. We didn't get to all of our people in time, of course. Of the thirty-nine women sent to France, twelve perished in the camps, but at least we *knew*. We could give their families closure."

Meg fixed me with tired, gray eyes. "I hate that word. Closure."

With some difficulty, I fought back tears.

Meg reached for the box.

I swallowed hard. "Before you put it away, do you mind if I take a photograph?"

"Not at all." Meg unfolded the scarf, draped it over both arms and turned her body sideways so the scarf's impressive length would fit in the frame.

"Ironic, really," she said as I fiddled with my iPhone and set up the shot. "Hans Kieffer was tried for his war crimes and condemned to death by a British military tribunal. They hanged him in 1947."

I snapped one photo, then another. "Why ironic?"

"When Veronique and I saw one another again, many months after the Armistice V-E Day, she confessed that she'd often fanaticized about wrapping this scarf around Herr Kieffer's neck, and pulling it tight, then tighter..."

She began to giggle. "In the end, it was the information she encoded here that helped dispatch that monster to Valhalla," she said, once she'd reined herself in. "Veronique's scarf did him in. It hanged him good and proper!"

Behind the Magic 8-Ball

ALMOST A YEAR had gone by since Tommy had dressed in his track suit, laced up his Nikes, and jogged into the path of a late-model SUV and out of my life forever.

But his things remained.

"It's amazing how much stuff you accumulate in a five-year relationship," I said to Missy, my coworker and best friend. Only eleven o'clock on a Saturday morning, but I'd already liberated a bottle of Moët from the fridge, left over from the office Christmas party, the last time we three— and seventy of our closest friends—had been together.

I poured a glass of bubbly for each of us, then sat down next to her at my kitchen island. I raised my glass. "To Tommy!" I said, clinking my glass against hers. "May there be thirty-six-hole golf courses in heaven."

"Or wherever," Missy added.

"Don't be mean," I said, narrowing my eyes. "It's not Tommy's fault that you lost the Barton account. If that asshole, Parker, hadn't gotten stinking drunk and thrown up all over the—"

Missy held up a hand, cutting me off. "I'm sorry, Lisa. You're absolutely right. But Tommy egged Parker on, you have to admit that. Cheers to this, cheers to that, cheers to that other thing," she sing-songed, waving her wine glass like a conductor's baton.

"Apology accepted," I said and drained my glass. I peered into the bottom, wondering if it had sprung a leak, then reached for the bottle. "And thanks for the moral support today."

"You had to get around to it sometime," she said, offering her glass for a top up.

"It" was going through Tommy's closet and getting rid of his things.

Missy had turned up that morning, armed with cardboard boxes, heavy-duty lawn and leaf bags, and a can-do attitude. Saint Columba's was having a clothing drive for victims of the earthquake in Uzbekistan, she announced. Perfect timing, in her opinion. Two and a half glasses of champagne later, I agreed with her.

We emptied Tommy's dresser drawers in short order—socks, undershirts, BVDs, and tees—then turned our attention to his closet. I bundled up sports jackets, chinos, belts, and ties without a qualm, but when it came to his dress shirts, I paused. I reached for the sleeve of one of Tommy's signature light-blue oxford cloth button-downs, pressed it against my nose, and inhaled, savoring the familiar spring-washed scent from We Mean Clean in the village. "I don't know about these," I said, glancing helplessly at my friend.

"Ruthless," Missy said. "If it doesn't spark joy—"

"I know, I know. Out it goes." I closed my eyes, slipped the shirts off their hangers, and handed them over.

My husband, the victim of an unsolved hit-and-run, had been buried in his best blue suit, of course, but what would an Uzbekistani peasant do with his tuxedo? I consulted Missy.

She held a bag in both hands, jiggled it for emphasis.

In went the tux, fancy garment bag from Nordstrom and all.

"What's on the shelves?" With a sidewise nod, Missy indicated the stacks of boxes that, in spite of their differing sizes (or perhaps because of it: Tommy had been kind of a neat freak), were slotted together like blocks in a Jenga game.

"I don't know," I said truthfully. "They've been sitting up there since Tommy moved in. Let me get the stepstool from the kitchen."

By the time I got back, Missy—who was a good six inches taller than I was—had successfully slid a box from the bottom of one of the stacks and, propping it up against her chest, lifted the lid. "Term papers," she announced, digging deep into the pile with her free hand. "Who holds on to these things?" She produced a thick, spiral-bound document and, squinting, read from the cover: "'American Magic, Technology, and Popular Science in the Machine Age with Special Reference to—' My gawd! I didn't know Tommy went to Duke."

"Yeah," I said, taking the box from her outstretched hands and setting it down on the dresser. "Here, let me." I motioned Missy aside, positioned the stepstool in front of the open closet door and climbed aboard. One at a time, I handed boxes down to Missy, who arranged them on the bed. The last item, a hard-sided aluminum case with snap locks, required extra effort but with Missy's assistance, was relocated to the bed as well.

I dusted off my hands. "Well, where to begin?"

"This suitcase looks promising." Missy pressed the appropriate button, but the locks didn't pop up. "Damn. It's locked."

"Why don't you check out a couple of boxes while I fiddle with the combination?" I grinned. "Tommy's repertoire in that department was limited. He used to drive the IT techs crazy."

Tommy's case flirted with the maximum size the airlines count as carry-on and had a three-digit tumbler lock. While I experimented with Tommy's go-to combinations, Missy threw herself into her assignment with enthusiasm, snatching lids off boxes willy-nilly.

"Jigsaw puzzles," she announced. "A box of Legos! Another box of Legos! A shoeshine kit! And this one has a pair of hiking boots."

I was hunched over the case, setting the dials to our wedding date when Missy said, "Ta-da! How do I look?"

I glanced up. Missy was wearing a top hat and waving a magic wand. "Watch closely. In the blink of an eye, all these boxes shall vanish! Abracadabra!"

I laughed out loud.

"Tommy dabbled in magic in high school," I explained. "By the time he got to college, he was a hot property on the corporate, restaurant, and birthday party circuits." I paused. "He billed himself as The Amazing Thomaso."

Missy giggled. "I would pay extra to see that. Did you?"

"Did I what?"

"See Tommy's act?"

I shook my head. "No. That was before my time."

Still wearing the top hat, Missy wandered over to supervise my efforts on the case. "I'll bet that's his magic kit."

"I bet you're right," I said as I pressed the button and the locks popped open.

"Wow," she said after I raised the top.

Nestled inside the case, each in a customized, padded compartment, were the tools of The Amazing Thomaso's trade. Ropes. Colored scarves. Sponge balls and cups. Gold coins. Half a dozen boxes of Bicycle playing cards. "What's that?" Missy wondered, pointing.

"I think it's a balloon pump. For making balloon animals."

"That's sweet," Missy said.

"Yes," I said, swiping a tear from my cheek with the back of my hand. "Tommy was the real deal." After a moment, with a sideways glance at the closet, I asked, "Is that everything?"

"Let me check." Missy plopped the top hat on the dresser,

mounted the stepstool, and swept each shelf with her hand. "Wait a minute! There's something way in the back." She stood on tiptoe, leaned far to the right, and hauled out an object wrapped in a brown-and-green-plaid flannel shirt.

"I always hated that shirt," I said, reaching for the bundle. "Tommy wore it fishing."

From her perch on the stool, Missy turned, wobbled, and lost her grip. Something black, round, and heavy slipped out of its flannel wrapping and bounced off my toe. "Ouch!" I cried, hopping around on one foot as whatever it was rolled across the carpet and under the bed. "What the hell was that?" Nursing my bruised toe, I hobbled over to the bed, bent down, and lifted the dust ruffle.

"Holy cow," I said as I retrieved a black plastic sphere the size of a softball. "I haven't seen one of these in years."

"What is it?"

"A Magic 8-Ball."

Missy's brow furrowed.

"Don't tell me you've never seen a Magic 8-Ball."

Missy shook her head. "I must have lived a sheltered life."

"Remember the movie *Toy Story?* When Woody asks the Magic 8-Ball if Andy is going to take *him* to Pizza Planet rather than Buzz Lightyear?"

"Nope. So, what did the ball tell him?"

"Don't count on it!" I laughed. "It's a magic oracle," I whispered, channeling a Gypsy fortune-teller. "Past, present, or future, the 8-Ball knows all." I held it in front of her. We watched as from a sea of deep-blue liquid a message gradually materialized in a clear round window set into the bottom of the ball:

Concentrate and ask again.

"The least you can do is say you're sorry," I said, addressing the 8-Ball, although my toe had already ceased to throb. "Ask it any yes-or-no question, Missy. Go ahead."

Missy took a step back, shaking her head so vigorously that the silver hoops in her ears bounced against her neck.

"C'mon," I said. "There's nothing to be afraid of. It's nothing but a fancy-dancy paperweight." I leaned over the ball. "Will Missy get the Barton contract back?" I intoned, then shook the ball, turned it over, and waited for a message to appear.

Don't count on it.

"Win some, lose some," I said, grinning up at my friend. "Isn't there something you want to ask? That little gizmo floating inside the ball has twenty sides, so there are twenty possible answers. Go ahead, ask it something."

Missy stared out the bedroom window, as if a suitable question were written on my backyard bird feeder. "Will I get a raise this year?" she said at last.

I shook the ball and showed her the answer.

You may rely on it.

"See! Good news. Ask it something else."

"This is silly, Lisa." Missy frowned. "Don't tell me you actually believe that thing's talking to you."

"Not really," I said. "But I think Tommy did. He once told me that the Magic 8-Ball was invented back in the forties by the son of a famous clairvoyant." I leaned over the ball, made my voice deep, dark, and spooky. "Is there a ghost in the room trying to communicate with us?"

"Stop it, Lisa! You're creeping me out!" Missy snatched up the stepstool and headed toward the bedroom door.

"Thanks for your help," I called out after her. "I really mean it."

"No problem," she said. "I gotta get going. Book club night, you know. But I'll be back in the morning to help load up the car."

* * *

After Missy left, I wandered into the kitchen still carrying the Magic 8-Ball. I placed it on the countertop, then rummaged through the freezer, looking for something to nuke for dinner. While my mac and cheese revolved in the microwave, I opened another bottle of wine, poured myself a glass, and sat down to wait.

I stared at the Magic 8-Ball.

The Magic 8-Ball stared back.

I picked it up and turned it over.

Yes, definitely.

Wait a minute. What was the last question I asked? I took a sip of wine, closed my eyes, and ran an instant replay: "Is there a ghost in the room trying to communicate with us?"

Some more wine, I thought, drinking deeply from my glass of merlot, the perfect tonic to take the edge off whatever was running its cold finger along my spine.

I took a deep, steadying breath, exhaled, and asked the question again, just to be sure. "Is there a ghost in here, trying to communicate with me?"

As I watched, hardly daring to breathe, the die floated to the window, wobbled on one point, then settled.

It is decidedly so.

"Who *are* you?" I asked. "Wait a minute. Scratch that, Lisa. Yes-or-no questions, remember?"

My house had been built in 1946, so any number of individuals could have died here before I moved in. Best to narrow it down. "Do I know you?" I asked.

Without a doubt.

"Tommy? Are you Tommy?"

Yes.

My heart beat a quick rat-a-tat-tat. Could this be true? I had to be sure.

My husband had grown up in rural Pennsylvania, so I tested the 8-Ball, asking, "Were you raised in Cleveland, Ohio?"

My sources say no.

When I could breathe again, I went deep and personal. "Did we first make love at a Holiday Inn Express in Savannah, Georgia?"

Yes, definitely.

"Tommy, oh, Tommy" I realized I had been stroking the ball with my fingertips, tenderly, the way I used to brush dark, wayward tendrils away from Tommy's forehead after he returned from his jogs. "I miss you terribly," I said. "Do you miss me?"

Better not tell you now.

"What?" I gasped and repeated the question.

My reply is no.

I glared at the ball. "Have I wasted almost a year of my life mourning your death for nothing?"

Signs point to yes.

"You bastard!" Behind me, the microwave dinged, but I ignored it. I knocked back my wine instead, thinking. This put an entirely new spin on the late-night client meetings, the paintball weekends, even that river rafting trip to West Virginia. I took a deep, steadying breath and cut to the chase. "Were you cheating on me, Tommy?"

Yes.

I grabbed the damn ball in both hands and shook it vigorously. "With who, I mean whom, you dirtbag!"

I thought about the office, about that new receptionist, so young, fresh-faced, and relentlessly perky. About the cloying way she answered the telephone—"Carter, Bookman and Associates. Branding It Better. How may I direct your call?"—as if auditioning for a role in *Gone With the Wind.* "Was it Penny?"

My reply is no.

Okay, I thought. Let's try again. "Is she with the office?"

As I see it, yes.

"Do I know her?"

Yes, definitely.

Armed with this information I tried out a half-dozen names, before thinking to ask the 8-Ball if Tommy had been fooling around with Missy.

It is decidedly so.

But that didn't make any sense. After the Christmas party Missy had been furious with Tommy. I'd overheard them arguing in the break room. If I'd called Tommy all the names she'd called him that day, my mother would have washed my mouth out with soap. Missy worked partially on commission and blamed Tommy personally for the loss of the Barton account. She had other clients, of course, but she'd hoped to buy a new car, so the loss still stung. She'd replaced her ailing Subaru not long thereafter, I knew, so perhaps her anger that day was all for show.

I covered the 8-Ball with a tea towel.

I had to think.

It would take something stronger than a glass of wine to sort out this problem.

I shuffled to the fridge, fumbled some ice into a glass, tossed in a big, fat olive, and drowned it all in a generous helping of gin. I couldn't locate the vermouth, but the hell with it. I staggered back to the kitchen counter, plopped my butt down on one of the high stools, and scowled.

I may have been buzzed, but one thing was clear: no self-respecting ghost comes back from the dead to confess to cheating on his heretofore unsuspecting wife. Something else had to be keeping Tommy up at night, wandering the dark, sepulchral halls.

I snatched the tea towel away, skewered the 8-Ball with my eyes, and asked, "Is this about your accident?"

Without a doubt.

Now we were getting somewhere. The police couldn't tell me who'd run over my husband, but perhaps his spirit could. "Do you know who hit you?"

Yes.

Magic 8-Balls have their limitations. How I longed at that moment for an Ouija board, for its tear-shaped planchette sliding easily around the board, spelling out the murderer's name, letter by incriminating letter. Instead, I took a break to mix another martini, then ran through the litany of names, one by one until... "Missy ran you down? *Our* Missy?"

Yes, definitely, the Magic 8-Ball confirmed, not being one to quibble.

* * *

Sunday morning, I awoke with a headache the size of Chicago. I staggered to the bathroom, where I dosed myself with aspirin and a hot shower, then wandered into the kitchen, in pursuit of the restorative powers of strong black coffee.

Missy showed up as promised. Still seething with rage, I offered her coffee, wishing I'd thought to lace a mug with rat poison. "Thanks, I'm good," she said, making a beeline for the bedroom. "If we hurry, we can get Tommy's things to Saint Columba's parish hall before services begin."

I followed close behind.

"You still playing with that silly thing?"

Until she spoke, I didn't realize I was holding the Magic 8-Ball, passing it silently from one hand to the other like an oversize worry bead.

Not waiting for an answer—perhaps none was expected—she bent to pick up a cardboard box labeled with black permanent marker: Underwear.

I'll never know what made me snap. Perhaps it was Missy's jegging-clad derriere in such close proximity to Tommy's Fruit of the Looms. I brought the 8-Ball down with a satisfying crack on the back of Missy's skull. She collapsed to the carpet like a rag doll.

"It makes sense to me now," I informed my ex-friend. "The affair, the fight and—big light bulb going off for me here, Missy—your shiny new Subaru. Are you listening to me, Missy?"

I stared at her back, willing it to rise and fall, but not particularly caring when it didn't.

"Are you happy now, Tommy?" I yelled at the ceiling, the walls, the open door, wherever his spirit might be wafting.

Reply hazy, try again.

"Don't you dare wimp out on me, Tommy! What the hell am I going to tell the police?"

Cannot predict now.

"What kind of an oracle are you, anyway," I snarled at the 8-Ball, "if you didn't see this coming?"

Concentrate and ask again.

"On second thought, why bother," I hissed. I sat on the foot of the bed, reached for my iPhone, and dialed 911. "There's been a terrible accident," I told the dispatcher.

Then I dropped the Magic 8-Ball on the carpet, stepped over Missy's body, and wandered outside to wait for the police. As far as I was concerned, Tommy and Missy could spend eternity haunting each other in the afterworld. But in this life, I was happy to leave them lying together on the floor, where they belonged.

The Island Boy Detective Agency

"JACKSON!"

I hear my mother calling from the deck of the marina lodge. I'm in the mangrove. My hammock is hung between two cork trees and I'm working on what Sherlock Holmes calls a two-pipe problem, so I don't answer. She'll call again in a couple of seconds.

"Jackson!"

Didn't I tell you? As long as she doesn't use all three of my names— James Jackson Judd—it's cool. Mom'll shrug, tell Miz Dee to fix me a plate of the blackboard special, and say, "He'll show up when he's hungry," and Miz Dee will click her tongue and say, "There's not much trouble a boy can get into on this island, Miz Laura," and she'd be right.

Mom and I have lived on Bonefish Cay for as long as I can remember. According to Miz Dee's husband, Constable Fergus, Bonefish Cay is eight miles long and only fifty yards wide at the Low Place, a strip so narrow that Hurricane Floyd cut the island in two. A couple of weeks later—Miz Dee says, and shows me pictures because I was only three when it happened—a barge turns up loaded with a Bobcat backhoe tractor and half a dozen construction workers from Texas to fix it.

Uncle Charlie hired them.

He owns the joint.

We have a grocery store, a bakery, two fancy souvenir shops, a beach bar, and a couple of restaurants like the one at the Bonefish Lodge where Mom is the manager, and he owns all of them, too. The last Tuesday of every month, Uncle Charlie thinks it's cool to buzz the lodge in his Piper Aztec before he touches down on the landing strip near the island's big generator and stays for a while. He's already got his shoes off when he climbs out of the pilot's seat carrying the mail bag and a copy of the Sunday *New York Times*.

He's not really my uncle.

"Jackson, be polite!" Mom says, so I try not to make faces over my cornflakes when Uncle Charlie wanders out of the bedroom in his boxer shorts, pats me on the head, and says, "How's it hanging, dude?" on his way to the coffee pot.

He's not my dad, either.

I had a dad once, but I never knew him.

When I was seven, I asked Mom about my father, but she just turned her mouth down at the corners and said, "Water under the bridge, Jackson. We'll talk about it when you're older." I keep getting older, and I keep asking, but nine isn't old enough, I guess.

I imagine my father was an explorer, a hero like James Stanfield or Dean Conger, guys I read about in the *National Geographic* magazines we've got in the lodge that go back—way back—to when Uncle Charlie's grandfather built the place, so long ago that the issues cost ten cents and had only writing, not photos, on the cover. Maybe my dad died in a fiery plane crash in Kenya, flying low while filming migrating elephants, I think. Or, maybe he froze to death near the summit of Mount Everest and will stay there until global warming uncovers his body.

Mom is supposed to be homeschooling me, but she gets busy and forgets. Nobody back in the U.S. is checking up on us, though, so it's no big deal. When I grow old and famous, my entry in the *Encyclopedia Britannica* is going to say, "J. J. Judd was self-educated," and that'd be the truth. We've got an *Encyclopedia Britannica* set in the lodge library. Even though it's old and the bindings are falling apart, there's all kinds of interesting stuff in there. My favorite volume is number nine, "Extradition to Garrick." I've read the article about fencing a million times, and practice with a machete—J. Jackson Judd versus a coconut hanging from a rope—unless there's a boat in the marina with kids on it I can play with.

There're shelves of *Popular Mechanics* in the library, too. I built a transistor radio from instructions in *Popular Mechanics*. Constable Fergus once helped me build a boxcar racer out of a shipping pallet, wheelbarrow parts, and an old golf cart battery.

And if I ever get bored with science and geography, I can grab one of the Reader's Digest Condensed Books that Miz Dee keeps dusted, their spines lined up all neat and even.

"You let him read *The Stepford Wives?*" Miz Dee asks my mom one day at lunch. I have a volume from 1973 propped up like a wall around my fish sandwich and fries. I'm actually reading *The Odessa File*, but Miz Dee can't see that.

Mom laughs her happy laugh and says, "It's condensed, Dee. They cut out the naughty bits."

Mom means sex. She thinks I don't know about sex, but I do. *National Geographic* has stories about the family life of apes, and I can't see how apes are much different from humans.

"Condensed!" Miz Dee huffs, as she gets up from the table. "Condensation is for soups, not for books." She collects my mother's empty plate and says, "In the sixth grade, I didn't realize they had us reading a condensed version of *Little Women*. When I got into high school, I was talking with a friend and she said, 'It's so sad, like the part in *Little Women* where Beth dies,' and I was, like, '*What?!*'"

That makes my mother laugh.

Not all the books in our library are condensed. We have a zillion copies of last year's best-sellers like *The Da Vinci Code*, *Midnight in the Garden of Good and Evil*, and every Harry Potter book that J. K. Rowling ever wrote, and in different languages, too, like *Harry Potter und Der Stein der Weisen* and *Harry Potter à l'école des sorciers*. They get left behind by cruising sailors who don't want them anymore. Miz Dee hung up a sign—TAKE ONE, LEAVE ONE—so I'm always on the lookout for something new to read. I really hit the jackpot last summer when a big, fat volume with a brown-and-yellow cover caught my eye, sandwiched between a spiral-bound *Cruising Guide to the Abacos* for 1980 and a book called *Two Stroke Engine Repair and Maintenance*. The cover said: *The Complete Sherlock Holmes, containing four novels and all fifty-six adventures*. I snatched it up quick and took it back to our cottage. From the Condensed Books, I'd read Dick Francis, lots of Grafton and Grisham, all of *The Cat Who...* books and some good stories by Mary Higgins Clark and Elizabeth Peters. Agatha Christie is awesome, too, but *The Complete Sherlock Holmes* totally blew my mind. It's my bible.

It'd be cool to be the son of Sherlock Holmes, I think, but I know he's just a fictional character dreamed up by Sir Arthur Conan Doyle. Besides, as far as I can tell, the Great Detective never had sex so a son was out of the question. Miz Dee goes on and on about how impressionable young boys need a strong male role model, and what a blessing it is that Uncle Charlie is in my life. But, as role models go, you can't get much better than Sherlock Holmes.

I've already solved my first case—The Missing Quarters Affair.

Someone had broken into the dollar-bill changing machine in the laundry room at the marina. If they'd jimmied the lock to get at the money, it might have taken me longer to solve the case, but the criminal was a moron—he used a key, and the only spare key was kept in Miz Dee's office, hanging behind the door on a hook under her apron. Only a handful of people knew about that. I had a closed circle of suspects!

I was hanging out at the Thirsty 'Cuda playing a foosball game with a twelve-year-old kid from a cruising trawler, when one of my suspects wandered in. Manny was Miz Dee's nephew from Baltimore, staying on the island for the summer to keep him away from "bad influences" in the city. Manny did odd jobs around the lodge—cleaning the hot tub, sifting leaves out of the swimming pool, making sure the golf carts were plugged in at night, washing glasses behind the bar—but that was his day off. I'd just served and made a wall pass with a push kick that whizzed past the visiting kid's goalie, when I saw Manny sidle up to the slot machine next to the bar and start feeding it quarters. Bells rang, lights flashed, and a fistful of quarters tumbled into the coin tray. Manny rubbed his hands together, scooped up his winnings, then fed the quarters back into the machine, one by one, until he was empty-handed. What a dope. Didn't he know the odds? The February 1960 issue of *Popular Mechanics* had been a real eye-opener about slot machines for me. "In Las Vegas," they wrote, "Electronics Keeps the Gamblers Honest."

After I beat the boat kid best-three-out-of-five, I went looking for Constable Fergus and fingered Manny for the laundry room job. That night, Miz Dee and Constable Fergus had a big pow-wow, and after that, Manny spent his days off at the dump, hosing out trash bins.

As an aspiring detective, I can't just sit back and relax. I have to practice my powers of observation. Here's what I deduced when Uncle Charlie showed up this morning for breakfast.

He's just had a shower because his hair is slicked back. He dyes it black, because the hair on his chest doesn't match—it's salt-and-pepper gray. His chest is bare, so you can see the knotted scar over his left nipple, about two inches long. I asked him about it once and he'd laughed and said, "Shrapnel." But I knew it wasn't an old war wound. "Charlie has a pacemaker," Mom told me, and when I mentioned that I'd read about the first artificial pacemaker in the March 1933 issue of *Popular Mechanics*, she said, "That's nice, Jackson. Now run along."

I note that Uncle Charlie's shaved off his stubble, leaving a speck of blood on his cheek and a dab of shaving cream behind his ear. He's wearing long pants but carrying a pair of Docksiders in his left hand. A green polo shirt is draped over his arm.

"I deduce that you're flying back to Texas early," I say.

"And what brings you to that conclusion, my man?"

I explain my reasoning. "You're all dressed up. And you always go barefoot," I add, pointing to the shoes. "Except on the plane."

"Guess again, Sherlock!" He pats me on the head. "Quick trip to the mainland and back. Got an important business meeting today."

Around ten o'clock, Uncle Charlie's powerboat zooms back from the mainland with him at the helm. He ties up at the end of the fuel dock and climbs out, followed by two city slickers. The taller one is carrying a briefcase; the other a canvas tube, too short to be a fishing rod.

I'm sitting in the window seat of the library, reading a mildewed copy of *N is for Noose,* and I see them out the window, strolling up the dock. I figure they're heading to the bar, like city slickers always do, but after a few minutes, Uncle Charlie opens the library door and they all come through. "Spread it out over there," Uncle Charlie says, pointing to the table in the middle of the room. It's made from an old ship's door and has currency from all over the world laminated to the top.

Children should be seen and not heard, the Victorians in Sherlock's time used to say. I figure the opposite might also be true: Kids who aren't heard can't be seen, so I scrunch down behind my book and keep mum.

The short guy is wearing a Hawaiian shirt with guitars all over it. He upends the tube over the table and a map falls out. He rolls the map out and anchors the corners with some heavy glass ashtrays nobody uses since Miz Dee nailed a THANK YOU FOR NOT SMOKING sign on the wall. He stabs at the chart with a fat, hairy finger and says, "The casino will go here, where the old lodge is now."

"I thought you planned on expanding the lodge," Uncle Charlie says.

The other guy shrugs. "No can do. Our architect says it'll break the bank. The place is a total teardown."

"Then where's the—" Uncle Charlie begins, but the tall guy cuts him off.

"I'm way ahead of you there, Chuck. We're siting the hotel over here, where the mangrove is now."

Mangrove? My ears begin to burn. Sherlock Holmes has 221B Baker Street. Hercule Poirot lives at 56B Whitehaven Mansions. Even Nero Wolfe has a brownstone on West 35th Street in New York City. There is only one mangrove on Bonefish Cay and that's where my personal hammock hangs between two sturdy cork trees and my plastic tub of treasures is stashed in the crook of a buttonwood tree. My best friends live there, too. Schools of yellow jack and sergeant majors. Jade, the green heron who *skeow-skeows* at night. A curly-tail lizard I named Izzy who nibbles on my big toe if I'm too slow tossing banana bits his way. Randy the manatee sometimes cruises by. I recognize Randy by the notch in his fluke from an unfortunate encounter with a power-boat. Mangroves are crucial to our island's ecosystem, everybody knows that! They absorb wave energy, like during hurricanes. They are nurseries for our fish and wildlife! I remember a May issue of *National Geographic* from 1977 that explains all about mangroves. I decide to find it and show it to them.

"Let's go to the bar and talk details," Uncle Charlie says as he shakes the hand of the guy in the Hawaiian shirt and pounds the other guy on the back.

After they leave, I put down my book and go over to check out the map. I know how to read maps—every issue of *National Geographic* has a centerfold. It's clear from their plans that the Bonefish Hotel, Casino, and Marina would take over one-quarter of the island. The channel would be dredged to accommodate yachts up to two hundred and fifty feet. Although I look hard for it, the cottage where my mother and I live is nowhere in the plans.

It's a disaster.

But, what is a nine-year-old detective going to do about it? I have a three-pipe problem on my hands.

The city slickers eventually leave, laughing like hyenas, stag-gering down the dock after one too many of Miz Dee's frozen Bahama Mamas. Uncle Charlie walks with them, making sure they don't fall into the water.

Later, I find the *National Geographic* from May 1977 and show the article to Uncle Charlie. He takes the magazine out to the patio to read, I give him points for that. "Well?" I say after an hour goes by. "What do you think?"

He lays the magazine down on the deck next to his chair, adjusts his sunglasses, and closes his eyes. "I hear you, Jackson. But ..."

"But what?" I ask.

"Progress, my boy," he says. "You can't stand in the way of progress."

* * *

Three weeks later the city slickers come back. They have lunch with Uncle Charlie who's dressed more like his normal self, in shorts and a Grateful Dead T-shirt, bare feet and all. Manny's doing his gig at the garbage dump, so I'm helping Miz Dee. Kids aren't supposed to serve alcoholic beverages, so she's got me loading the dishwasher in the kitchen when we hear the *whoop-whoop-whoop* of the Bonefish Cay Fire and Rescue boat. Everyone rushes out on the dock to see what's going on.

The city slickers are standing at the fuel dock, looking stupid.

Uncle Charlie's sprawled on the floor of his powerboat and Constable Fergus is pounding on his chest.

My mother starts to climb down the boarding ladder, but Miz Dee reaches out and drags her back. "What happened?" Miz Dee asks.

"Heart attack, Dee baby," Constable Fergus says. "Dead when he hit the deck. Not a thing anyone coulda done about it."

"Not a heart attack," I pipe up.

"What do you know about it, kid?" the constable says.

"Jackson?" My mother raises her head from Miz Dee's shoulder. "Nothing. He knows nothing, Fergus. He's only nine years old, for heaven's sake."

"I've read about this," I say. "Uncle Charlie's been electrocuted. Check out his hands."

Constable Fergus frowns, but does what I ask. Behind me, one of the city slickers sucks air in through his teeth. We all see the burns on Uncle Charlie's palms.

"Jesus!" the city slicker says. "I saw him! He put both hands on the pump. He was pushing the boat away a bit so we could get on."

Mom begins to sway and reaches for the fuel pump to steady

herself. I knock her hand away. "Nobody touch that pump until an electrician checks it out! Probably okay if you're wearing shoes, but . . ." I let my voice trail off and I see that everyone is checking out the burn on Uncle Charlie's foot. "Shock like that probably fried his pacemaker," I add.

"Kid might be right," Constable Fergus says. He reaches up from the boat and gives the pump a cautious tap. "Yipes!" he yells, jerking his arm back real quick. "Step away, everybody. That bastard packs a wallop!"

Eventually, Fire and Rescue takes Uncle Charlie's body to the hospital on the mainland. My mother, Miz Dee, and the city slickers go along. While they're gone, I do what needs to be done. The architectural plans are in itty-bitty pieces, flushed down the toilet in Buoys, the tiki-shack men's room behind the swimming pool. The March 2006 issue of *Popular Mechanics* with the article on "How to Avoid Electric Shock" is back on the library shelves.

"Reason backwards," Sherlock Holmes always says.

And that's exactly what I'd done.

* * *

Uncle Charlie died without a will, my mother says, so while his ex-wives, seven children, and their lawyers squabble over his estate, things on Bonefish Cay are returning to normal. I miss Uncle Charlie, of course. Everybody does.

Mom seems happier these days. I see her sitting at the bar, laughing with a guy named Joe who came in on a Nordhaven 42 for a few nights, then decided to reserve the slip for a month.

Meanwhile, I'm back in my hammock, working on a case. Overnight, someone ran into Miz Dee's golf cart, smashed the *Queen Bee* up good.

The game is afoot!

Somewhere on Bonefish Cay there's a vehicle with yellow paint on its bumper, and it won't be long before J. Jackson Judd, Island Boy Detective, tracks it down.

A Fine New York Whine

MY HUSBAND IS a couch potato.

No, potato isn't the right word to describe Daniel. A potato can at least aspire to greatness, like hashbrowns, or cheesy baked, or mashed and fluted onto the top of a hearty beef stew and browned under the broiler. Daniel just lies on the sofa like a dead man, barely blinking, the only clue that he might still be alive the slight motion of his thumb as he surfs through the channels. If the channels aren't flashing by like a slide show at the Y, I check to see if he's breathing.

Daniel wasn't always like that, of course. I met him over a glass of complimentary champagne at an art show on the Caribbean Princess, two-hundred miles out to sea. We danced the nights away between Cozumel and Grand Cayman, and by the time we reached the Turks and Caicos, I'd spent what remained of the night in his cabin.

Mama wasn't amused. "Slanders cluster thick around a widow's door, Marjorie Ann," Mama said, quoting an old Chinese proverb. Sour grapes, if you ask me. Mama had picked Daniel out of the crowd for herself, I suspect. Like Mama, he'd aged well. Daniel had the lean, tight-butt physique of a matador. He combed his abundant dark hair straight back, and Mother Nature had dusted it attractively with gray at the temples. Fortunately, long before the ship docked at Nassau, Mama'd got her freshly-manicured claws into a retired banker—one of those guys who are paid to dance with widows on cruise ships and aren't supposed to get romantically involved with the passengers. Sadly, the management hadn't figured on Mama, and the banker—for the duration of the cruise, at least—was a goner.

Daniel used to be full of life . . . back then. We played pickleball on the Sports Deck every morning, duplicate bridge in the afternoon, and he matched me shot for shot around the ship's putting green. On the day a stockbroker from Hong Kong with a tiger embroidered on his cap challenged Daniel to a cut-throat game of Ping-Pong, I sat it out. Daniel won, four games to three. Just watching the action from the sidelines left me weak with exhaustion. "Fancy a mojito?" Daniel grinned as he wiped his brow with the towel I'd handed him. That same night, at Sabatini's Italian Trattoria down on Deck 7, he leaned across his tiramisu, grasped my hand and asked me to be his wife.

It's two years later, and I'm lucky if I can get my husband to take out the garbage. "Don't be too hard on the man," Mama chided when I complained to her about it. "He works hard and deserves his rest."

Exactly what Daniel does that's so exhausting at Anderson's Auto-Mall, the used car dealership he owns in Elkridge, Maryland, is a mystery. When we first married, he worked long hours, but after a few exhausting months, he hired an office manager who spruced up the showroom with blood-red leather armchairs, a big screen TV and an automatic espresso machine. She even managed to jump start the two lackadaisical salesmen Daniel had inherited from the previous owner by increasing their earnings to twenty-five percent over MSRP.

By she, I mean Angela Martinelli. Angie was the complete no-nonsense package. Flat black hair as uptight as she was, tortured into a twist at the back of her head and held in place with a tortoise-shell claw,. Hazel eyes quick and sharp behind red reading glasses, the frames round as saucers. Within a month, Angie had the dealership running like a well-oiled machine, so all Daniel had to do was show up every day from one to three and go over the daily sales figures.

Our two year anniversary was coming up. With Angie firmly in charge, I figured we could afford time away on a celebratory trip. When I suggested it to Daniel over breakfast one morning, surprisingly, he balked.

"What's wrong with a staycation, Marjorie Ann?"

"And do what?" I asked as I flipped his eggs from sunny side up to easy over. "Binge-watch all eight seasons of *Game of Thrones*?"

"Don't be silly, Marjorie Ann. Nice weather coming up. I could start work on that water garden you've been nagging me about."

"But you never take me anywhere!" I whined. "I want to *go* somewhere. *Do* something fun. Like we used to."

Daniel grunted and spread some cherry jam on his toast.

I slid the eggs onto his plate and stood over him until I caught his eye. "Read my lips, Daniel. I. Want. To. Go. To. New York City."

Daniel frowned. "I hate New York."

"It's bright, fast and fun," I rattled on. "We could stay at Times Square. Eat some good food. See a few shows."

"Too expensive," Daniel grumped.

Money, as Daniel well knew, was not a problem. Twice tragically widowed, I'd been left fairly well off when Stephen, my late husband . . . Sorry, give me a minute. It's been three years, but it still stings.

"How about a compromise?" Daniel suggested after a moment. "Philadelphia?"

I sucked in my lower lip, shook my head. "If you've seen one cradle of liberty, you've seen them all."

"Williamsburg?"

"You know I'm not much of a history buff."

At least wherever we decided to go, we weren't obliged to visit family. Mama was all I had, and Daniel was an only child, orphaned as a kid, he told me, when his parents were killed in a high speed crash on Interstate 95. Strapped into the back seat, young Daniel had survived, but the ragged scar that snaked down his left cheek remained a stark souvenir.

"New York City. Please?"

"Whining is so unattractive, Marjorie Ann."

I softened my tone. 'Pretty please?"

"No, just no," Daniel muttered, and dug into his eggs.

"No is not the right answer," I informed him flatly.

The following afternoon, shortly after Daniel returned from the dealership and before he had time to completely meld into the sofa, I pounced. Carrying a plastic folder, I pushed his legs aside to make room for myself and sat down. I removed the TV remote from his hand and tossed it onto the coffee table.

"I've got it all planned," I began. "We can take the *Acela* to Penn Station," I said, opening the folder. "Next Thursday," I added firmly, producing the ticket. "Then, Friday and Saturday nights we stay at the Marriott at Times Square. And this . . ." I waved a printed receipt under his nose where he could read it even without his glasses. "Two tickets on Friday night for *Spamalot!*" I took a breath and barreled on. "And on Saturday, we're going to see *Sweeney Todd!*"

"But . . ."

"No buts about it, Daniel," I said, laying the folder down on the coffee table next to the remote. I snuggled up, nibbled playfully on his earlobe in the way that drove him wild. "Happy anniversary, darling."

He relaxed into me. "Times Square, you said?"

"Where else?"

"Mmmmm," he murmured into my hair. "I guess that'll be okay, then."

* * *

The following Friday, as we surged out of the St James Theater on a wave of theater-goers, all laughing, I linked my arm through his. "I don't know about you, but I'm starving! Let's find someplace to eat."

While we waited at the corner of West 44th and Eighth Avenue for the light to change, a watery-eyed urchin accosted us, waving a fistful of flyers. She thrust one in my face. I took it, just to be polite.

I tilted the flyer and read it in the light pouring out the window of The Shake Shack. "It's an advertisement for a new restaurant called Cacio e Pepe," I informed my husband. "Just around the corner. A grand opening, according to this, designed to attract the after-theater crowd." I grinned up at him. "Like us. Two entrees for the price of one," I read. "And eggplant parmesan is on the menu," I added. "Shall we? I know you love eggplant parm."

DON'T WALK changed to WALK. "Sounds promising," Daniel said as he steered me over the curb and hustled us across the busy street. A few minutes later, inside Cacio e Pepe, a blast of overheated air propelled us forward and deposited us at the hostess station where a young woman leaned over a touch screen, stabbing it with a forefinger. The badge pinned to her black, open-necked blouse read: TINA.

Daniel cleared his throat. "Table for two . . ."

Tina glanced up, beamed a thousand-watt smile in Daniel's direction. "Sure . . ." she began, then her eyebrows disappeared under her bangs. "Oh my God! It's Marco LeDuca, isn't it?"

Next to me, Daniel stiffened. "Sorry. Who?"

"Marco LeDuca. Damn! You probably don't remember me? I used to wait tables at Camille's in Providence. Bradford Street? On the Hill?" She aimed a finger. "*Involtini di melanzane*, am I right?"

"You're obviously mistaking me for somebody else." Daniel flashed a smile right back, winked. "I think I'd remember a waitress pretty as you."

"I could swear . . ." Tina looked puzzled, shrugged.

"Tell you what," Daniel said as he glanced around the crowded restaurant, packed with customers and bustling waitstaff, eager to please. "Why don't we come back when it's less busy."

Tina's eyes flicked to the computer screen. "I can find a quiet table for you upstairs, Mr. Le . . . Gosh, sorry, it's just . . . I swear you could be his twin."

"They say everyone has a doppleganger," I chimed in helpfully.

Daniel waved Tina's offer of a table aside. "No, no. But thanks. Perhaps another time."

Back on the sidewalk in front of the restaurant, Daniel linked his arm through mine, leaned close and whispered, as if Tina could still overhear, "I wasn't really in the mood for Italian anyway. How does Chinese appeal to you, Marjorie Ann? We passed a Dim Sum Palace on the way here."

"Sure," I agreed, although my mouth had been all set for the seared scallops I'd seen pictured on Cacio e Pepe's flyer. I sighed and folded it into my coat pocket. Anything to keep Daniel happy. "Shrimp with cashew nuts, here I come!"

* * *

Early Monday afternoon, after picking up our car at the BWI parking garage, Daniel dropped me and our luggage off at home before dashing off to check in at the dealership.

I took a long, hot bath, then—wearing my bathrobe and still basking in the glow of our romantic weekend—I curled up on the sofa to watch a movie. The Hallmark channel was showing *The Wedding Veil*, but I'd wept buckets over that story at least a dozen times, so I surfed around a bit before landing somewhere in the middle of *Murder on the Orient Express*. Not the old version with Albert Finney playing Hercule Poirot, but the remake starring Kenneth Branagh and his preposterous mustache. I stayed with it all the way to the Big Reveal, where Poirot solves the crime and virtually no one, including the victim, turns out to be who they claimed to be.

Somewhere in the deep recesses of my brain, a bell began to clang.

I switched the TV off and reached for my iPad. Who was

it, that guy in Providence, Rhode Island, the guy that Tina said looked so much like my husband? Mark something? Luca? Duca?

I tapped in my search terms and an article popped up right away. According to the *Providence Journal*, three years ago, Marco LeDuca, a certified public accountant known by his nickname, the Wizard of Odds, pleaded guilty to protecting the local mob's illegal casino profits in exchange for immunity from prosecution. The black and white photo that accompanied the *Journal* article was disappointing. With his head bowed and turned away from the photographer, the man being led away from the federal courthouse in Providence by U.S. Marshals could have been anyone—the postman, the produce manager at Safeway, even our priest at St John's.

I followed a link to another article dated a week later. It had appeared in the *New York Times*, however everything but the headline was locked tantalizingly behind a paywall. I groaned, but the fix for that was simple: I logged onto the Howard County Library web portal using my library card and tapped into their comprehensive newspaper archives.

In a color photo that popped up, Marco LeDuca was again spotted leaving the federal courthouse, but this time he was accompanied by a woman described in the caption as his long-time girlfriend, Valentina DeAngelo. In spite of facing federal charges of her own for harboring a fugitive, Valentina beamed at the camera, as if she didn't have a worry in the world. It had been wintertime—snow was piled up against a fire hydrant in the foreground—and she wore a fashionable faux fur jacket, with a hood.

> *Marco LeDuca*, the article continued, *had cooperated with the government in a high-profile organized crime trial that led to the conviction of former mob boss, Nicodemo Pizzo, age 77. DeLuca, 52, pleaded guilty to hi-tech wire fraud and money laundering and has been sentenced to ten years in federal prison, but has been spared prison time by Supreme Court Judge Chester McNitt in exchange for his cooperation. LeDuca is being held in an undisclosed location and will be given a new identity and relocated under the Witness Protection Program (WITSEC).*

I flopped back against the sofa cushions, seeing everything more clearly than I had in years. Daniel didn't really love me, he'd married me for my money. Then, after settling into his new life, he'd managed to persuade the Feds to relocate his mistress, too.

I closed my eyes and pictured Angela as I'd last seen her, perched on a stool behind the chest high counter in the service bay, issuing orders to one of the mechanics. Mentally, I peeled off the no-funny-business black blazer, removed her eyeglasses, let down her hair, and gave it a skillful bleach job. The result? Valentina. I thought about the countless afternoons he spent at his dealership, "going over the figures" when apparently the only figure he'd been "going over" was hers.

I'm not stupid. I watch TV. Dealing with the mob could be dangerous business, so I had to be sure. I flicked my fingers on the screen to enlarge the image. The man in the photo was definitely Daniel, no doubt about it. The scar, his beautiful scar, was all the confirmation I needed.

Still in denial, I googled on and on. More articles followed, more photographs: in the *New York Times*, the *Boston Globe*, the *Washington Post* and *USA Today*, confirming my suspicions. I could forgive Daniel, the double-dealing, ratfink mobster, but Daniel the lying, two-timing husband? Never.

I padded barefoot to the hall closet where I'd hung the coat I'd worn in New York City that weekend. The Cacio e Pepe flyer was still in its pocket. "Call for reservations!" the flyer invited when I smoothed it out on the kitchen table, helpfully providing a number with a 212 area code.

I checked my watch. Tina should be manning the hostess station about now, busily seating the lunchtime crowd.

I had a phone call to make.

Grandpa Minds the Baby

TANSY STANDS IN the open doorway of her condo next to an over-stuffed wheelie carryon. A garment bag from Nordstom is draped over her arm.

"Are you sure?" my daughter asks, looking worried. "It's not too late to change your mind."

I open the door wider, keeping a hand on the knob. "Don't be silly," I tell her. "You've got the dress and the shoes and that feathery thing for your hair." I pause, trying to remember what it's called.

"A fascinator," she supplies.

"Go, go ..." I say, making shooing motions with my free hand. "The Uber's waiting. Charlie and I will be just fine. Don't worry."

From the infant seat where he's been so recently smothered with kisses, Charlie agrees. "Blurp," he says.

"I could always take Charlie with me . . ." she offers for the third time that morning.

For the third time, I cut her off. "To a Las Vegas wedding? Married by an Elvis impersonator crooning 'Love Me Tender?' Not on my watch."

Tansy frowns in mock exasperation. "It's not *that* kind of wedding, Dad. It's a class act. On the terrace by the fountains at the Bellagio."

"No Elvis? How can the marriage even be legal?" I lean forward and kiss her cheek. "You'll be the prettiest bridesmaid at the ceremony, wherever they decide to hold it."

"The only thing missing is Peter," she says, hooking the strap of her handbag securely over her shoulder.

"It's only a week," I remind her. "Charlie and I will be fine, won't we Charlie? We'll hang out with the guys at the Strike Zone, bowl a few games, chow down at MickeyD's . . ."

She leans in, gives my cheek a peck. "No funny business now, boys. Not like the last time."

I once took my grandson to a NASCAR race in Richmond and a car spun out into the stands. Tansy's memory is long. "No worries," I promise. I grasp my daughter firmly by the shoulder and escort her into the eighteenth-floor vestibule of the high-rise apartment she shares with my son-in-law. Peter's deployed to the Persian Gulf with the USS Eisenhower carrier strike group. Indefinitely. She waggles her fingers at her baby boy, blows him a kiss. "Be good for Grandpa," she coos, "and Mama will bring you a surprise from Las Vegas."

"Bye-bye, bye-bye," Charlie says.

I watch from the window until my daughter's Uber exits the horseshoe in front of Lighthouse Towers and heads north along Shore Drive toward the Norfolk Airport. Then I fix Charlie a bottle of milk, pop the top on a can of Bud Light and settle onto the sofa with my grandson. I reach for the remote and aim. "Let's see how the Ravens are doing, buddy."

We tune into the game, swigging happily. I cringe when Lamar Jackson fumbles and Steelers linebacker T.J. Watt picks up the loose ball.

Charlie belches, equally unimpressed.

Charlie and I are wrapping up dinner—microwave mac and cheese for me and spaghetti hoops for Charlie—when Tansy FaceTimes from the Bellagio, reporting in. "All's good here," I tell her, "but the Ravens blew an early lead and lost to the Steelers 17 to 10."

"Pity," she says flatly. Tansy says that watching football is like being stuck in heavy traffic—stop and start, stop and start. She's not a fan.

While we're talking, I'm holding my phone in one hand and rummaging through the freezer with the other. I find a pint of rum raisin ice cream tucked behind a plastic bag of frozen teething rings. "All right if I give Charlie some ice cream?"

"There should be some plain vanilla," she tells me, then asks to speak to Charlie. I aim the phone in my grandson's direction while she waves and coos, "How's my big, big boy?"

Charlie blows tomatoey bubbles and offers his mother a soggy stick of toast. She blows goodbye kisses and hurries off to get dressed for the rehearsal dinner at Spago.

I can't find the vanilla, so I pull my chair up close to Charlie's highchair and dig the rum raisin directly out of the carton. I pick out the raisins for myself and spoon what's left into Charlie. The instant the cold hits his tongue, he grimaces, screws his eyes tight and quivers. Then, his eyes fly open, he smacks his lips and says, "Muh, muh."

"Sure thing, pal," I say and keep shoveling until between the two of us, the carton is empty.

According to my daughter, Charlie has slept straight through the night since he was three months old, so I'm surprised to be awakened a little after eleven by pitiful crying coming through the baby monitor Tansy had installed on the end table next to my bed. As I throw off the covers and pad barefoot down the hall to Charlie's room, I'm thinking maybe all that ice cream after dinner was a bad idea.

I push open the door to Charlie's room. "What's up, little dude?" I begin, but Charlie doesn't say. He's sound asleep, lying spread-eagle on his Elmo sheet. He doesn't even stir when I feel inside his onesie to check his Pampers, which are dry as dust. Maybe a nightmare, I think as I tuck his blankie-bye snugly around him, then wander back to bed.

Around midnight, Charlie awakens me again, wailing. I rush to his room, but whoever's bawling, it isn't Charlie. My grandson's out like the proverbial light, sleeping as soundly as … well, as a baby.

Back in my bedroom, I perch on the edge of the mattress and glare at the baby monitor, a Kinder-Kare V. It's whimpering now, and I hear *shhh-shhh-shhh* and the tinny, tinkly sound of "It's a Small World." Kill me now, I think, as I turn the damn thing off, flop back and burrow under the covers.

The following morning, I relocate the Kinder-Kare V to the kitchen counter while I fix breakfast for Charlie and me. Charlie's deep in concentration, pinching up Cheerios from his highchair tray, closely inspecting each "O" for flaws before conveying it to his mouth. I pop a slice of whole wheat bread into the toaster. "It's picking up signals from somewhere, Charlie," I say as I butter the toast and sprinkle it with cinnamon sugar. I tell him about a woman in Hampton Roads driven nearly mad by Hispanic music playing in her head twenty-four-seven. Turned out she was tuned into AM1050 on her fillings.

"Um," says Charlie.

I slice the toast into strips and hand one to Charlie. I nibble on another strip while I consult my iPhone for the Kinder-Kare

V manual I'd googled online. The units were manufactured in Stuttgart, I learn, and come in eight "playful" colors.

"Eureka!" I tell my grandson after a moment. "The manual says the unit can be tuned to five difference frequencies. Some crybaby around here has a monitor tuned to the same frequency as you, but God only knows where," I continue, scrolling quickly down the page, "'cause the damn thing's got a range of anywhere from five hundred to a thousand feet." I take a break to wipe buttery crumbs off Charlie's chin with the tail of his bib. "A thousand feet, Charlie. That's the length of three football fields. Think about it."

Charlie leans forward, not thinking about anything except the slice of banana still left on my plate. I hand it over and continue reading.

According to Professor Google, the fix is super easy—tune to another channel.

I reach for the Kinder-Kare to do just that when a cell phone starts ringing and I know it's not mine because I'm holding it. Mine wouldn't be playing the theme song from *Titanic*, either. A woman, her voice pitched low, answers without saying hello.

I can't keep doing this, Matt. It's tearing me apart.

Whatever Matt thinks about this remains a mystery. Charlie and I are hearing only her side of the conversation. *I can't live this lie anymore. Every moment with him seems like a betrayal,* the woman continues, her voice shaky. *Sometimes I wonder if he suspects anything. If he can see the truth in my eyes.*

Then she moans. *It's just getting harder to pretend, to carry on like nothing's happened.*

After a moment, she takes a deep, shuddery breath and says, *Just promise me this will all be worth it.* And then, after a long pause, *I should go before he gets back from the gym. If he hears me...*

I stare at Charlie and Charlie stares back. "Well, what do you think, pal? Should I fiddle with the frequencies, or make popcorn?"

"Pah," Charlie says.

I tip an imaginary hat. "You got it, dude."

* * *

Two days go by before the Kinder-Kare V tunes in on another episode of "As the Lighthouse Turns." Charlie and I'd listened to endless renditions of "It's a Small World" and "Twinkle, Twinkle

Little Star" and enjoyed a reading of "Good Night Moon," but he'd already been asleep for two hours and I was twenty-three-percent into *Shogun* on my Kindle, when the monitor piped up, a man's voice this time.

Hello? Is this, uh, the person I'm supposed to talk to? He's speaking low and gravelly. *Uh, yeah,* he says. *Got your number from this guy, Freddy, down at the Bent Cue. My wife, uh, she's having an affair,* he stammers after a moment, and I'm thinking, poor schmuck, he's got that right. But what he says next makes me sit up straight and drop my Kindle. *She's leaving me and taking the baby. No way that's gonna happen.*

The guy's whispering now and I'm perched on the edge of the mattress, leaning close to the monitor. Could be talking to an attorney, I reason, but hardly at this late hour, and when he says, *Money's not an issue, man. Whatever it takes, I'll pay,* I know it's serious. I'm wondering what's the going price for a hit job these days. Whatever, they agree on the amount way too quick. *Half now and half when the job's done, okay?*

As I listen in, the husband gives the guy directions to the fitness center on the third floor of the south tower of our complex and explains that his wife works out at ten on Tuesday and Thursday mornings when the gym's practically deserted.

Promise me you'll make it look like an accident, he says, and after a couple of beats he adds, *It's Pilates, man. All those springs, straps and pulleys. You're a pro, you'll think of something.*

I feel cold, sick to my stomach. I want to curl up in the crib with Charlie and pull his blankie-bye over my head.

Jesus, I can't just PayPal you, ya'know, the husband is grumbling. *Yeah, yeah. I know the place. First thing in the morning. Yeah.*

I don't realize I'm holding my breath until I hear quiet rustling and a whispered, *Sleep tight, Princess.* A door opens and closes. Everything goes quiet.

I gulp in air and reach for my cell phone. My finger's poised over the screen, and then I think, what do I say after the operator answers—*nine-one-one what is your emergency?*

It's only Thursday, so I wait till the next morning to hash it out with Charlie. I spoon applesauce into his mouth, scrape the excess off his chin and say, "Who *are* these people, Charlie? Except for that boyfriend, Matt, and some pool hall bum named Freddy, I got no names, nothing. Think about it, kid. A transmitting range of a thousand feet—up, down and sideways. In this high rise, that other baby's monitor could be just about anywhere."

After breakfast, Charlie and I decide to check out the playground. On weekday mornings, it's usually crawling with kids, their moms sitting watchfully on eco-friendly benches made of recycled soda bottles. I strap Charlie into his stroller and we take the elevator down to the lobby. I tell Charlie to be on the lookout for a Yummy Mummy with an infant daughter. We walk around for a while, then I buckle Charlie into a bucket swing and give him a push while I survey the playground, acting casual. Merry-go-round, slide, seesaw, climbing rocks all lousy with kids, but none of them young enough to be our "Princess."

Charlie and I are strolling back across the quadrangle when we spot a pretty twenty-something sitting on a bench under a poplar tree rocking a baby buggy. My spirits lift. When I lean in and make *goo-goo-gah-gah* noises over her daughter though, she laughs and says, "His name is Michael."

Suddenly, locating our baby's mother seems like mission impossible.

I've been retired for more than five years, but not by choice. Mandatory retirement sucks when you're feeling fit, still in your prime as to knowledge and skills. I decide to handle the situation myself.

On Tuesday morning, early, I tuck what we need into Charlie's diaper bag and park him at Puddle Ducks—the day care center in the basement of north tower. I cut across the quadrangle to south tower, punch in the access code and ride the elevator to the third floor. The doors open directly into an expanse of polished wood that gradually gives way to the gleaming tiles that lead to the swimming pool. Water's splashing and the voice of the noodle aerobics instructor is echoing off the ceiling of the solarium—*right arm, left arm, both arms, squeeze, squeeze!*—but the swimming pool is tucked behind a glass block wall, so I can't see it from here.

To my immediate right, blue foam puzzle mats designate the area where the exercise equipment—treadmills, exercise bikes, rowing and Pilates machines—have been arranged in double rows. Dumbbell racks line the walls beneath floor-to-ceiling windows that offer a panoramic view of the Chesapeake Bay.

A woman encased in pink spandex is working one of the elliptical trainers like an Olympic cross-country skier. With short, tightly-curled gray hair, she seems too old to be the mother of an infant, although with hormones and invitro, I figure anything is possible these days. I give her a polite nod and step up on a treadmill. Panting, but not missing a beat, she nods back. I've walked about a half mile before the woman steps down, wipes her face with a scrap of towel and heads for the showers.

I walk another quarter mile before *she* comes in. Instinctively, I know it's her. Not yet thirty, surely, her dark hair is styled in a shaggy pixie cut streaked with purple. She's wearing gray leggings and a sports bra. The only splash of color—other than her hair—comes from a pair of tangerine New Balance slip-ons. She's carrying a gym bag decorated with Disney princesses. She drops the bag on the floor next to a Pilates machine.

I could stick around but if I do, the hit man might not show. So, I smile, wave politely and head for the men's side of the locker room.

I find what I need in the janitor's closet, a neon-yellow tricone with CAUTION—WET FLOOR printed on one side and CUIDADO—PISO MOJADO on the other. I use it to prop the locker room door open, then move just inside to wait.

Almost right away, I hear a door open. "Mia!" It's the skier, popping out of the ladies.

"Hey, Jan," Mia calls out. "Great timing. Can you help me hook up? I'm starting with my hamstrings today." While Mia lies flat on the sliding carriage of the machine with her neck between the shoulder blocks, Jan stretches the pulleys out one at a time and hooks a strap around each of Mia's feet. Mia's legs start to scissor. The women chat for a while, but too softly for me to hear. Eventually, Jan checks her Apple watch and chirps, "Gotta run. My turn to host book club," and she's gone.

Mia continues to scissor.

I wait.

At ten minutes past the hour, a maintenance worker dressed in dusty blue coveralls shambles into the gym, pushing a broom along a floor already so clean you could eat off it. There's a Lighthouse Towers logo embroidered on his pocket, so he seems legit, until he sweeps past the locker room door and I get a closer look. The trousers are too short, barely covering the top of his socks, which are lime green with a Nike swoosh. The shoes aren't right either—Gucci canvas low-tops? Last time I saw a pair like that was at Neiman Marcus. Priced—on sale—a smidge south of a thousand.

Mia's moved on to working one leg at a time. Her back is to me, left foot resting against a bar and flexing, moving the carriage of the Pilates machine rhythmically out and back, out and back. I hold my breath, watching as the maintenance guy props his broom against the wall and approaches her silently from behind.

Out and back, out and back.

I wait, calculating, praying my timing isn't rusty.

He's looming over Mia like a malevolent vulture when I spring. Muscle memory kicks in as I launch myself out the door and across the floor, closing the space between me and the hitman in seconds. I tackle the guy from behind, knocking his feet out from under him. In four seconds flat, I have his hands behind his back, zip-tied and trussed up like a rodeo calf.

"What the fuck?" he begins, followed by a string of profanity that was breathtaking in its originality.

"Shut up," I say, "or I'll have to wash your mouth out with soap."

Mia is sitting up on the Pilates machine, eyes wide, hugging herself.

"You got a phone?" I ask.

Tight lipped, silent, she nods and points to her gym bag.

"Call nine-one-one," I tell her, then I turn to the hitman and say, in a voice husky from lack of practice, "You're under arrest. Anything you say can and will be used against you in a court of law . . ." When I yank him to his feet, I recognize the guy, a two-bit thug from Diggs Town who's apparently graduated from vandalism and unlawful possession to murder for hire. You'd think two years in juvie would have straightened the kid out.

Now he's back in custody, singing like a teakettle to my former colleagues in the Norfolk Violent Crimes unit. Mia's husband, whose name is Doug, has a lot of explaining to do, and he's doing it down at the station, too.

My name never comes up, and that's fine by me.

* * *

From his infant seat on the sofa, Charlie uncorks his pacifier and offers it to me, his face solemn.

"Thanks, pal. But I think I need something a bit stronger." I know where Tansy stashes the booze, so I leave Charlie with Peppa Pig on the TV for a few minutes while I fill a glass with crushed ice, top it up with gin and a splash of vermouth, then rummage in the fridge for the olives. I'm stirring my drink with a chopstick from last night's take away when I join Charlie again on the sofa. While Peppa Pig attends a birthday party, I take some time to reprogram the Kinder-Kare V, then set it aside. "Now what?" I ask my grandson.

"Bah boo," Charlie begins, but he's cut short by the front door banging open. "Hello, boys! I'm home!"

"I couldn't stand Vegas one … more … minute," my daughter says, as she leans over and expertly extracts her son from his carrier. "There was an empty seat on an earlier flight, so I grabbed it," she explains as she folds Charlie into her arms.

She kisses the top of his head. "So, what have you and Grandpa been up to while I've been away, huh?"

"Not much," I say, grinning. "Watched the game. Knocked back a few beers. Kinda quiet around here, wasn't it, Charlie?"

Comfortably straddling his mother's hip, Charlie grabs a fistful of her hair, skewers me with his baby blues and agrees, "Gah."

That's my grandson for you. Always has my back.

Sources

"With Love, Marjorie Ann," *Murderous Intent Mystery Magazine,*
    Fall 1999
Nominee, Agatha award, Best Short Story

"For Sale by Owner," *Murderous Intent Mystery Magazine,* Winter
    2000

"Conventional Wisdom," *Malice Domestic 9* (Avon, 2000).

"To Catch a Fish," *Death by Horoscope* (Carroll & Graf, 2001).

"Too Many Cooks," *Much Ado About Murder* (Berkley, 2002).
Winner, Agatha award, Best Short Story
Winner, Anthony award, Best Short Story
Nominee, Macavity award, Best Short Story

"Safety First," *Blood on Their Hands* (Carroll & Graf, 2003).
Nominee, Agatha award, Best Short Story

"Vital Signs," *Chesapeake Crimes* (Quiet Storm Publishing, 2004).

"Miss Havisham Regrets," *Death by Dickens* (Berkley Prime Crime,
    2004).

"The Queen is Dead, Long Live the Queen," *Thou Shalt Not Kill*
    (Carrol and Graf, December 2005).

"Driven to Distraction," *Chesapeake Crimes II* (Tidewater Publishing,
    December 2006).
Winner, Agatha award, Best Short Story
Nominee, Anthony award, Best Short Story

"Home Movies," *Baltimore Noir* (Akashic Books, May 2006).

"Two Sisters," *Chesapeake Crimes 3* (Wildside Press, 2008).

"Can You Hear Me Now?," *Two of the Deadliest: New Tales of Lust, Greed, and Murder from Outstanding Women of Mystery,* (HarperCollins, 2009.)

"Night and Fog," *Murder Most Historical:Malice Domestic 12,* (Wildside Press, 2017).

"Behind the Magic 8-Ball," *Chesapeake Crimes: Magic is Murder,* (Wildside Press, 2022)

The Island Boy Detective Agency," *School of Hard Knox,* (Crippen & Landru, 2023);

"A Fine New York Whine,:" *Agatha and Derringer Get Cozy,* (Down & Out Books), November 11, 2024.

"Grandpa Minds the Baby," *Shamus and Anthony Commit Capers, ,(*Level Best Books*), September 17, 2024.*

Forthcoming Stories
"Everybody Ought to Have a Maid," *Every Day a Little Death: Crime Fiction Inspired by the Songs of Stephen Sondheim,* edited by Josh Pachter. (Level Best Books), March 25, 2025.

"Dead Man's Chest," *Hooked on Urban Legends–And Murdert!* edited by Andrews, Goffman and Talley. (Wildside Press), April, 2026.

Other works:
A Second Helping of Murder: More Diabolically Delicious Recipes from Contemporary Mystery Writers, by Jo Grossman and Robert Weibezahl (Poisoned Pen Press, 2003).

"Detectives Have Weaknesses, Too," *Now Write! Mysteries,* by Sherry Ellis and Laurie Lamson (Tarcher/Penguin, 2011).

With Love, Marjorie Ann and
Other Dangerous Stories

WITH LOVE, MARJORIE Ann and Other Dangerous Stories is printed on 60-pound paper, and is designed by Jeffrey Marks using InDesign. The type is Caslon. The cover is by Gail Cross. The first edition was published in a perfect-bound softcover edition and a clothbound edition accompanied by a separate pamphlet of "Manny and the Square Grouper" was printed by Southern Ohio Printers and bound by Cincinnati Bindery. The book was published in March 2025 by Crippen & Landru Publishers.

Crippen & Landru, Publishers
P. O. Box 532057
Cincinnati, OH 45253
Web: www.Crippenlandru.com
E-mail: orders@crippenlandru.com

SINCE 1994, CRIPPEN & Landru has published more than 100 first editions of short-story collections by important detective and mystery writers.

This is the best edited, most attractively packaged line of mystery books introduced in this decade. The books are equally valuable to collectors and readers. [Mystery Scene Magazine]

The specialty publisher with the most star-studded list is Crippen & Landru, which has produced short story collections by some of the biggest names in contemporary crime fiction. [Ellery Queen's Mystery Magazine]

God bless Crippen & Landru. [The Strand Magazine]

A monument in the making is appearing year by year from Crippen & Landru, a small press devoted exclusively to publishg the criminous short story. [Alfred Hitchcock's Mystery Magazine]

Subscriptions

SUBSCRIBERS AGREE TO purchase each forthcoming publication, either the Regular Series or the Lost Classics or (preferably) both. Collectors can thereby guarantee receiving limited editions, and readers won't miss any favorite stories.

Subscribers receive a discount of 20% off the list price (and the same discount on our backlist) and a specially commissioned short story by a major writer in a deluxe edition as a gift at the end of the year.

The point for us is that, since customers don't pick and choose which books they want, we have a guaranteed sale even before the book is published, and that allows us to be more imaginative in choosing short story collections to issue.

That's worth the 20% discount for us. Sign up now and start saving. Email us at orders@crippenlandru.com or visit our website at www.crippenlandru.com on our subscription page.

THE HANNAH IVES mystery novels
BY MARCIA TALLEY
(IN ORDER)

SING IT TO HER BONES
UNBREATHED MEMORIES
OCCASION OF REVENGE
IN DEATH'S SHADOW
THIS ENEMY TOWN
THROUGH THE DARKNESS
DEAD MAN DANCING
WITHOUT A GRAVE
ALL THINGS UNDYING
A QUIET DEATH
THE LAST REFUGE
DARK PASSAGE
TOMORROW'S VENGEANCE
DAUGHTER OF ASHES
FOOTPRINTS TO MURDER
MILE HIGH MURDER
TANGLED ROOTS
DONE GONE
DISCO DEAD
CIRCLES OF DEATH

SERIAL NOVELS BY Marcia Talley, author/editor
NAKED CAME THE PHOENIX
I'D KILL FOR THAT

www.ingramcontent.com/pod-product-compliance
Lightning Source LLC
Chambersburg PA
CBHW060559190726
48283CB00003B/1076